JOHN HOWARD AND THE TUDOR DECEPTION

John Howard Tudor Series

Book 3

J.C. JARVIS

Get a FREE Book!

Before John Howard found sanctuary on the streets of London, Andrew Cullane formed a small band of outlawed survivors called the Underlings. Discover their fight for life for free when you join J.C. Jarvis's newsletter at jcjarvis.com/cullane

To my wife, Glenda, who is my biggest supporter and my bedrock. Without her support and encouragement none of this would ever have happened.

WHERRY ROAD PRESS

John Howard and the Tudor Deception

John Howard Tudor Series Book 3

Edited by https://safewordauthorservices.com/

Cover Design by http://www.jdsmith-design.com/

Quotes

"Never attempt to win by force what can be won by deception."

Niccolò Machiavelli

Foreword

Welcome to the third and final explosive adventure in the John Howard Tudor Series.

Early on in my research, I made the decision to write my books in modern (British) English. If I'd kept it wholly original, nobody would have wanted to read it. So, to make it applicable to today's young adult population, I kept the Tudor period words to a minimum.

I used a few original Tudor words to help with the atmosphere of the novel, such as the terms "rascal" and "knave." Even though they don't illicit the same reaction today, the words reach back through history to a time when words such as these carried more power and demanded more attention than they do in the modern world.

To keep things authentic, I kept the street names in their original spellings, including the term "strete" instead of "street."

Marriages in Tudor times didn't always require a priest. A young couple could simply agree to take the other as their husband or wife, preferably before a witness. Once they had done this, they were legally married, and as there were no possibilities of divorce, they were married for life.

The one thing I didn't change was history itself. Any authentic events I describe are as historically accurate as possible, and when using real characters from history, I didn't have them doing anything they would have found impossible to do.

I hope you enjoy the epic adventures of John Howard and the Tudor Deception . . .

J.C.Jarvis

John Howard and the Tudor Deception

By J.C. Jarvis

Chapter 1

January 1537

THE WINTER of 1536 had been one of the coldest in living memory, and on this freezing cold morn, there was no sign that it was losing its grip on the frozen wasteland stretching out in every direction.

It was so cold that even the mighty River Thames in London had succumbed to the thick sheets of ice covering virtually every inch of England. The ice was so thick that traders had set up shoppe on the frozen river and were even now selling their wares to the patrons crossing from one side to the other with their horses by their sides. In contrast, London Bridge was as quiet as anyone had seen it for months, and the wherries that normally filled the busy river with goods and passengers sat silent, their operators cold and hungry for lack of work.

Even the great king wasn't spared from the clutches of the big freeze. For the first time since his inauguration in 1509, Henry VIII and his queen, Jane Seymour, had to alter their arrangements for the annual ceremonial procession that formally opened the Christmas season. Instead of taking part in a grand procession of boats from London to Greenwich, Henry rode on horseback to St Paul's with his entourage to hear mass before crossing the Thames on foot with their horses. This was the only time during Henry's reign that the great river would freeze over during the winter.

One hour after the bells rang out to end the curfew on this bitter wintry morning in late January 1537, seventeen-year-old John Howard tucked his long wavy dark hair under the hood of his velvet-lined cloak and pulled it tightly around his shoulders. He shivered, not so much from the cold, but from the bitter events that had led him to be where he now stood on this frigid morning.

He gripped the outstretched hand of his beloved wife, Catherine Howard, and gazed at her rosy red cheeks that looked as red as ripe beetroots. The deep hood of her cloak hid her long blonde hair, but her green eyes shone through and calmed John's soul.

It was just what he needed on a day like today.

John surveyed the scenes unfolding around him, each new vision reminding him how much his life had changed since the last time he was here. He was standing at the exact spot where just eight short months ago he'd watched on as Anne Boleyn, England's queen, had lost her head. The memory made him shiver as he stared at the scaffolding stretching out before him at Tower Green inside the grounds of the famed Tower of London.

He'd used the distraction of Anne's execution to escape from his father, Robert Howard, Earl of Coventry, and his stepmother, Margaret Colte, who had accused him of poisoning her son. They had been about to banish him to a life of exile in France. Instead, John had run away and lived on the rough stretes of London while he tried to prove his innocence.

He shivered as the memories poured back to him.

Today, he was here for a different reason. A just reason. After a tortuous existence that he couldn't have survived without the help of his new friends from the lowly stretes, John Howard, heir to the earl's estates, was about to witness the final chapter from his life on the run.

He had defeated the evil that was Margaret Colte and proved his innocence to both his father and to his king. Now he was a free man again, and although Margaret herself was dead, her confessions had helped John bring about the demise of the wealthiest nobleman in England - William Asheborne, Duke of Berkshire.

Today was William Asheborne's day of reckoning.

The scaffolding stretched out before him, draped in black, and raised about four feet off the ground. The block lay directly in front of where John and Catherine stood, its presence a sombre reminder of what lay in store for the disgraced duke.

Shadows emerged from the growing crowd and joined them to witness the duke's execution. John tore his gaze away from the ominous scene to greet them.

The first to arrive was an old man with a long grey beard. Or at least it was normally grey. Today it was frosted over and covered in a thin layer of ice. John thought Gamaliell Pye looked frozen to death, but the old man didn't even seem to notice. Instead, he reached out a grizzled old hand to greet John and Catherine.

"Hello, Gamaliell," John said. "It's so good to see you again."

"You're looking very well, John," Pye said. "It looks like being a nobleman is doing you good. You too, Lady Catherine, you look stunningly frozen under that hood."

John smiled at the man who had done more than any other to help them the previous year when they had been in serious need of help. A wealthy meat merchant who owned several of the slaughterhouses in the Shambles, Gamaliell Pye regularly gave food to the poor, but he had risked everything when he went above and beyond in helping John survive when the rest of the country had wanted his blood.

"You single-handedly kept us alive, and for that we will be eternally grateful," John said, grabbing Pye's ice-cold hand and shaking it as hard as he dared to get some circulation going.

Pye nodded at the scaffolding in front of them. "Isaac would have been proud of you," he said. "He never stopped believing in you, and he died knowing you would survive to see this day."

"That he did." John agreed, wishing the best friend he'd ever had was with him now. "Never a braver man have I met, and I shall mourn my friend for the rest of my days."

More footsteps crunched on the icy ground, and John turned around to see who it was, although he already knew.

Two young men approached, their appearance disguised under the new cloaks John had provided with his newfound wealth.

Stephen Cullane was instantly recognisable by the long scar that ran down the right side of his face. Even under the cover of his hood, the scar glistened in the morning light, making him look even more dangerous and ominous than he normally did.

Which, in the wrong company, he most certainly was.

The other man remained quiet, which was no surprise to John and Catherine. Tall and muscular, eighteen-year-old Edward Johnson had joined them the previous autumn after Lord Asheborne's men had murdered his wife and unborn child, as well as his employer and his wife, in a place called Burningtown Manor in the English Midlands.

Raised as a warrior, Edward was built for war, and he had proven himself more than worthy during their adventures in Yorkshire and London the previous year.

John trusted Stephen Cullane and Edward Johnson with his life.

"You look very well in your fancy new clothes," Stephen said, pulling at John's new cloak. "Mine's not bad either," he added. "You gave it to me at just the right time."

"It was the least I could do," John said. "What have you both been up to since we last met?"

"It hasn't been that long," Edward said. "It's only been a few weeks. We've been looking for Gare, but so far, we've not had much luck in finding the murdering knave. Believe me, when we do, everyone will know about it."

"I have no doubt," John said. "And it won't come a moment too soon."

He bowed his head as memories of the small but incredibly powerful man with the coldest grey eyes he had ever seen entered his mind. Grotesque images of Oswyn Gare murdering the poor beekeeper in Malton, as well as poor Jane Stanton in Burningtown invaded his inner thoughts, and he shook his head to clear them before they mingled with the many other nightmares that kept him awake at night.

"Today is indeed a good day. It is the day we finally put the past behind us and move forward with our lives. Lord Asheborne will pay for his many sins, and I wouldn't miss it for the world."

"It is indeed a great day for the duke's execution,"

Catherine said. "Did any of you know that today is John's day of birth? I think it a sign that Lord Asheborne should perish on the very anniversary of John's birth."

"We didn't know," Stephen said, "and indeed it is a good sign. I hope he suffers just as much as Andrew did when he hanged for crimes he didn't commit."

"Today is a day of justice for so many," John said. "And not a day too late, either. William Asheborne is an evil man who deserves no mercy."

Although a large crowd had gathered outside the Tower, the gates were closed this frozen morn. The execution of William Asheborne was to be a private affair, which was normal when a nobleman was to be executed. "The last time I was here, they were executing Anne Boleyn," John said. "This time it's a duke, but at least this one deserves it. I never thought Anne guilty of anything they charged her with."

"She wasn't." Edward frowned. "Neither was Master George."

Edward was referring to George Boleyn, Anne's brother, who had been executed before Anne for adultery, incest, and conspiracy against the king.

"It was all lies," he said.

Nobody argued, because every one of them thought the same way.

"It's different this time," Stephen said. "The duke deserves everything that's coming to him this day."

John looked around for his father and sister, Sarah Howard. He spotted them near Beauchamp Tower, so he led the way towards them and the green where the scaffolding was waiting for its next victim.

It won't be long now.

Robert Howard's tall and slender frame stood to its full height when he saw his son approaching. Ice covered his thick moustache, and his cheeks were as red as John had ever seen them.

"Good morning, Father," John said. "It's good to see you again."

Robert remained silent as he cast his eyes around the entourage that accompanied his son. "Did you have to bring them with you?" he snarled. "Whatever else Asheborne was, he was a nobleman of the highest order, and his execution is not a public spectacle."

"You mean like Queen Anne's wasn't, either?" John shot back.

Robert shook his head and turned away.

"John!" Sarah Howard, John's fourteen-year-old sister, leapt forward and hugged him tightly. "It's so good to see you again. I've missed you, and I wish you would spend more time with us."

"That's hardly likely," John said, nodding his head towards his father's back. "He doesn't approve of my new life."

"He'll come around," Sarah said, although John knew she didn't mean it.

After greeting the rest of them, Sarah returned to her father's side and fell silent. The crowd had grown to a considerable size, and John noticed that the atmosphere had become darker and more sombre in anticipation of what was to come.

Noblemen from all over the country nodded curtly at Robert Howard, but none stopped to speak to him. Instead, most of them threw John a look of disgust and moved as far away from him as they could.

"I see you're popular with your own people," Stephen said with a grin. John could tell he was enjoying himself today.

"They believe it is I who should be on those gallows

today, and not Lord Asheborne," John said. "They will never forgive me for what I supposedly did last year, but what they are really worried about are the confessions Margaret left behind. The nobles are fearful that I will find their names and expose them for the scoundrels they are."

Silence fell as a group of men approached the scaffold from the direction of the frozen waters of Cold Harbour Gate. John could feel the tension rising in the frigid air, and all eyes were on the balding and overweight forty-year-old disgraced duke, who slithered towards the gallows like a broken man. The once-powerful lord looked a pale shadow of his former self, and John almost felt pity for him.

Almost.

The guards had to help Asheborne onto the scaffolding, and John shivered when he saw the executioner with the large axe that was glinting in the weak winter sun. Lord Asheborne must have seen it too, because he moved sharply to the side and made his way towards the front of the scaffold.

"I know you all come here this day to witness an execution - my execution. But all of you gathered here this morn know that it is not I who should be standing here condemned to die like a common thief. Good nobles of England, you all know it should be Lord Robert Howard and his murderous son, John Howard, who should be executed before you today. Was it not John Howard who reigned terror on England last year? Was it not Robert Howard that protected him and helped him escape justice all that time? All of us gathered here today know the answer to that question. No, my good Lords, rather than allow his son to face the consequences of his actions, Robert Howard instead blamed his wife - the same wife his son brutally murdered in her carriage on her way to my home in London. Margaret Colte was no more guilty than

I am, and neither of us deserved to die. But fear not, my fellow lords, for I know many of you fear the wrath of the so-called confessions will be brought down upon you by the murdering knave. Fear not, for even in death I have the matter in hand. A day of reckoning is coming for Howard and his son, and when it does, it will be swift and just. So, my friends, pray for my soul, and I shall see you all again in the eternal gardens."

John shuddered as heads stared at him from all directions. The anger and resentment were so strong he could almost touch them, and at that moment, he knew the nobility would never again welcome him. Even in death, Margaret Colte had won. She had condemned him to a life on the stretes whether he liked it or not.

Even his father stared at him like he was a venomous snake, and John knew he would never again have a close relationship with the man he had once idolised.

It was time. William Asheborne fell to his knees and placed his head over the block. The crowd fell silent, and everyone stared intently at the duke as he faced his final moments.

The executioner stood over the kneeling body of William Asheborne. John felt tingles going up his spine, and he clutched Catherine's hand tightly as he steeled himself for the blow to land. It was so quiet that John could hear Asheborne anxiously panting with his eyes closed on the scaffold.

Thud!

A sickening scream came from Asheborne as the executioner struck as hard as he could, but he missed Asheborne's neck and instead hit him on the shoulder. Strange noises came from those gathered, and Catherine turned away and buried her head in John's chest. John held onto her tightly as the second blow screamed down onto the hapless nobleman.

Yet again, the executioner missed, this time hitting Asheborne squarely in his back. Asheborne screamed, and even the hardiest of witnesses turned their heads. John could hear people throwing up at the bloody sight, and many people turned away, unable to watch any more of this terrible cruelty.

Two more heavy blows, and it was all over. William Asheborne, Duke of Berkshire, was dead, finally put out of his misery by the inept executioner who had made his final moments such agony.

John felt his stomach retching, and he pushed Catherine out of the way so he could bend over and throw his guts up.

The execution of William Asheborne was yet another terrible event that would haunt John Howard for the rest of his life.

Chapter 2

John led the way past Baynard Tower and over the moat, forcing himself through the crowds in a hurry to get away from the gruesome events they had just witnessed.

Once they reached the clearing at Chicke Lane, John stopped and waited for Edward and Stephen to catch up.

"The old man got exactly what he deserved," Stephen said when they joined together.

"Even in death, he made sure that you could never rest," Edward added. "Everything he said was a lie, but the nobles are so afraid of the confessions that they will believe every word he said. You need to be careful, John, or they will find a way to get you on that scaffold next."

"I know," John said. "Margaret will win in the end, no matter where I go or what I try to do to prove my innocence."

"That was horrid," Catherine finally spoke. "I wish I'd never seen it."

"I'm sorry, my love." John stroked her hair under her cloak. "I wish none of us had seen it."

"What are we going to do?" Catherine asked. "I'm not going back into those crypts again before you ask."

John shook his head. "No, Catherine, we're not going back to the crypts. In fact, we're not going to do anything. If we go back into hiding now, the nobles will assume we're guilty and have something to hide. We don't, and we will not hide. We paid a high price for our freedom, and we won't allow a disgraced, dead duke to ruin it for us now."

"John, look." Edward gestured with his head to a group of young nobles stood on the corner of Towerstrete, staring at them.

"They won't do anything," John said. "They won't have the guts. But let's go before more join them."

John led the way into the thinning crowds along Towerstrete and away from the Tower.

The group of around six young nobles followed them, so when they reached the junction with Estchepe, John stopped and huddled them all together.

"I think they're following to frighten me and to see where I am heading. If they find where we are living, they will make life difficult for us. So, here's what we're going to do: Stephen and Edward, take Catherine back to the little white house, but go a long way around, making sure you're not being followed. These mumpers are following me, so I'll lead them away from you and re-join you later."

"No, John," Catherine protested. "I don't want you to go anywhere right now. Stay with us, please."

"We need to be there in case they catch you." Stephen said.

"The last thing we need right now is an altercation with a group of nobles." John said. "That'll get us in the Tower quicker than anything. In any case, I want to study the confessions some more, so I'll see you later. It's me they're following, so you should be safe."

"Please be careful," Catherine said as John pulled away.

He headed down Estchepe, keeping a close eye on the group following him. He had been right - they all followed him, and they made sure that he knew they were there.

"You're a murderer, John Howard, and we're going to see you kneeling before the executioner," one of them shouted.

John hurried his steps as the six young nobles gained ground on him. Fearing an altercation that he didn't want, John searched around for somewhere to hide. An image of his great friend, Isaac Shore, came into his mind.

He remembered Isaac once telling him about his time with Andrew and the Underlings before John had joined them. Isaac said they had hidden in a secret passageway between two churches that were close to where he now stood.

John wracked his brain to remember the name of the churches. He burst into a run, taking his pursuers by surprise. Before they knew it, he had gained enough ground on them to create space for him to dart into one of the many buildings on either side of the strete as he ran past them.

With a glance over his shoulder, John darted to his left down New Fysshestrete, and then ran up a narrow lane called Crokyd Lane. By now, his pursuers were in full sprint, but the houses along the sides of the filthy stretes gave John the cover he needed to get away from them.

He darted into the church at the end of the lane and hoped he had remembered Isaac's words correctly. If not, he was safe inside the church for now. It was too cold for the nobles to hang around outside for too long, so John knew he'd be safe whatever happened.

A large tapestry adorned the wall on one side of the

church. John ran to it and pulled it to the side. A small door set into the stone wall stared back at him. It looked old, like it belonged to a forgotten age, and John knew he had run into one of the two churches that Isaac had described to him.

He turned the handle on the door, and it opened just enough to reveal a musty, dark space that had been long forgotten. He didn't have time to ponder what lay in the darkness, so he ran inside and closed the door behind him.

He didn't leave a moment to spare, because the nobles burst into the church just as the tapestry settled back into its resting place. John was nowhere to be seen.

John fumbled about in the total darkness, trying to get his bearings. He had no candles to light his way, so all he had were his vague memories of what Isaac had told him about the narrow tunnels.

I wish I'd listened harder.

Luckily, the stone tunnel was narrow enough for John to touch both sides, and even though the walls were slimy from years of damp and neglect, it somehow comforted him to feel the cold, clammy walls on either side of him.

The sounds of tiny feet scurrying over the stone floor penetrated the deep silence. All around him, John could hear the rats getting closer. One ran over his foot, and he had to stop himself from crying out in fear and panic.

For the love of God, get a hold of yourself. It's only a rat, and you've seen lots of those in this filthy city.

John took a deep breath and composed himself.

The air was frigid and stale, and John buried his face deep inside his hood as far as it would go. Each step took an age as he carefully felt ahead with each footstep before committing his weight forwards. He reached in front of him with his hands to make sure the way was clear, and after what felt like an eternity, he felt emptiness where the floor should have been.

He reached down with his foot and found a step.

This must be the steps that go under the strete that Isaac told me about!

Rough steps were hewn into the stone, created in a bygone age when it wasn't safe to be on the stretes outside the church.

Not much has changed, then.

John took his time, making sure he didn't stumble into the black abyss ahead of him. He knew that if he suffered a serious injury down there, nobody would ever find him.

I don't want to die down here.

Finally, he felt solid ground beneath his feet. The tunnel was cramped and low to the ground. It forced John to his knees, and he reached out before each slow, painful movement to make sure he didn't crawl headfirst into solid stone.

The air was so stale and cold that it stung John's lungs as he struggled to breathe under his cloak. It had probably been centuries since any fresh air had reached these tunnels, and John couldn't wait to feel the wind whipping his face again, no matter how cold it was.

The tunnel was barely wide enough for a single man to pass through, and it was slow going as John tested the space in front of him before each movement.

Eventually, he reached more steps leading upwards, and heaved a sigh of relief. He slowly climbed the steps that led to another dark, cold, narrow corridor.

He grabbed onto the side of the walls as he inched forward and was beyond grateful when he finally felt a thick wooden door in front of him.

Panic rose inside his chest as he fumbled around for the handle.

What if it won't open? What do I do if the door is locked?

The last thing John wanted was to go back through these eery, dank passages ever again without a candle to light his way. Finding the handle, John took a deep breath and turned.

It opened!

John stepped out from behind a tapestry and sat on the nearest pew while his eyes adjusted to the sudden injection of light. He took deep breaths, and the freezing fresh air burned his lungs as he gratefully gulped it in as hard as he could. He shivered and wrapped his cloak around him as tightly as he could to ward off the freezing temperatures and took stock of his surroundings.

He was sitting in the rear right-hand corner of a small church, and it was exactly as Isaac had described to him. As it had been for Andrew Cullane and the Underlings before him, John knew it would make a good hiding place should the need ever arise. He made a mental note to leave a supply of candles at both entrances in case they ever needed them in a moment of crisis.

It was far too cold to sit around for long, so John gave a silent prayer of thanks and cautiously opened the door to the church. There was no sign of the young nobles that were hellbent on making his life a misery, so he stepped outside to get his bearings.

A narrow road separated the two churches on either end of the underground tunnel, and John thought it a genius move from whoever built the tunnels all those centuries ago. While any pursuer would search for them in one place, they could quietly slip away from the other.

John was glad he knew about tunnels such as this in different parts of London. They had saved his life many times before, and he had no doubt after Asheborne's final words that they would probably save him again before this was all over.

John shivered and huddled under his cloak and made his way north through the city towards Aldersgate and the crypts that had given them safe shelter during their darkest hours, and which now hid the precious confessions left behind by Margaret Colte that scared almost every nobleman in England.

And with good reason.

Chapter 3

Cheppes Syed was unusually quiet, even for a day as frigidly cold as this one. John stopped and looked around, trying to work out what the faint noise was in the distance.

As he got closer to St Paul's, he realised why Cheppes Syed was so quiet. The town cryer was in full voice at St Paul's Cross, giving the news of the day to the frozen residents of London.

He hurried to hear what the cryer had to say, and as he got nearer, his heart jumped into his throat as his body filled with an all too familiar sense of dread. He made sure his cloak was tightly over his head and moved to the back of the gathered crowd.

Oh yeah, oh yeah, oh yeah. Hear yea, people of London. Lord William Asheborne, Duke of Berkshire, executed at the Tower this morn. His final words spoke of the coming reckoning for Lord Robert Howard and his murdering son, the disgraced John Howard, who spread a reign of terror upon the good people of England throughout the year of our Lord, 1536. Lord Asheborne's last words promised vengeance for all the suffering wrought on England by John Howard, and he promised that his time would soon be over. Rejoice, good people of London, that the murdering nobleman, John Howard, will soon face the executioner's axe for his many crimes. Oh yeah, oh yeah, oh yeah . . .

John shuddered as so many terrible memories flooded back to him.

Not again. I thought this was all behind me. Even in death, Margaret and Asheborne have won. I can never live a free life ever again.

He backed away slowly, being careful not to bring any attention to himself. The murmurings in the crowd gave a strong sense of anger, and John needed to get away as quickly as possible. It seemed London would never forgive him for the crimes he had never committed.

John quickly made his way through the almost deserted Shambles into the quiet grounds of Grey Friars, and from there he walked to the cemetery at the side of the church. After stopping for a moment to make sure nobody was following him, he opened the closed gates of a large family tomb and crouched behind a gravestone.

Satisfied nobody was around, John pulled a key from around his neck and unlocked the solid oak door that was hidden from view inside the family tomb. Once inside, he closed the door behind him, leaving himself in total darkness for the second time that day.

He reached around the side of the door and quickly found the sack of candles he had left there for times such as these, and once one was lit, he began the long, lonely walk he knew so well.

No matter how many times he walked through the crypts, John always felt as if he was an intruder. He apologised to the tombs sealed long before in a bygone age for his intrusion and focused on the ground in front of him. The candle cast long shadows on the walls, and his spine tingled when he saw them dancing through the corner of his eyes.

He would never feel comfortable walking through these crypts.

Eventually, he reached the other side, and he stopped in front of one particular tomb and fell to his knees. This was the spot where Isaac had spent his last moments in the dying days of Autumn the previous year, and John could never walk past it without offering a silent prayer for his fallen friend.

He stood and searched for the steps leading up to the storeroom where the Underlings had spent so much time in hiding the previous year. Unlike the crypts, John had fond memories of the storeroom, and he looked forward to feeling the sunlight from the window on his face again, no matter how cold it was going to be.

Climbing the steps, John silently unlocked the door to the storeroom and ran up the steps into the small room they had called home. It was exactly as he had left it a few days prior when he had been here to study Margaret's confessions. In fact, when he thought about it, he spent more time here than he did at the little white house with Catherine.

He'd thought about keeping the confessions at the white house on Watelyng Strete, but the risk was too great. He was sure that the noblemen had spies everywhere looking for where he kept them, and once they discovered where he was living—if they hadn't found it already—they would turn the place upside down until they found them.

The risks of keeping them there were too great, so for now at least, until he could find somewhere better, the crypts were where they lay hidden. The crypts had kept the Underlings safe when the whole of England wanted their blood, and now they would keep Margaret's confessions safe for as long as they were there.

John went back into the crypts and walked to the second tomb on the right-hand side. At the rear of the tomb, where the head lay near the wall of the crypts, he pulled a stone away from the base, exposing a hole. It was large enough to conceal his mother's jewellery box, which Margaret had at one time so cruelly stolen to store her confessions in. Being careful not to disturb the tomb, John gently removed the box and carried it into the daylight of the storeroom.

Before he opened the box, John made sure for the umpteenth time that the door from the storeroom to the inside of the church was locked. He ignored his freezing fingers and took a second, smaller key from around his neck.

The large box laid out before him was about ten inches long by eight inches wide, and the sides had intricate carvings with dolphins spouting water from their mouths. Two of them adorned each side, one on each side of the lock, with both facing inwards.

A carved top showed a red shield with a white diagonal stripe running from left to right, and each side of the stripe held three white crosses, which followed the diagonal line down the shield.

It was the family crest of the Howard family.

John closed his eyes as he remembered his mother, Jayne Howard, proudly showing him and Sarah her jewellery box in better times before Margaret Colte had ruined their lives.

John bowed his head and said a silent prayer for his mother.

A large bundle of documents sat inside a pouch in the box. The handwritten letters Margaret had left behind after her death were the most dangerous documents in England, and John knew that as long as they existed, his life would be in grave danger.

And yet he knew he could never give them up. Too many people had committed serious crimes against not only him, but also against the king himself, and the proof was right there in front of him. John was just waiting for the clamour of his pardon to die down before reopening the gaping wounds with Margaret's confessions.

One set of letters in particular haunted John's thoughts more than any other, and he didn't know why.

Perhaps it was the mystery surrounding the poor girl's death. Who was she? Why did Margaret kill her? What was her life story? John didn't know, but for some reason, he couldn't let it go. He had to find out who Isobel was and why she had some strange hold over Margaret.

He leaned over the jewellery box and scattered the confessions over the cold floor in front of the window that cast daylight on Margaret Colte's dark past.

My confessions begin in April 1520. I was thirteen years old, and I remember it was only a handful of weeks before I turned another year older.

On the day my life changed, I was walking along the banks of the river enjoying a rare dry day after the heavy recent rains. The small path along the side of the now raging river soothed my soul and made me feel alive. More importantly, the solitude I found by the river's edge calmed the inner anger that was never far from the surface, and it helped me hold my tongue when I returned to the village and the normal life that I detested so much.

I deserved more, and I knew that one day I would have all that I wanted, and more.

I remember singing to myself as my feet sank in the muddy, waterlogged path. Thick filth clung to my shoes, and I watched it climb up my legs like a dark shadow. I love remem-

bering this moment because it reflects the most personal, innermost feelings that have haunted my mind since I was a young child.

I was lost in my own little world, enjoying the solitude I so craved, when a voice I was all too familiar with startled me so much I almost tumbled down the banking into the raging waters.

"What are you doing here?" Isobel snarled at me. She might have only been ten years old, but she hated me with the passion of a thousand suns. I thought only I was capable of such deep hatred, and yet here she was, sneering at me yet again, her mere presence reminding me how superior she was.

Except she wasn't. She wasn't even my equal, and we both knew it.

"Shouldn't you be cleaning out the privies or something?" Isobel taunted me.

I thought about turning away and ignoring her, and I tried. I honestly tried. But my heart had had enough of this little bitch, and we were alone.

It was time to teach her a lesson and show her I was more than her equal.

The first words I ever spoke against the likes of her happened on that very day, and the more I think of them, the prouder of myself I am for standing up to her.

"You might get away with that back at the Manor House, but out here where it's just you and me, you can't. You're a spoiled little girl who needs a good slapping."

Those are the exact words that will remain etched into my heart for the rest of my life.

I felt alive! I had finally stood up to one of the two sisters who made my life so miserable. Even though I knew I would pay for it later, not least with my own mother, I knew I had crossed a line I could never go back over.

Isobel yelled and screamed at me, and all I did was stand there and take it. Until she told me that my mother would pay for my inso-

lence. That's when I truly crossed the line and began the journey that brought me to the woman I am today.

Strong and firm.

I raised my fist and slapped Isobel as hard as I could across her face. The look of shock was worth a thousand lashings, especially when I saw the red finger marks down the sides of her cheeks.

"You will hang for this, or your mother will. Nobody strikes me, not even my father."

Isobel ran past me, but by now the mists of rage had taken control. I grabbed her and pulled her back towards me. Isobel struggled, and the next thing I knew, she had lost her footing and was sliding down the banking towards the rushing water.

Isobel pleaded with me to help her as she grabbed for all she was worth at the undergrowth, but the river was too ferocious this day, and she wasn't strong enough to haul herself out of the strong current.

Her anger changed to fear. I could see it in her eyes, and I admit I was enjoying it. She grabbed my hands after I offered them, and I stood as if to pull her up.

Then I let go.

I felt joyful as the raging river dragged Isobel deep into the rapid, muddy waters. The last thing I saw was her face as it disappeared beneath the surface.

I stood there, frozen to the spot for a long time, before I gathered myself together. I had never felt such a powerful feeling before, but I knew I had to act quickly if I was to save my own life.

She slipped down the banking. I tried to save her, but it wasn't my fault. The river was just too strong.

To make things believable, I found a sturdy branch overhanging the river's edge and gripped tightly so I wouldn't join Isobel in her watery grave at the bottom of the river. I lowered myself into the water as far as I dared and made sure the water soaked me to the skin. I held on as the water washed away all my sins, but I was tired.

My fingers slipped, and water was rushing up my nose and into my mouth. I panicked and had lost control.

What had I done? I was going to die, and I didn't deserve to die like this. My life was only just beginning, and yet I felt myself being washed away to my demise. My back thudded into a large rock, and the back of my head cracked open as it collided with the heavy stone. I was pinned to the rock by the fast current, and water poured over my head in torrents. I reached up, convinced I was going to die, and grabbed hold of another overhead branch. With one almighty heave, I pulled myself towards the riverbank with the last strength I had, and I collapsed onto the muddy banking, glad to be alive.

I lay there for what seemed an age before I gathered myself and got my story straight in my mind. My head ached, and I was cold and tired, but the thrill was something I wouldn't feel again for a long time. Not until Malton, but that's a confession for another day.

I ran as fast as I could back to the village and played the best part I have ever played. Everyone believed me, and everyone felt sorry for me. Everyone, that is, except Isobel's mother and sister, who both hated me as much as Isobel did.

At least now they had good reason for that hatred . . .

Chapter 4

John put the confessions away and walked through the church to the unmarked graveyard in the rear corner of the cemetery. He fell to his knees and touched the frozen earth that covered the best friend he'd ever had.

"My friend, I miss you every day. We all do, and even though we struggle day to day, we are in a much better place than we used to be, and that is all down to you and your bravery. Without you, none of this would have been possible."

He prayed silently for Isaac's soul and then stood up. He spoke as though Isaac was still there, listening and giving his opinion as he always had when John felt troubled.

"I always valued your opinion, my friend, and I would do anything to hear it now. Why am I so intent on finding out who Isobel was? Why does her life story affect me so much? It isn't as though we don't have enough problems to solve right now, is it?"

He stopped as though waiting for an answer. When none came, he continued.

"We have plenty going on right here, so I don't really have the time to be searching for Isobel, but I can't help myself. Who was she, Isaac? Why did Margaret kill her? What was Isobel to Margaret? How did she get away with her murder, and after she did, how many more people did she kill? I guess I'll find out if I keep reading her confessions."

A gust of wind brushed past John's face as if Isaac was comforting him from beyond the grave. "I know we need to be careful, and we will be. Oswyn Gare roams free, and the nobles are worried about the confessions. The people of England remain convinced I'm a murderer, and I doubt I'll ever be able to make them believe otherwise. Don't worry about us, Isaac. You know we're resourceful and can take care of ourselves. I'll take my leave now and return to Catherine, but until next time, rest easy, my friend."

He clasped his hands together and closed his eyes, allowing the emotion to rise inside his heart as he recited the words that had always brought so much comfort to Isaac during their time together.

Pater noster, qui es in caelis,
sanctificetur nomen tuum.
Adveniat regnum tuum.
Fiat voluntas tua,
sicut in caelo et in terra.
Panem nostrum quotidianum da nobis hodie,
et dimitte nobis debita nostra,
sicut et nos dimittimus debitoribus nostris.
Et ne nos inducas in tentationem,
sed libera nos a malo.
Amen.

John touched the earth on top of Isaac's grave one more time and headed back inside the church.

Figuring it was safer to avoid the city gates this day, he

headed back through the crypts, emerging inside the gated family tomb. After making sure he was clear, he walked through the Shambles towards St. Paul's Cathedral and the little white house he and Catherine called home—for now, at least while the sale of Saddleworth was being negotiated. John headed down Watelyng Strete until he reached the junction with Soperlane.

Rather than entering the house from the main entrance on Watelyng Strete, John dodged around the corner onto Soperlane and entered the grounds of the house from the double gates that led into the small courtyard. He locked the gates behind him and entered the stables that backed onto a high wall at the rear of the house.

By now it was late afternoon, and the frosty tentacles of dusk were taking over as the weak winter sun faded. John was frozen inside his cloak, and he looked forward to sitting in front of a roaring fire with his beloved Catherine once he had completed his last task of the day.

There were eight stalls inside the stables, and three of them were empty. Four stalls were occupied by horses, and the one on the far left was full of horse droppings and old straw. The two stable boys who worked for him had just about finished feeding the horses and making sure they had enough straw and hay for the frosty night ahead.

"Good work, boys," John said. "Go to the house and warm yourselves by the kitchen fire. It's too cold to be out here tonight."

"Thank you, John. It's going to be a freezing night again." Edmund, the older of the two boys, led the way out of the stables and across the courtyard to the inviting house with the warm fireplace.

John watched as the two boys disappeared through the door at the rear of the house and stared as their shadows disturbed the light from the candles glowing dimly through the windows. Edmund was about fourteen years old and was tall and skinny. His long dark hair ran down to his shoulders, and he had the biggest feet John had ever seen. Edmund was fast, which was a skill that Ren Walden, the once cruel leader of the strete gang, had coveted in his young runners.

The other boy was called Thomas, and he was around twelve years old. He was much smaller than Edmund and was unusually quiet. Thomas was sickly and physically weak, and although he, too, had been a runner for Walden, boys like Thomas usually ended up dead or missing after Walden had taken what he wanted from them.

John had never regretted killing Walden for a single moment.

After Walden's death, homeless boys like Edmund and Thomas had few options for food and shelter. The church and the Almshouses helped, but after King Henry clamped down on the church with his reformation, a lot of the help for the homeless disappeared along with the churches and monasteries the king claimed for himself. The only option left for many of them was the generosity of Gamaliell Pye, and he alone couldn't feed every homeless person in London.

It was against this backdrop that Pye had asked John to take in Edmund and Thomas and give them shelter in return for work. It kept them honest and away from the unscrupulous men who were filling the void left behind after Ren Walden's death.

And it gave John a sense of purpose. As much as his father hated it, this is what he wanted from his new life. He wanted to give back and use his status to help the homeless strete kids. He would do his best to make sure these kids didn't suffer the same fate that had befallen Isaac and all

the other Underlings who had saved John's life the prev
year.

The sounds of shod horses clattering along the rough cobblestones of the normally busy stretes had quietened to barely a whimper by the time he walked into the last stall at the far end of the stables. The stretes had been quiet most of the day because of the freezing temperatures, but now the sun was dropping, and the oncoming night promised death-bearing temperatures. London had become almost like a ghost town. Ever since he had taken to the stretes in May of the previous year, John had never known the city to be so quiet.

If only the putrid smells would vanish as well, we'd be much better off.

John stood silent for a few minutes inside the stall. His breath froze on the inside of his hood, and he watched the steady stream of steam as his chest went in and out. His feet felt like blocks of ice, and he was more than ready to feel the comforting warmth of the fire on his frozen body.

Happy that he was completely alone, he dropped to his knees and began digging in the huge mound of horse droppings and hay he'd instructed Edmund and Thomas to pile up in the stall. He felt around with his fingers until they clamped around a frozen metal ring that was set into the stone in the middle of the floor that was hidden by about a year's worth of horse shit.

This was the place where Edward had found a box of Margaret's confessions the previous autumn, and although it hadn't been the full collection, it had eventually led John to the discovery that had cleared his name and brought about the execution of Lord Asheborne.

It was also the reason many nobles wanted him dead.

After clearing a path to the stone, John reached for the rope hanging on the stable wall and wrapped it through the metal ring. He pulled with all his might and lifted the stone from its resting place. He reached inside and removed a wooden box that contained a leather pouch and pulled out a wad of letters from inside his cloak.

These were Margaret's confessions pertaining to Isobel. Against his better judgement, John was so fascinated by her story that he'd brought them back to the little white house so he could study them without having to go back to the crypts.

The rest of the confessions remained where they were.

After he'd put the stall back to the filthy state it had been in prior to his arrival, John finally entered the rear door of his home in London. The warmth immediately hit him, and he felt sharp needles attacking his face, feet, and arms as the warmth got his blood circulating again.

He walked into the kitchen to grab some bread and cheese, and then strode through the narrow hallway to the largest downstairs room, where he knew a roaring fire was waiting for him.

Edmund and Thomas shouted greetings at him as he walked past their room next to the kitchen, and as he approached the parlour, the door flew open, and Catherine ran out to greet him.

"John! Where have you been? You've been gone all day, and I was worried about you. I thought those nobles had captured you, or that you'd frozen to death somewhere."

"I'm sorry, my love, for I went to the crypts and forgot myself in the confessions. I lost the nobles easily enough, but I do admit to needing a roaring fire to warm myself up."

Edward and Stephen were sitting inside the room, and once they'd all taken their seats, Stephen spoke up.

"Those young nobles didn't give you any trouble, then?"

"No, it was too cold for them to remain outside for long. They were trying to scare me, but you know me better than that."

"What have you been doing, then?" Catherine asked. "I'll wager you've been reading about Isobel again, haven't you? What is it about her that fascinates you so much?"

"I don't know," John replied honestly. "But I feel a powerful urge to discover her story and find out what happened to her. Once the weather thaws, I'm going to find out who she was and where she lived."

"We don't have time for that," Edward spoke up. "We still have to find Gare and make him pay for what he did to my wife and many others. That is our agreed priority."

"You are right, of course," John said. "What news do you have of him?"

"We've gone to every known place where Asheborne owned houses around London," Edward said. "Nobody had any clue who we were even talking about, much less admitted having seen him. And believe me, once you've seen Gare, you never forget him."

"That much is true," John said, remembering the coldest grey eyes he had ever seen. "And now, he must have a large scar on his face from the wound Edward inflicted upon him at Burningtown."

"We need to talk about what happened today," Stephen said. "We all saw the looks on the faces of the nobles when Lord Asheborne was giving his last words. It was true what he said, and you know it as much as anyone, John. They will never rest until the confessions are destroyed, and as long as you have them, you are a target for execution."

"I don't think they want them destroyed so much, as they all want them in their possession so they can hold power over the rest of the nobles," John corrected him.

"But yes, you're right. I'm their enemy right now, and we all need to be very careful. I listened to the cryer at St Paul's on the way to the crypts, and he was telling everyone what Asheborne said."

"What was the reaction?" Catherine looked like she didn't dare ask.

"He told them I would soon face the executioner's axe for all the suffering I have wrought on the people of England. And he's probably right."

"So, what do we do next?" Edward asked. "Do we go back to hiding again?"

"No." John replied. "We can never convince anyone of our innocence if we go back into hiding. If we did, we would remain that way for the rest of our miserable lives. No, we have done nothing wrong, and we must act that way. I'm going to find out what happened to Isobel, but as for the rest of the confessions, we need to leave them be and allow people to forget about them. Once the nobles realise that I present no danger to them, they will leave us alone."

"And if they don't?" Edward asked.

Before John could answer, a loud bang on the front door shook the foundations of the house.

Chapter 5

Edward and Stephen leapt up from their chairs and drew their blades. John gestured to Catherine to stay where she was and reached down for his sword as well.

Another loud thud from the door.

Before John could reach the door, Willis, his personal guard, and the man who had helped him so many times in his hours of need, got there before him and gestured for John to stand back out of the way.

John did as Willis asked, but he drew his sword and waited behind him, ready to pounce at the slightest sign of trouble.

"Willis, it's me, Drayton. Thank goodness you're home, because I don't think I'd get back through the gates before curfew."

"Drayton!" Willis's voice rattled in his throat as though he were gargling with rocks. "What are you doing here at this hour?"

Willis had been badly injured during the fight with Margaret the previous year. It had been Stephen, of all people, who had rammed his sword through Willis's chest, thinking he worked for Margaret. Willis had barely survived and had helped track down Margaret's confessions after her death at the hands of Catherine.

Now he was the sole loyal guard who worked for John, who thought the world of him.

"Drayton, come in and get out of the cold," John ordered.

"Thank you, Master John. I bring urgent word from your father."

"He sent you here at this hour? What is so important that it couldn't wait until tomorrow?" John asked.

Willis ushered Drayton into the parlour and stood as close as he dared to the crackling fireplace. Installing a chimney into this old house was one of the first things John had done after he'd taken over it a few months earlier, and now he was glad he'd done it. Most of the houses in this area didn't have chimneys, and John often thought of them sitting on the straw-covered ground, coughing and choking as the smoke rose to the ceilings.

"Well?" John asked. "What is so important that my father sent you at this hour?"

"Sir Robert orders you to come to the Stronde tomorrow for a meeting, as he has news for you."

"What news?" John asked.

Drayton shrugged. "Master John, your father doesn't tell the likes of me what news he has for you. He just sent me here to inform you to attend."

"Fair enough," John said. "You must stay here tonight and leave in the morn. Tell my father we will be there."

Drayton shifted uncomfortably. "There is one more thing, sir."

John looked quizzically at Drayton, but he already knew what he was going to say.

"Your father ordered you to go alone."

John pursed his lips. "Tell my father that Lady Catherine is my wife and that he will treat her with the respect she deserves. Inform him we will either both be there, or I shall not attend."

"Yes, sir." Drayton bowed his head.

"Tell me, Drayton," John said. "Is my sister in attendance?"

"I believe the Lady Sarah is indeed still at the Stronde." Drayton looked happy to change the subject. "I'm sure she will be delighted to see you."

"Wonderful," John said. "I look forward to seeing my sister tomorrow, then."

After Drayton had been dismissed, John turned to the others in the room. "I wonder what he has found out? I hope it's the whereabouts of Oswyn Gare."

"What will you have us do?" Edward asked.

"You're coming with us," John said. "We're all going. I told my father how it was going to be when we agreed I would reclaim the heirdom to his titles and estates. He might hate me for it, but he knows how it is. He'll probably make you wait in the stables, but you're going and that's it."

"I don't mean to overstep," Edward said. "But do you trust him? He didn't seem to be too happy with you at Lord Asheborne's execution, and after what Asheborne said, he might not want you around anymore."

"The thought has crossed my mind," John answered. "The other nobles are shunning him and making life difficult for him, and he blames me for that. I don't trust him, so I propose we leave early and make sure he isn't setting a trap for us."

Four raised glasses confirmed they all agreed.

Early the next afternoon, John, Catherine, Edward, and Stephen slipped out of the rear gates, leaving Willis in charge of the two boys working the stables. The wind bit through their thick cloaks, and John shivered in the frigid weather. He hurried his step so he would warm up a bit.

The cryers at St Paul's were quiet this day, and the normally crowded stretes were almost deserted compared to warmer times when there would be heaving masses of humanity filling the stretes like ants in a flower bed.

Ludgate was almost deserted, and the guards on duty scowled as John and his gang crossed through the city gate.

"It seems everyone knows who you are," Stephen remarked after they had safely passed through. "There's no hiding for you anymore. All of London knows what you look like now."

"And every one of them hates me," John replied. "Perhaps for different reasons, but the whole of London, indeed the whole of the country, seems to hate me. So, Margaret has won, no matter what I do in the future."

"That's not true," Catherine said. "Not everyone hates you. We all love you, and so does Sarah. It's just everyone else that does." She punched John in the ribs playfully.

Everyone laughed at Catherine's humorous remark, although they all knew it was true.

The smell hit them long before they saw it. The River Fleet never failed to invade their nostrils with the stench of centuries of filth and waste. Edward heaved as he always did when he went near the wretched river.

"I swear I don't need enemies to kill me," he said. "If I keep crossing this dreadful river, I shall die from the foul stench."

The stench thankfully dissipated as they got further away from it, and it had gone by the time they reached Temple Bar, where the Stronde broke off from Fletestrete and Halywell Strete.

Stopping to make sure they weren't being followed,

John led them as they cut off the strete at the Bishop of Exeter's Inn and made their way through what should have been the muddy fields where fresh vegetables grew during the growing season. But today the ground was frozen solid beneath their feet, making each step painful underfoot.

They clambered over the wall onto Milford Lane and crossed the narrow strete to the other side, where another wall separated Milford Lane from the large estate. This was the Stronde, the London home of the Howard family, and the largest estate in the high-class area reserved for the elite.

They jumped over the wall and crouched next to the stables, the freezing weather both a blessing and a curse. It was a blessing because nobody was anywhere to be seen, but it was a curse because it was so cold that John was convinced he was going to get frostbite on his fingers and toes.

John looked longingly at the tallest tree in the entire estate, which sat in the middle of a row of trees separating the different garden plots that grew their vegetables during the warmer months. When the leaves were in full bloom, the large tree became a safe hiding place that John had used during his time on the run. The branches high in the tree disguised the treehouse in the winter, but in the summer the leaves obscured it completely, making it the safest place John knew outside of the hated crypts when they needed somewhere safe to shelter.

The house was quiet, and after watching for any unusual activity, John decided they were safe.

"If father is planning on doing me harm this day, then whoever he has hired is inside the house," he said.

He stood up and moved around to get some circulation going in his frozen limbs. He glanced over at Catherine and winced when he saw how cold she was. Catherine knelt with her head tilted down as if in prayer, but her whole body shivered from head to toe. John resisted the urge to reach for her and hold her close, and instead helped her to her feet and got her moving again.

"I think we're safe, so let's get inside where there is a warm fire waiting for us."

Smoke bellowed from the four chimneys, which were in stark contrast to those on the large house that sat empty on the land next to his father's estate. When he thought about it, John couldn't remember ever seeing anyone at the house next door. It sat as empty today as it had since the day the building had been completed the previous year.

The roof was frosted over with ice, and the weak morning sun reflected off it, creating a calming, picturesque view that would have been good to sit and watch if it wasn't so cold.

John shook his body and pulled his mind back to the problems at hand. He led the way back over the wall onto Milford Lane, and quickly made his way back to the Stronde, where he turned left and approached the large gates that protected his father's estate from the rest of the city.

Two miserable-looking guards prowled around the gates, and they scowled as John and his rough looking companions approached.

"What do the likes of yea want 'ere?" one guard asked gruffly. "This part of London isn't for the likes of yea."

John took a long look at the rude guard, although he couldn't see much under his thick hood. All he could see was a long, pointed nose that was dripping from the cold.

"I'll be sure to tell my father how welcoming you were to the future earl." John pulled the hood down from his cloak and instantly regretted it. His ears just about froze on the spot.

"What is your name, guard?" he demanded, using his best upper-class voice.

"Master John," the guard spluttered. "I'm sorry, sir, I didn't recognise you. Please forgive my insolence."

John enjoyed the guard's discomfort for a few minutes before replying. "Well, open the gates and let us in. We'll freeze to our deaths out here waiting for you."

The guard ran to the gates and opened them, allowing John and the gang to pass. John stopped before he crossed into the grounds of the estate.

"I asked, what was your name?"

"Barton, sir. My name is Barton."

"I don't recognise you, Barton. How long have you worked for my father?"

"Not long, sir. I'm new, and that's why I didn't recognise you."

"Well, Barton, I suggest you learn to recognise both myself and my friends here, because I shall not tolerate your insolence again. Do you hear?"

"Yes, sir. I'm sorry."

"Did you have to treat that guard like that?" his wife asked. "I thought you despised the way the nobles treat people like us, and yet there you were doing the exact same thing."

"I know, and I shouldn't have done it," John replied. "I just get so angry when people treat you like that. It's my way of getting my own back. Anyway, he deserved it."

"Whoa," Stephen stopped and pointed at the imposing manor house dominating the view in front of them. "It's enormous, John."

"You should see Broxley if you think this is big," John replied. He stopped in the middle of the empty circular drive and looked at the house he knew so well. This was the first time he'd entered the front of the house since he'd run away in May the previous year. The house looked the same, but John had changed enormously, and what used to be a happy home that flowed with love and harmony was now a lumbering shell that harboured nothing but sad memories of his mother's death and the exile that followed.

"The only good part of this house is the treehouse in the gardens behind it. The house can rot as far as I'm concerned."

"I don't feel comfortable going in this way." Catherine said. "We should be at the back of the house."

"Don't worry, my dear," John said. "As soon as my father sees us, he'll make sure that's where you shall be."

John knocked loudly on the overly large, solid oak door. After a few minutes, it creaked open, and a face John instantly recognised appeared in the doorway.

"Evans, it's good to see you again," John said. "It's been a while."

Evans was the trusted family steward, and although he was balding and plumper than John remembered, he had fond memories of Evans.

"Master John, it's good to see you again. Come on in out of the cold. You must be freezing."

Evans ushered them inside and guided them to a small room that had no fireplace. "Your father sends word to wait here, and he will call for you shortly."

"This doesn't look good, John," Stephen said. "Your father despises us being here together. He doesn't want the likes of us anywhere near this place."

"I know, but if he wants to maintain a relationship with me, then he'll have to accept it. It's the least he owes me after all he's done to me."

An hour or more passed before Evans reappeared. He looked uncomfortable, and John knew his father had taken his rage out on poor Evans.

"Your father is ready for you now, Master John."

John stood up and gestured for the others to follow suit.

"Your father insists only you are to attend, Master John. It's a private matter that is between you and him."

"What about my wife and friends?" John asked. "We have been here for hours, and we are all hungered and thirsty."

"They are to wait here until you are done. I will bring refreshments for them while they wait."

"Very well," John said, turning to Catherine. "Wait here and I will be back as soon as I can."

Chapter 6

Evans ushered John into the sumptuously laid out dining room. It was lunchtime, which was traditionally the biggest meal of the day, and Robert Howard had left no expense spared on this occasion.

Swan, peacock, oxen, wild boar, and deer meat filled the table in front of him, and John's stomach rumbled as his senses were overwhelmed. He hadn't seen this level of opulence in a long time, and he knew deep down that a part of him missed it.

"John, it's good of you to join us," Robert Howard, the Earl of Coventry and prominent member of the king's privy council, stood up to greet his son. In his mid-thirties, Robert was tall and lean. His chin was clean shaven, but he had a thick moustache, and had long dark hair that grew down to his collar. He looked every inch the powerful lord that he was.

"Father." John nodded towards his father, shunning his outstretched hand. "Why did you not allow my wife and friends to join us? You know that was a part of our arrangement when I agreed to come back into this family."

"We agreed you would live with your peasant friends. There was no such agreement that I would allow them to trample all over my estates like vermin scampering in the kitchens. I shall never accept them in places I frequent, and you know that, John. You are fortunate that I allowed them in the house at all, so leave it there before the situation gets out of hand."

"Catherine is my wife, and you shall treat her with respect."

"This conversation is between us and nobody else. Catherine is perfectly safe where she is."

John glared at his father but didn't say another word.

"What is so important that you ordered me here this day?" John asked after a brief pause. "And where is Sarah? I'd like to see my sister."

"Ah, yes, Sarah. Evans, please inform Lady Sarah we are ready for her."

Evans nodded and left the room, leaving John alone with his father.

"You know there will be trouble after Asheborne's outburst yesterday," Robert started. "You were there and heard every word he said, and you must have seen the reaction from the other nobles after he'd spoken. It was a ghastly death, and the executioner deserves to be killed himself for the terrible job he performed on poor William."

"Poor William? After all he'd done to us?" John couldn't help himself. "He deserved all he got and more."

"Your time on the stretes has hardened your heart, son." Robert said. "There was a time you would have had sympathy for him. And remember, he was a noble of the highest order, and as such, he deserved a cleaner death than the one he received."

"Why am I here, Father?"

"I would think that's obvious. The nobles are turning against us—against me. I am shunned in the court, and none of them will speak to me anymore. Whispers have reached the king's ears that I now possess Margaret's confessions, and that I am scheming to bring down many of my esteemed peers. They are worried that her confessions will implicate them in one of her devious schemes and lead to them facing the executioner's axe. I have many enemies, John, and they are gathering to bring me down."

"That may be so, and I am sure you are correct, but what does that have to do with me? You still haven't told me why I'm here?"

"Don't you see? You must give me those confessions so I can destroy them before they destroy us."

John's lips curled into a wry smile.

"Now I see why I'm here. You want me to hand over the confessions so you can do the right thing and destroy them?"

"Exactly. That will show the nobles they have nothing to fear, and that whatever was in them has gone forever."

"You really think it's that simple?" John asked. "You know better, Father. There will always be doubts and rumours that some survived and are being held back for leverage somewhere down the line. The finger of suspicion will never go away, not until everyone of this generation is dead. The confessions are a curse to whoever has them, and even if they no longer existed, the nobles would still believe they did."

"That is true, but if I destroyed them at the court, the nobles would see that I am genuinely trying to make amends for what Margaret did, and when they see their destruction, at least some trust can return."

John shook his head. "That won't happen, Father, and you know it. If you took them to court to destroy them, there would be schemes of all kinds to steal them and take them from you. Having the confessions is having power over the nobles and that is what they fear. If they weren't so corrupt and dirty, none of them would have anything to fear, would they?"

John saw the anger flash in his father's eyes. "I insist you hand the confessions over to me, so I can do the right thing." He almost spat the words out.

John rose to his feet.

"If that is why you ordered me here today, then you shall be disappointed, Father. I shall not give you the confessions any more than I shall give them to anyone else. You would do what everyone else would—you would destroy all those that reference you and use the rest as leverage against your enemies."

"How dare you?" Robert Howard thundered. It was obvious to John that he wasn't used to being challenged. But John wasn't backing down.

"I dare because I have suffered the most at the hands of Margaret Colte and her scheming allies. You are as complicit in my downfall as she was, and yet you sit here today telling me how difficult it is for you at court? Try living on the stretes for a year as a beggar and then we'll be even."

Robert's face flushed deep red, but John would not back down. There wasn't much love left between father and son.

"You realise that if I don't destroy those blasted confessions, then the nobles will most likely destroy me? I am doing this for your future, John. Yours and Sarah's."

"What about Arthur?" John was referring to his half-brother, who was the child born to Robert and Margaret in April 1536.

"What about Arthur? He isn't my son, and you know

that better than anyone. I wish he was, so I wouldn't have to put up with your insolence any longer, but Margaret made it very clear in her confessions that Arthur is the son of William Asheborne, not me. I shall raise him, but not as a Howard, and he cannot inherit my estates."

"Where is he?"

"He is safe, and that is all you need to know."

After a pause, Robert once again looked at John. "I need those confessions, son. They will be the death of both of us if we don't hand them over."

"I'm sorry, Father, but you have wasted your time if you thought I'd agree to hand them over to you. Half the nobles will die if I hand them over. They might be dangerous to us, but they are far more dangerous if we release them. They will remain hidden until long after we are all dead."

"Which won't be long if we don't act." Robert was almost pleading now.

Before either could speak again, the door opened, and Evans announced Lady Sarah Howard.

Sarah, tall and slender as she approached her fifteenth year, entered the room with all the regency befitting a lady of her stature. John adored his younger sister.

"John!" Sarah's bright hazel eyes lit up when she saw her brother. She ran over to him, her dark collar-length hair waving around behind her as she ran. "John, it's so good to see you."

After a brief hug, their father spoke up. "Please sit down, Sarah. I have some big news, and it concerns you."

They ate in silence, and John made a mental note to fill a bag of food for the others so they could all have a feast later that evening when they were safely back at the little white house.

Once the meal was over, Robert cleared everyone from the room except John and Sarah.

"Here's why I have brought you here today." Robert looked at John. "I have some good news to share, and I wanted you here to hear it first."

John sat in silence, exchanging glances with Sarah.

"There is to be a wedding," Robert announced after a suitable pause for dramatic effect.

"Oh, no," John groaned. "Please don't tell us you're getting married again, Father. I barely survived the last one."

Sarah giggled, but Robert threw a dark stare at his son.

"No, John. I'm not getting married. Sarah is."

The colour drained from Sarah's face when her father's words sank in.

John sat speechless, staring at their father.

"Sarah is soon to be fifteen, which is a good time for her to be married. We need her to provide a close alliance with another noble family, and her sons will bring unity where before there was animosity."

"Who are you marrying me off too, Father?"

John knew there was no point arguing with his father. Marriages were arranged all the time, and Sarah was the right age to be married. He just hoped it was someone they could all get along with.

"I have several in mind, and I shall choose the one I think is most suitable. I hoped that John would grace us with his presence in Broxley when the time comes."

"You want me there for the wedding, or for when you parade my sister to the highest bidders?" John felt sorry for Sarah, who he knew had no say in who she was to marry.

"You know how this works, John. This is how it's always worked. It would have been the same for you had circumstances been different."

"You mean if you hadn't tossed me out with the pig swill?"

Robert Howard's cheeks flushed again. "I shall not tolerate your insolence, John. Whatever happened between us, you are still my son, and you shall show me some respect."

John looked at Sarah and remained silent.

"When is this going to happen?" Sarah looked as if she was about to cry.

"It will take me a few months to arrange the wedding, but I am hoping for September."

"That's wonderful news, Father." John said, still holding Sarah's gaze.

Sarah sat and said nothing. After an awkward silence, she excused herself from the room. John stood up to follow her, but his father stopped him.

"Leave her to her thoughts for a while, John. You'll have time to speak to her later, for you must remain here for the night. We have more to discuss."

"I'm not giving you the confessions, Father, so there is nothing for us to discuss. I'd like to spend some time with my sister."

"Those confessions will be the death of us, but there is more to discuss than just them. Please, sit down."

John did as he was asked.

"Considering what happened yesterday, and because I know the reaction of the nobles, I would like to increase the guards who protect you. I know you trust Willis, but he is old and injured, and he won't be able to protect you in times of need. I propose to give you a dozen of my best men to take care of you, especially while you are here in London."

"Thank you, Father, but I have no need for extra

guards. Between myself and my friends, we are more than capable of taking care of ourselves."

"John, you are a nobleman by birth right. You are the heir to a substantial fortune and titles, and yet you live like a peasant, and it irks me so much. You allow stable boys to call you by your first name and let them live in the same rooms that you do. If the king finds out, he will punish you all for breaking sumptuary laws and the rules of nobility. Surely you don't want that to happen?"

"Of course not, but how will he find out if nobody tells him? Surely the king has much better things to do than wonder what I'm doing."

"You forget that we have many enemies, and they will grow stronger the longer you hold on to those confessions."

"Is that why you are marrying Sarah off now? So you can find noble allies that will stand by you?"

"Sarah is the right age for marriage, and you know that, John. It's the perfect time for her union, and it won't hurt us to have a few more allies on our side during these troubling times."

"I don't want any guards, thank you Father." John knew his father was right, so he changed the subject. "What news do you have of Saddleworth? I'd like to move there in the spring if possible."

Saddleworth Manor was the residence in Horsham, Sussex, that Robert had promised to purchase for John after their reconciliation a few months earlier. Ironically, it had once been the home of Margaret Colte before she'd unleashed her wrath on the Howard family.

"I am in final negotiations with the cousin of Lord Henry Colte, who is the guardian of the estate until Colte's son is old enough to take over. Once we complete the sale, I shall let you know."

"Thank you, Father. We are done here. Curfew will be

called soon, and we don't have time to get back to the white house before dark, but I'm staying with my friends wherever you have placed them. I shall not abandon my wife and friends."

John rose to leave the room.

"I need those confessions, John, and I shall have them."

John turned as if to say something and then turned away.

Chapter 7

William Asheborne paced around the ancient undercroft of his makeshift home in Yorkshire. Tall and athletic, with long brown hair and deep blue eyes, William looked nothing like his recently executed father, William Asheborne Senior, the deposed Duke of Berkshire.

The younger William Asheborne had foreseen the demise of his father and had warned him repeatedly about his close relationship with Margaret Colte, but his father hadn't listened. He never did. He was so used to giving orders that by the time he'd reached his final years, he'd completely given up listening to anyone.

And that had been his downfall.

William Junior considered himself smarter than his father. In fact, at twenty years old, he considered himself to be smarter than any other man alive, and he'd proven that when he'd taken the actions necessary to save himself during the last days of his father's life.

Over several weeks, he had secretly sent carriage loads of his family's wealth to his allies in the north so he wouldn't be penniless when the king inevitably confiscated his father's lands and estates after the trial.

In return for his father confessing his many sins, the king agreed not to charge his son with any crimes, although the good Lord knew he was just as guilty.

But Henry VIII had been far from benevolent with William Asheborne Junior. Stripped of his heritage, estates, and his wealth, William hadn't even been allowed to keep a single property for himself, leaving him homeless, and in the eyes of the crown at least, destitute.

But William was smarter than that.

He'd beaten the king at his own game.

An acquaintance of the duke had reached out and offered the hand of friendship in their darkest hour, and this is how William Asheborne Junior had ended up in the smallest town he'd ever heard of in the middle of nowhere in Yorkshire.

The manor house he called home—for now at least—was tiny by his standards, and it certainly didn't keep him to the levels of comfort he was accustomed to.

Originally built in the twelfth century during the Norman times, Erikson Hall, as its owner had proudly renamed it after his favourite Viking explorer, stood quiet and alone in large grounds outside of the town William could never remember the name of. Whatever Erikson Hall lacked in terms of comfort and prestige, it more than made up for in privacy and solitude, and it was the perfect place for Asheborne to hide out of sight while he regrouped and gathered the men who had remained loyal to his family.

Now he was ready, and he was impatient. He'd been in hiding for too long, and it was time to strike back at the hated Howard family and teach them a lesson they would never forget.

The sounds of horses disturbed the silence and echoed off the ancient walls of the undercroft. William ran up the spiral stairs into the largest room in the house on the first floor that was used as the great hall. He watched from the window as a carriage surrounded by a dozen horsemen approached the old house down the frozen lane.

A large fire crackled and roared in the centre of the room, and William warmed himself while he gazed around the great hall, wondering how many skilled knights of the past had stood in the same spot he was now occupying.

The present owner had added several windows, but otherwise it looked how William imagined it would have in its halcyon days. A high, wooden beamed ceiling towered overhead, and although the room was much smaller than the great hall at Whitehough Court—the sprawling mansion near Windsor that had been his family home for centuries until Henry VIII had taken it from them—it had a character that appealed to the masculine ego that William possessed in abundance.

The stone walls were bare, except for one large painting that adorned the wall directly opposite the fire-place. It depicted a nobleman with short legs and a long body wearing his armour on a great white horse. The noble warrior—for that was the image the painting was going to great lengths to depict—faced towards the artist, and he was instantly recognisable to anyone who knew of him.

The coat of arms was one William instantly recog-nised, and it left him wondering how the Tudor king would react if he saw it.

The nobleman carried a shield with a bright red back-ground with a large white rose painted in the centre. The rose had a gold centre with five green stalks spreading out from the middle to separate the petals of the rose at its outer edge.

This was the symbol of the House of York that had fought a thirty-year war with the House of Lancaster for the throne of England. Three of the Yorkist Plantagenets had held the crown before Henry Tudor, a nephew of the last Lancastrian king and father of the current king, ended the conflict at the battle of Bosworth in 1485 and united the houses once and for all with his marriage to Elizabeth of York in January 1486.

The painting troubled William because it went against everything he knew of the man it depicted, who was the current owner of Erikson Hall. His family had fought alongside Henry Tudor at the battle of Bosworth, and indeed, it was Henry VII who had granted the lands and titles he now possessed to his grandfather as a mark of gratitude for his service to him.

So why was this painting that supported the House of York, and by definition the Plantagenets, on full display in his great hall?

William wondered what Henry VIII would think if he knew of its existence.

Approaching footsteps dragged him back from his thoughts.

Chapter 8

Alexander Carlyle strode purposefully into the great hall like a man who enjoyed his own sense of power and purpose.

Not unlike my own father, then.

Carlyle cut an unusual sight, and William had to stifle a smile when he strutted into the room as if he owned it.

He did.

Of below average height, the forty-two-year-old Viscount Richmond had a rounded, clean-shaven face and brown hair that was cut unfashionably short. But that wasn't what made him an unusual sight. Alexander Carlyle had the shortest legs William had ever seen in an adult. He compared them to those of a child of perhaps seven or eight years old, but Alexander's body compensated by having an elongated torso that seemed to stretch for eternity, until his oversized, rounded head topped off what was the most unusual physical sight William had ever seen.

However, William knew better than to underestimate his friend and ally.

Well, I wouldn't exactly call him a friend. Ally is enough.

Carlyle had a reputation with those who knew him of being hot-tempered and ruthless. William had heard stories of servants and guards who had scoffed at his physical appearance and had been dragged outside and gutted for giving nothing more than a mere snigger when he walked into a room.

"Good afternoon, Alexander. I trust your journey here was uneventful?"

"It was long and boring, and I'm parched. Steward, fetch me some ale." Carlyle's voice was high-pitched and sounded more like a girl's than any man's William had ever heard.

William nodded at his steward to do as Carlyle requested. As the steward bowed and made his way from the room, Carlyle stepped forward and barred his way.

"When I give an order, Steward, I expect you to obey it. I don't want to see you look to your master for confirmation. This is my house, and while I am here, you will obey my orders. Do I make myself clear?"

"Yes, sir," the steward stammered. "I'm sorry, sir."

Carlyle looked at Asheborne as though he wanted him to say something, but he remained silent. There would be time to put Carlyle in his place later.

Once the ale arrived and they were alone, William turned to his benefactor.

"I trust we are ready to talk now?" He barely disguised his growing distrust of Alexander Carlyle.

"Are you not enjoying my hospitality, William?" Carlyle squeaked with his high-pitched voice.

"I am, Alexander, and I do not mean to sound ungrateful. You have given me shelter and protection and allowed me to gather both myself and my men at this location, which is the perfect place for such an endeavour."

"Then we are ready to proceed with our plans?" Asheborne's squeak filled the room.

"I am, or at least I would be if I knew what our plans actually were. You still haven't told me anything, and I don't even know why you are helping me. You realise you will lose everything if they catch you assisting me, including your life?"

"I am aware of the consequences, Asheborne, which is why we must ensure that we do not fail."

"Please forgive me, Alexander, but I have only survived this long because, unlike my father, I think before I act. I plan everything ahead of time and only then decide to act if the odds are in my favour. Although you have shown me kindness, I shall do nothing until I know exactly what our plans are and how it will benefit me. You have yet to tell me why you are risking so much to help, and until I know that, I'm sorry to say that we're not doing anything together."

Alexander Carlyle's piercing stare cut right through William and made him shudder. The only other person who made him so uncomfortable with his stare was Oswyn Gare, but he was an abomination that would make the devil himself uncomfortable.

Carlyle's top lip curled upwards, exposing his rotted teeth, and for a moment, William thought he was going to attack him.

"Straight to business, which is just how I like it." Carlyle's snarl turned into a smile. "I understand your reluctance, and I would feel the same if our roles were reversed. What do you want to know, my young friend?"

"Everything. Why did you offer to help me, and how does it benefit you? What do you have against the king and the Howard family to risk so much?"

"So many questions. Where would you like me to start?"

"Let's start with that painting." William pointed at the painting that had caused him so much confusion.

Carlyle looked at the painting and burst into a high-pitched laugh. "You noticed my painting then," he said. "I commissioned it many years ago and hung it on the wall here to remind me every time I see it, how the Tudor king and the scheming Howards betrayed my family. Believe it or not, I have waited for an opportunity such as this for a long time, and now you are here, we can work together to seek our revenge."

William took a moment for Carlyle's words to sink in. "You want me to help you bring down the king?"

"It would be the greatest pleasure of my life to see the usurper's son brought down and dethroned, but alas, I can't see any way to do that. No, my young friend, we are working together to bring down the Howard family and show them once and for all that they must pay their sins of the past in blood. By the time we're finished with them, they will repent every action they have ever taken."

"What do you have against the Howard family? And what does that have to do with this painting? Your family fought alongside Henry Tudor and the Lancastrians at Bosworth, and if my history is correct, it was Henry Tudor who granted the lands and titles here in Yorkshire to your grandfather for helping him win the battle."

"That is true. Your history is correct."

"Then why does the painting display the Yorkist crest? They were the enemy of the Tudors in that battle."

"Indeed, they were. I had that painting done to remind me of the injustices done to my family by Henry VIII and Robert Howard, not Henry VII, who remained true to his word throughout his life."

"Pray tell." William said. "If we are to be allies in the battles ahead, I need to know who I am fighting alongside."

"You are wise beyond your years, young Asheborne. Your father told me you'd be a great ally one day, and he was right. My father held the position as head of the king's privy council, which is the position Robert Howard now enjoys. I was promised that role after my father passed, and I spent most of my younger years preparing for it so I could serve our king to the best of my abilities. When my father died and the titles and estates passed down to me, I was summoned to the royal court for the king to bestow upon me the honour that was supposed to be mine. It was the proudest day of my life."

William watched as Carlyle clenched his fists and raised his shoulders in the manner that young boys do when they throw a temper tantrum.

"Instead," Carlyle continued, "it turned into the worst day of my life, and one that I shall never forget. Henry VIII laughed at me when he saw me. He actually laughed at me and mocked my physical appearance. After that, every noble in the court laughed alongside him, none more so than Robert Howard. Their mocking grew louder as I left the court, never to return. I heard Howard above all the rest, and when I returned home to Yorkshire, I learned Henry had appointed Robert Howard to the position promised to me." Carlyle's head dropped.

"I have never forgotten that day, and I vowed there and then I would have my revenge. The painting depicts which side my grandfather should have taken at Bosworth, especially as we are now noblemen in the county of Yorkshire. King Richard would never have betrayed me as Henry VIII did, but even if he had, Robert Howard wouldn't be where he is today. His family would have been defeated at

Bosworth and stripped of their wealth by Richard III, and he would live in exile, as I do today."

Alexander Carlyle looked into William's eyes.

"That is what the painting means to me."

A long silence followed as William digested what he'd just heard.

"The Howard family has a history of betraying other nobles for their own gain and benefit." William broke the silence. "Like father, like son. John Howard is no better than his father."

"Robert betrayed his own son, never mind what he did to me." Carlyle spat out Robert's name. "There are no limits to his depravity, and we must be avenged. I know you want revenge on the wayward son, but I want Robert Howard. Together, we can bring them both down and destroy the entire family."

William clasped hands with the older Alexander Carlyle. "Well, now we know the reasons we are here, have you any news of the Howard family? What plans do you have?"

"I do. And I have something that I think you'll recognise."

"What would that be?" William asked. "Is it the head of John Howard? Or maybe you've discovered the whereabouts of those infernal confessions the bitch left behind?"

"As it happens, I might be able to deliver both to you." Carlyle showed his rotted teeth again as his lips parted to form a sinister smile. "I have spies everywhere, as you well know. How else would I have known to reach out to you during your times of need?"

William opened his mouth to ask him how he'd known about that, but Carlyle cut him off with a wave of his hand.

"I have learned from a reliable source where John

Howard and his whore are living. He only has one old guard to protect him, and he refuses to allow his father to send more. He thinks this is all over now your father is dead. John Howard thinks he's safe."

"How do you know this?" Asheborne asked. "Is this fact, or merely speculation?"

Carlyle stared at his ally for a long moment before answering. "I'm not in the habit of making unfounded statements, and I never act on anything unless I know for certain the information is correct. Rest assured, my young friend, the information I give to you today is indeed accurate."

"You didn't tell me how you know about this." Asheborne pressed, although he knew he would not get a straight answer.

"I have my sources, and that's all you need to know."

"Where is he?" William asked. "Tell me and I shall be there."

"Have you gathered all your men together?" Carlyle asked. "If this is to work, we shall need them for what lies ahead."

"I have thirty loyal men waiting for my orders." Asheborne answered. "I have eleven in London, and the rest are here in Yorkshire. If that isn't enough, I'm sure you have more that would be happy to join us."

"That is more than enough for what I have in mind," Carlyle said. "But before I reveal my plans, I have one more thing for you."

"What is it?"

Carlyle raised his voice to a high-pitched shout. "Gardiner!" he yelled. "Gardiner, get in here."

The door opened, and one of Carlyle's guards entered the great hall. "Gardiner, bring him in," Carlyle ordered.

William Asheborne's eyes grew wide as Gardiner

stepped aside to allow the aberration to enter the great hall. He felt the colour drain from his face as the life was sucked out of the room when the man stepped forward.

The man—the devil was more appropriate—approached them wearing a monk's grey robes. He was small, but even under the robes, it was obvious to Asheborne, and no doubt to everyone else, that he was in perfect physical shape.

The dullest grey eyes he had ever seen stared straight through him as if sucking his soul from his body, and William shivered in fear and trepidation. A huge, fresh scar running down the left-hand side of his face made him look even more sinister, and William had to remind himself that he was only a man made of flesh and blood just like everyone else.

The scar was a wound the monk had picked up the previous year during the battles with John Howard and his friends at Burningtown Manor, when Gare had been sent by William's father to kill them. Asheborne knew the monk would relish another meeting with them.

William was staring into the face of death itself.

He was staring into the face of Oswyn Gare.

"How . . . ?" Asheborne's words trailed off as he forced himself to look away from Gare.

Anywhere but Gare.

"I told you I had spies everywhere," Carlyle said. "Did you think that you and your father were the only ones who knew of Gare's existence?"

"I . . . I . . ." William stammered. He was stunned. Gare was the closest kept secret he and his father had ever maintained. Or so he had thought.

"Gare has worked for me for a long time," Carlyle said, his voice raised in triumph. "Now he's here to work for both of us."

"Gare." William regained some of his composure. "It's good to see you again."

"Sir William." The monk nodded. He was never a man of many words.

Carlyle looked around the room and indicated for Gardiner to close the door.

"Now we're all here, it's time to outline our plans."

Chapter 9

The guard with the long, pointy nose watched in the cold early-morning fog as John and his band of misfits walked out of the gates and turned right onto the Stronde, towards the gated city. Visibility was poor, and Barton could only watch for a few minutes until the fog enveloped them and made them invisible.

Dawn had barely broken, although it was almost impossible to tell with the thick fog that looked as if the sky had fallen down to earth. The servants would soon start their day, and the chambermaids would get to work cleaning the bedchambers where the lord and his family slept.

Barton didn't have long.

Avoiding the stairs at the front of the house that were reserved for the family and their distinguished guests, Barton ran up the staircase reserved for the servants. He stopped on the second floor and turned along the narrow hallway, being careful to avoid making any sounds.

The hallway was dark, so Barton used a candle to light his way and make sure he entered the right room. The first door was the entrance to Lord Howard's bedchamber, so Barton took particular care to avoid making even the slightest sound as he crept past it.

The second door had been the entrance to Lady Margaret's bedchamber, but as that was now empty after her demise, Barton hurried to it and scanned the two doors on the opposite side of the narrow hallway.

Lady Sarah's was the first door, and John's was next to it. Being careful not to disturb the sleeping girl, Barton slipped into John Howard's room.

The first thing he did was make sure the dividing door between John and Sarah's chambers was closed, and then he got to work.

The room didn't look like anyone had disturbed it since the last time it had been cleaned.

Did Howard even sleep in here last night?

Barton cursed under his breath. He'd been certain that John would have slept here. *If not here, then where?*

Barton slapped himself on the forehead. Of course! The nobleman-turned-peasant would have stayed with his friends last night, and as the lord wouldn't allow them on this floor, John would have slept wherever they were.

The stupid mumper should have done what he was supposed to have done and slept in 'ere. Now I'm not goin' to find anything.

Leaving no trace that he'd been in John's room, Barton searched under the bed, in the bed, in the drawers, and even behind the curtains. He checked for loose floorboards where documents could be hidden but found nothing.

Damn his blood!

The messenger Barton had met with two days prior had been adamant that John would try to conceal the confessions in his bedchamber after his meeting with his father. From what the messenger had told him, their master was certain the Howard boy was about to release some more of the confessions that would further hurt the nobility, and Barton had to steal them before they were released.

Wherever they are, they aren't here.

Barton slid into the hallway and got away from the bedchambers before he lost his life for stealing from Lord Howard.

Chapter 10

Driving sleet stung John's face as he led the way back towards the city. The freezing fog was so dense he couldn't see more than a few footsteps ahead. His teeth chattered, and he buried his head as deep into his hood as he could.

Fletestrete was nigh on deserted, and John could understand why. Nobody would be out on such a cold morn unless they had urgent business. Sleet and ice lit up the dull early morning, and John was sure it would have been a pretty sight if it hadn't been so cold. His fingers stung, and his feet felt like ice.

The wind was ferocious, and it drove the sleet through every small gap in his clothing. He turned his back to the driving wind to get some relief and looked into the eyes of his beloved Catherine.

What he saw broke his heart.

Catherine was sobbing quietly to herself, and although she buried her head deep inside her hood, John could see from the look in her eyes how much she was suffering. He slowed down to allow her to catch up to him, and when she did, he held her close so he could share what little body warmth he had left.

"This must be the coldest day in history," Catherine proclaimed through her frozen jaw.

"Not quite," John said. "But it's close. I think we were colder when we jumped into the river in Malton. What say you, boys?" John looked behind Catherine at the frozen figures of Edward Johnson and Stephen Cullane.

"Aye," Edward said. "I thought I was going to die that day."

"Me too," Stephen joined in. "Although we'll die this day if we don't hurry and get in front of a fire."

"I don't need eyes to know where we are," Edward said. "That stinking river is right ahead of us. I'm surprised we couldn't smell it from your father's house."

John knew exactly what he meant. The River Fleet was the foulest smelling river he'd ever encountered, and even when it was frozen solid and covered over with several inches of thick ice, the stench still penetrated his nostrils worse than the corpse of a decaying animal rotting in the summer heat.

"Fleet Bridge must be somewhere close by." Catherine's teeth chattered. "And then Ludgate. Please hurry, John, and get us home, for I fear I can't stand much more of this."

John smiled at the innocence Catherine still possessed, even after all she had been through since he'd met her. It was one of the many things that he loved so dearly about her.

"My dearest Catherine," he said. "The fog is so thick that you missed the bridge several minutes ago. We walked right over it and you never noticed. The city gates are right ahead of us."

John was correct. The combination of the thick fog

and driving sleet made the visibility so bad that Catherine had completely missed the manned bridge they'd crossed several minutes earlier.

"I'm too cold to care," she said, ignoring John's sarcastic grin.

As he spoke, the loud ringing of bells suddenly disrupted the early morning quiet. It was the familiar signal that told the people of London curfew was over.

John and his frozen comrades entered the city through Ludgate and then skipped through the grounds of St Paul's, saving some time. It took a moment or two to find Watelyng Strete through the sheets of sleet and fog, but they found it and walked down the normally thriving strete that would usually be alive with the sounds of men shouting and horses clattering on the rough cobbles.

But today it was silent.

A few hardy souls were out, but their horses were walking so slowly they were barely moving. The men didn't dare drive them any faster for fear of crashing into some unseen obstacle in front of them.

Catherine let out a loud yelp and fell. John caught her, but not before she'd hit the ground.

"Are you alright?" he gasped through frozen teeth.

"I'm fine. I slipped on the ice. Get me home, John Howard, and don't ask me to leave the house again until springtime."

"As you command, my lady." John helped Catherine to her feet. "Not long to go now. We're almost there."

Keeping to the side of the strete to get shelter from the overhanging eaves of the houses, John slowed down to make sure he didn't walk right past his own house. He knew the next junction would be Soperlane, and that was his cue to tell Catherine they had made it home.

"We're here," he announced finally. "We made it. I bet

there's a warm fire waiting for us inside." He squeezed Catherine's frozen hand.

Soperlane was a narrow lane that was normally filled with the signs of London life, but this morn it was eerily quiet.

Almost deathly quiet.

John flinched. *Something's wrong.*

Sensing it more than feeling it, the hackles on John's back rose, and suddenly he forgot his frozen hands and feet. Several sets of footprints in the frozen landscape disturbed the otherwise-untouched area around the gates at the rear of the little white house, and all of them either went in or came out from that direction.

John looked at Edward and Stephen, who indicated that they, too, had seen it. John leant into Catherine and whispered in her ear.

"I know you don't want to hear this, but something isn't right. Those footprints are all leading in and out of our home. Stay here, outside the gates, until I come for you and tell you it's safe."

"What do you think happened?" Catherine asked, her eyes fixed on John. "I want to go in there with you."

"It's probably nothing, but we have to be careful. We'll only be a few moments and then I'll come for you."

Catherine nodded and stepped aside. John looked at her, admiring her strength and courage. She was frozen to the core, and yet she didn't make a single complaint. John loved Catherine with all his heart.

Forcing himself away from his beloved, John stepped towards Stephen and Edward, who had both drawn their swords.

"Stephen, check the stables," John ordered. "Edward and I will check the house. It's probably Edmund and

Thomas, but by the looks of the footprints, there were at least eight or nine people here."

"More than that," Edward said. "They are coming and going, and when they left, they split up. Look at the footprints."

Edward pointed at the fresh footprints in the frozen sleet going in different directions, all heading away from the rear gates of the little white house. "Some go up Soperlane while others went towards Watelyng Strete. Edmund or Thomas made none of these."

"He's right," Stephen agreed with Edward. "These were not made by our boys."

John drew his sword. "We need to be careful, then." He looked at Catherine huddled at the side of the gate and took a deep breath.

John pushed the gates just wide enough to squeeze through and stepped inside the courtyard.

The fog was so thick that John couldn't see either the stables or the rear of the house. It made for excellent cover, but it also gave whoever was there an advantage as well.

John watched Stephen vanish into the mist and then silently made his way to the rear of the house. The door leading into the house was wide open, so John took a deep breath and stepped inside, his sword at the ready. He indicated that Edward should go to their left, towards the kitchens and the rooms where Edmund and Thomas lived.

John turned to his right and walked down the narrow corridor towards the largest room at the end, where there would normally be a roaring fire waiting for them.

The two doors along the corridor were both closed, and John slowly opened them as he got to them. Wet footprints and melted ice told him that whoever had paid them a visit had been in these empty rooms.

He moved on towards the parlour at the end of the corridor. The door was closed, but he knew as soon as he opened it that he was going to regret it. The sweet, sickly smell of blood hit his senses before he saw it, and even though he knew it was coming, it did not prepare him for what he saw.

The room had been ransacked. Items that were on the solid oak table lay scattered all over the floor, and the paintings that only a few hours earlier had adorned the walls had been torn down and shattered. Whoever had been here had been searching for something, and John knew exactly what it was.

Margaret's confessions!

His mind briefly wandered to the hiding place where he'd stored the confessions relating to Isobel, but only for a split second before the image that overwhelmed his senses came into view, forcing him to lurch forward and vomit all over the straw covered floor.

John closed his eyes and took a deep breath. He forced himself to approach the body that was laid out on top of the oak table. Whoever it was looked as though he had been sacrificed to one of the ancient gods.

Except he hadn't. Only one person on earth could be responsible for such evil, and he'd been here, in John's house this very morn.

Oswyn Gare!

John looked more closely at the mutilated body stretched out across the table and let out a stifled cry. It was Willis, his trusted guard, and the man who had helped him so many times during his struggles with Margaret.

Willis.

John fell to his knees and rocked back and forth. He threw himself forward, vomiting for all he was worth over the floor. When he stood up, he forced himself to look at the evil that had been perpetrated on his loyal guard.

Willis's clothes had been torn from his body, leaving him exposed and humiliated in front of his attackers. John knew it had taken several men to do this to Willis. He may have been weakened from his injuries, but Willis was no easy target for any man.

Any man, that is, except Oswyn Gare.

His chest had been ripped open, and his heart and entrails lay on the table by his side. There was more, but John couldn't look any further. He closed his eyes and prayed. Poor Willis had been tortured so terribly that it was beyond imagination.

How can any man be capable of such a thing?

But Gare wasn't a man. He was the devil himself.

John felt his stomach convulsing and threw up once again.

Knowing he'd made too much noise not to be heard, John threw caution to the wind. He ran out of the parlour and charged up the narrow staircase, screaming and shouting for all he was worth.

"Gare, where are you? Come out now, you evil villein. Come out from where you are and face me. You're a coward, hiding in the shadows and attacking innocent old men and women. Come out and die like the devil you are."

John shouted as loud as he could, but his voice was broken and disjointed. Through his grief, he could barely get a coherent word out.

He ran from room to room, and each of them looked the same. Someone had ransacked every room and smashed them almost beyond recognition. Whoever had been with Gare had obviously been angry they couldn't find the confessions.

When he entered the room at the far end of the corridor, a shadow approached him. John screamed a deep, guttural scream and ran headlong at the intruder.

"John, stop. It's me, Stephen!"

John didn't hear him. He screamed even louder and threw himself at the aberration in front of him.

A large hand caught John from behind him and yanked him back with the hood of his cloak. The hand wrapped around his neck, and he felt warm breath in his ear.

"John, it's Edward and Stephen. Stop what you're doing and look around you."

Edward loosened his grip, and John stood there, dazed and confused. He stared at Stephen in front of him.

"What happened down there?" Stephen asked. "The stables were empty, so I came over here, and the next thing I knew you were charging at me like a crazed animal."

John sank to his knees again.

"Down there, in the parlour." His voice cracked again. "Willis."

Stephen looked quizzically at Edward, who was standing over John.

"Gare has been here," Edward said. "I found Edmund and Thomas in the kitchen, and John obviously found Willis."

"Gare has been here?" Stephen spat out the words.

John's composure slowly returned, and he felt the colour slowly coming back to his face. "You are correct, Edward. It had to have been Gare, because no other creature on earth could have committed the evil that was perpetrated here today."

"It happened only a short while ago," Edward said. "The bodies of Edmund and Thomas are still warm, so we must have only just missed them."

"I bet they waited until first light to attack," Stephen said. "We must have missed them by minutes."

"Then we have no time to waste." John ran out of the room and down the stairs. "If we hurry, we might stop them before they disappear again."

Stephen and Edward ran after him.

Chapter 11

John charged out of the gates at the rear of the house, closely followed by Edward and Stephen. Catherine ran to him, frozen to the bone and looking for all the world like she was about to freeze to death.

"Go inside and get warm," John barked his orders. "But whatever you do, stay away from the kitchen and the parlour. Gare has been here, and you don't want to see what he's done. Go to one of the empty rooms we don't use and wait for us to return."

"What happened? I want to . . ."

"Please do as I ask," John spoke quickly. "They might still be in the area, and we have to find them."

Edward had already gone, following the frozen footsteps heading up Soperlane. Stephen was waiting impatiently for John to join him in the other direction.

John turned from Catherine and ran into the thick frozen mist. He followed the footsteps to the end corner of the house and turned right on Watelyng Strete to follow them.

The stretes were coming to life in the early morning

fog. Footsteps left behind in the ice and sleet came and went in every direction, and it was impossible to follow any single set. John ran as fast as he could, only stopping to approach anyone he came across to make sure it wasn't Gare.

Stephen crossed the strete and checked the people on the other side, but the fog was so thick that anyone who wanted to remain unseen would have found it easy to do so. John ran as far as Ludgate before turning north and running to Newgate.

Nothing.

John sighed and stopped running. He knew he wasn't going to find Gare this day. His thoughts turned to Catherine all alone in the house. What if Gare hid somewhere close by and saw them leave her behind?

Now panicked, John ran as fast as he could through the slippery ice, hoping and praying that Catherine was safe and sound.

By the time he skidded around the corner of Soper-lane, the sleet had turned into heavy snow. It was so cold that the snowflakes were freezing on John's clothing the moment they touched, and yet he hardly even noticed.

He ran through the gates and into the rear of the house.

"Catherine!" he yelled at the top of his voice. "Catherine, where are you?"

He stopped to listen for her calling, but his heart was beating so fast he couldn't hear anything over its roar. "Catherine, it's me, John."

Still nothing.

Now panicking, John ran down the corridor towards the parlour where the mutilated corpse of Willis lay waiting. He crashed into the two empty rooms he'd been in before, but there was no sign of Catherine.

Images of Gare torturing Catherine flooded John's mind, and his heart raced even faster. His skin was on fire, and his panicked state set his soul ablaze.

"Catherine!" he yelled repeatedly.

Nothing.

He ran into the room where Willis lay and shivered as the sight of his mutilated guard came into view. Surely Catherine wouldn't be hiding in here?

She wasn't.

He ran down the corridor towards the kitchens and searched the room where the stable boys laid their heads.

Empty.

He ran into the kitchen, and the sight of Edmund and Thomas filled his senses once again with sorrow and loathing. Like Willis, they had been stripped and mutilated.

John could look no more. He felt the familiar feeling of nausea returning, and he bent over and threw up for the umpteenth time that day.

He staggered out of the kitchens and ran upstairs, shouting Catherine's name over and over.

Nothing.

Every room was ransacked and destroyed, but John didn't care. All he wanted to see was his beloved Catherine, safe and sound.

But she wasn't anywhere to be found.

In full-blown panic, John raced down the stairs and ran across the courtyard to the stables. As soon as he entered, he heard voices from the far end where he'd hidden the confessions he'd brought back from the crypts two days earlier.

Afraid of what he might see, John hurried to the last of the eight stalls and peered inside, his sword raised and ready to kill whatever vermin Gare had left behind.

Catherine was sitting on top of the horse dung and

used straw. Edward was sitting next to her, his arm around her shoulders, comforting her as best he could. Her face was as white as the snow outside, and although she had seen John, her eyes didn't register his presence.

She must have seen the atrocities that Gare had committed in their home.

John fell to his knees and gathered Catherine's frozen hands in his. He rubbed them, trying to get her to respond, but all she did was stare through him like he wasn't there.

"I found her sitting under the table in the parlour." Edward spoke flatly. "I brought her over here because she refused to stay in the house once I'd coaxed her out from under the table. She's in shock, John. I've seen it before in the midst of battles."

John nodded. "Thank you for your help, my friend. I'll see to her from here. Perhaps you can find Stephen and inform the sheriff what happened here this day."

Edward nodded and left the stables.

John sat next to Catherine and placed his arm around her. She laid her head on his shoulder, and they sat in silence for several minutes. Eventually, Catherine moved her head and turned to face her husband.

"What kind of man can do such things? Poor Willis. John, he was . . ." Her voice cut off as she sobbed.

"Gare isn't a man," John said. "He's an aberration. He's the devil himself. Whatever else I do in this life, I shall not rest until he and the rest of the men who were here this morn are all dead. Gare must be stopped, and I vow to do it, even if it means my own death."

"I can't stay here." Catherine turned to face John. "After what happened, I can't ever come here again. I don't care where we live, but it won't be here."

"I know," John said. "They have forever tainted this

house with the blood of a great man and two innocent boys. It isn't our home anymore."

"Where will we go?" Catherine asked.

"I don't know. I haven't had time to think about that yet."

A plan was forming in John's mind, but he didn't have the heart to tell Catherine what he was thinking.

Chapter 12

After such gruesome murders, John knew the Sheriff would have his men swarming all over the little white house for days, and by the time he'd finished his investigations, the house would be as empty as the day he had moved in.

Edward and Stephen would return soon with the Sheriff, so John didn't have long. He piled some fresh straw against the wall outside the last stall in the row of eight and sat the shocked Catherine down so he could keep her in his sights.

He got to work moving the horse muck and dirty straw out of the way. Catherine sat and watched, but her eyes looked a million furlongs away. John knew he would have to be careful with her for the next few days while she processed what she had seen.

Gare and his men hadn't found the confessions because the stables hadn't been ransacked. *Why was that? Had the men been disturbed somehow? Did they come here to murder us all or to find the confessions?*

Or both?

How did they even know we lived here?

John had more questions than answers, but his priority was to find Isobel's confessions and get Catherine to safety. The questions could wait until later.

He dug out the pile of crap to expose the stone with the metal ring through it and threaded the rope through the middle. Catherine watched as he pulled as hard as he could, and she sat staring as the stone lifted, exposing the small hiding place below. John retrieved the confessions and hid them inside his cloak.

He'd just about put the stall back to how it looked normally when he heard the gates to the courtyard swing open with a loud creak, as the hinges protested against the severe cold weather.

"Don't move," John ordered Catherine. "Stay here where it is warmer, and as soon as the Sheriff is done, we'll leave here, never to return."

Catherine stared at the wall.

"Catherine, do you hear me?"

She nodded and bit the top of her lips that had chapped from the biting weather.

"Do not go outside these stables until I come and get you."

Catherine nodded again.

Four horses thudded into the courtyard, the echoes that normally bounced off the cobbles muffled by the heavy snow and ice. The man in the lead slid off his horse and approached John.

"You must be the infamous John Howard?" The man spoke with a deep voice that was full of authority. He was tall, but John couldn't see his face or eyes, as they were buried deep inside the hood of his cloak.

"I'm Sheriff Holley, and your men have told me a tale that's almost unbelievable. In fact, I wouldn't have believed it until they mentioned your name. When John Howard is involved, anything is possible."

"A pleasure to meet you, Sheriff Holley. Let's go inside the house and get out of the nasty weather." John spoke in his best cultured nobility voice. It was a voice that superseded the authority of the Sheriff and reminded him he was the son of a powerful earl.

"Yes, sir. That's a good idea." The Sheriff sounded immediately less commanding. "Constable, put the horses in the stables and then join us in the house."

The other three men with the sheriff did as they were commanded, while John led the way inside the rear door of his home. Edward and Stephen followed close behind.

"I'll warn you, Sheriff, that what you're about to see is evil beyond compare, and you must steel yourself before you see it."

"Master Howard, I have seen more violence than even you during my life, and I assure you that nothing can bother me anymore."

"As you wish, Sheriff. I just wanted to warn you."

The Sheriff pulled the hood of his cloak from his head, revealing a man in his thirties with long black hair not unlike John's, and a kindly face with brown eyes that darted around the room taking everything in. John knew he was dealing with a competent man who took his role seriously —which made him happy, because he wanted the outrage that had happened here to be felt throughout the city.

"Your men told me quite a story, Master Howard. Perhaps you can tell me again before we see for ourselves."

"Indeed, Sheriff. Last night, my men and I, along with my wife, Catherine Howard, who is waiting in the stables until we are done here, spent the night with my father and sister at our London home in the Stronde. My guard, Willis, and the two stable boys I employ remained here.

When we returned this morning, we walked into what you see here today."

"Did you see anything after you returned?"

"Several sets of footprints coming in and out of the rear gates, but that was all. My men and I split up and tried to find those responsible, but the heavy fog and sleet made it impossible."

"Do you have any idea who would do this to you? I suspect that after what happened last year, you have many enemies who have good reason to kill you."

"Good reason, Sheriff? What are you trying to imply?"

"Nothing, sir, and please accept my apology for my poor choice of words. I merely meant that you must have enemies out there who would want to see you dead."

"I am innocent of all the charges ever made against me, and you know that as well as anyone, Sheriff, and you would do well to remember that in the future. I know exactly who did this today, and I also know why."

"Pray tell, Master Howard."

"You are aware of the confessions my stepmother left behind, and I know you must have heard the rumours about what they contain. Every nobleman in England is worried that she revealed some dark secrets they would rather remain hidden. That is good enough reason powerful people would want to see me dead, but this is different, as you shall see. Only one man is capable of such horrors, and his name is Oswyn Gare. He worked for Lord Asheborne, and is probably now working for his son, who no doubt wants revenge for his father's death. Killing me, and taking the confessions were Gare's orders when the duke was alive, and I suspect they are the orders his son is now continuing."

"Do you have any proof of this?"

"They executed the duke for his crimes. What further

proof do you need? Gare murdered good people in the exact same manner last year, so it won't be difficult to tie him to these as well."

"What about the duke's son? Do you have any proof that he ordered this attack today?"

"No, I don't. I don't even know where he is after the king confiscated all his estates, but he's the only one I know who has access to Oswyn Gare and who also has good reason to want to unleash such evil on us."

"Who is this Gare you speak of? I heard rumours of animalistic brutality, but I never believed it. I thought it was like the rest of the story—exaggerated and made up."

"Believe what you like, Sheriff. You are about to see for yourself that it was neither made up nor exaggerated."

The Sheriff's men joined them in the small room on the ground floor.

"Am I to be allowed to see the crime scenes?" Sheriff Holley asked impatiently. "We have work to do here."

"I warn you, Sheriff. What you are about to see is inhuman, and we must stop Gare without delay."

John led the way to the parlour at the end of the narrow corridor where Willis lay mutilated. Stephen and Edward waited outside, but when the sheriff and his men entered the room, experienced men who had seen the results of many violent crimes during the course of their duties, fell forwards and heaved for all they were worth.

The constables ran out of the parlour, and Sheriff Holley looked pale and shaken. John watched as he closed his eyes and wretched, again and again. He didn't blame him, because he was doing the same thing, and he'd seen it several times by now.

He knew he never wanted to see the likes of this ever again.

"What kind of creature commits a crime like this?"

Sheriff Holley thundered after he regained some of his composure. "This is inhuman and a crime against God himself."

"I warned you," John said. "Only one man is capable of such a crime, and I know this because I've seen it before. Oswyn Gare did this to the Stanton family at a place called Burningtown Manor in the Midlands last year, when he was trying to kill me and my men. Verify it for yourself if you must, but I'm telling you the truth. We must stop Gare before he does this to someone else."

Sheriff Holley swallowed hard. "You say there are more like this?"

"My two stable boys in the kitchen. Young innocent boys who did nothing more than live here with us."

"And they were mutilated in the same way?"

"Worse, actually. See for yourself."

John could see that Sheriff Holley would rather not see for himself, but he had no choice.

Holley stopped on the way out of the room and spoke to his men. "This is an act of the devil himself. Send for the carriage to remove the bodies, but we need a priest to rid the house of the evil that was perpetrated here."

His men looked more than happy to find a reason to leave. John gestured for Holley to lead the way to the kitchen, and when they got there, John waited outside with Edward and Stephen.

It was too much for the Sheriff. A loud noise came from deep within his throat, and he forced his way past John, running out to the courtyard as fast as he could. He fell in the snow, praying hard between throwing his guts up.

"What kind of man does this?" he wailed. "I have never seen the likes of this in my entire life."

"I tried warning you, Sheriff. Gare is the evillest man there ever was, and he needs to be stopped."

"Rest assured, Master Howard. This Gare, or whoever you say did this, shall be stopped if it's the last thing I ever do. I shall dedicate my life to finding this monster and bringing him to justice."

"I'm glad we agree," John said. "Because that is the declaration I make before God. I shall never rest until we bury this evil monster in unconsecrated ground where he belongs, and where he can rot in hell."

"Do you have any idea where he is?" Holley asked.

"No, I'm afraid we don't. We have searched everywhere for him, and in fact, my men here spent all winter searching for the villein. The only thing we know is that he goes around wearing the robes of a monk, but as you can see, Oswyn Gare is no messenger of God."

"What does he look like? Does he have any outstanding features that would help me recognise him?"

"Believe me, you will know when you see him. His very gaze makes your soul shudder. He has cruel grey, lifeless eyes that suck the life from your body with just a glance, and believe me, Sheriff, I am not exaggerating. He's not a tall man, but he's extremely agile and strong, so don't let his lack of height fool you. Gare is the most dangerous man I've ever encountered, and he kills for the enjoyment of it."

"After what I've seen here today, I believe you, Master Howard. Is there anything else you can tell me about him?"

"He would have a fresh scar on his face from here to here," Stephen said, running his finger down the length of the left side of his face. "Edward did that to him last summer at Burningtown, right after Gare had murdered his wife and unborn child."

Sheriff Holley bowed his head. "All this is very useful information. Rest assured, gentlemen, that we will do all we can to find this evil man. The king himself will hear about this. I will make sure of it."

"Thank you, Sheriff," John said. "We are here to help in any way we can. Maybe together we can stop him before he does it again."

Sheriff Holley rose to his feet. "Where will you go? You need to be somewhere close so we can carry out our investigation. I ask that you do not leave London until we are done with this."

"You can reach me at my father's house on the Stronde. It's Lord Howard's residence, and you can't miss it."

"I know where it is," Holley answered. "And you will remain there?"

"I can be contacted there. As for my whereabouts, I shall keep those private because whoever was helping Gare today has a long reach, and I am not giving myself up that easily. I shall remain hidden where my wife and friends are safe, but rest assured, Sheriff, we shall remain in London. We are more committed than you to bringing Gare and his masters down, wherever they may be. As I said, you can reach me at my father's residence."

"Do you need protection? I can assign some of my best men to you until this is over."

"I appreciate the offer, but we are fine as we are. My father employs many competent guards should I need them, and my friends and I are more than capable of taking care of ourselves."

"So I hear, Master Howard, but we are not dealing with any ordinary man. We are dealing with the devil himself."

"Indeed, we are, which is even more reason we must work alone so we can act fast and catch him."

"Very well, Master Howard, as you wish. I shall be in touch, but in the meantime, please stay safe, all of you."

John watched as Sheriff Holley left the courtyard.

"What now?" Stephen asked. "Where do we look for this devil?"

"We need to stay in London to pay our respects and bury our dead," John said. "But first we need to talk. Wait in one of the empty rooms while I get Catherine and then we'll decide what we're going to do."

Chapter 13

Edward, who'd remained silent while the sheriff was at the scene, spoke up. "I don't know what you are planning, but I know what I'm doing. Gare killed my wife and unborn child, as well as Master Stanton and his wife. Now he has killed Willis, Edmund, and Thomas. I shall not rest until I lay him dead before my feet."

John looked at the pale faces as they sat in a circle on the straw in the first empty room on the ground floor. Catherine was the palest of them all, and her eyes looked vacant and empty as John squeezed her hand, trying to get her to join in the conversation and show that she was still with them.

He waited for a response to his touch, but there was none. She just stared at the wall, seemingly oblivious to everything that was going on around her.

John closed his eyes and took a deep breath. "I understand, Edward, and that is how we all feel, but first we must remain safe and recover from the shock of what he's done. Catherine especially."

Catherine never moved. She just stared at the wall in front of her.

"How did he know where we were?" John spoke the questions that were swirling around in his mind. "Was he hoping we'd all be here so he could kill us all at the same time? And what about the confessions? He must have been looking for them by the state of the house. Every room is destroyed, and even the floorboards are ripped up, so it's obvious they were searching for the confessions while Gare was doing the killing."

"Who is he working for?" Stephen asked. "Is it Lord Asheborne's son? He'd be the obvious one. If he is, where is he? Where did Asheborne go after he left London? If we find him, then we might find Gare."

"I think he came here this morn because the thick fog gave him the cover he wanted," John said. "Someone like Gare can't walk around a city like London unnoticed, so the heavy fog, along with the sleet and snow, gave him the best cover he could hope for, and that's why he attacked today. He probably thought we'd be home like everyone else, because nobody in their right mind would venture out in such conditions. And we would have been here if we hadn't stayed so late at the Stronde last night and missed curfew."

"I wish we were here." Edward slapped his oversized palm on the ground, causing dust and straw to rise in a small dark cloud. "It would be him laid dead on the parlour table and not poor Willis."

Still, Catherine said nothing.

"Willis was a good and loyal man who did more than most to help me," John said. "I shall never forget him."

"So, what do we do?" Stephen asked. "We can sit around feeling sorry for ourselves and mourn our lost friends, or we can stand together and avenge them. Which is it to be?"

"We stand and fight," Edward said. "We find the devil and kill him. I shall kill him with my own bare hands."

"I agree with both of you, and of course that is what we shall do," John said. "But we can't run around blindly, or we'll be easy targets. We need to be smart about it and find where they're hiding. Then we attack."

"I hate to ask," Stephen said, looking at John sheepishly. "And please don't take it as an insult, but do you think your father was involved? After all, it seems strange that the one night we aren't here is the night Gare attacked. With us gone, he could kill Willis, Edmund, and poor Thomas, who had never hurt a soul in his life, and he had the freedom to search for the confessions. If we'd been here, there would have been a fierce battle, and Gare knew that. He might be evil, but he isn't stupid."

John stared at Stephen for the longest time, weighing up what he'd just said.

"Your idea isn't without merit, and don't think it hasn't crossed my mind as well, but as much as my father doesn't approve of my life choices, I doubt even he would go this far. And I certainly don't think he'd associate himself with someone as evil as Gare. He would be happier if you two were dead, of that, I'm sure. Maybe even Catherine, although he would never dare say it out loud. But he wouldn't allow Gare to do what he did to Willis and the boys. That much I know to be true."

"How sure?" Stephen pressed. "It's not good if we have an enemy within who's reporting our every move to Asheborne or whoever is controlling Gare."

"I'm sure," John said.

"Nobody controls that animal," Edward snorted. "He is beyond even God's control."

John bowed his head and grasped Catherine's limp hand. He led them in prayer, reciting his words in the Latin language he'd learned as a child during the happy phase of his life at Broxley Hall in the Midlands.

"Amen," they all said together after he'd finished.

The atmosphere had lifted a little, but it did nothing to lift the dark mood of the four stunned and spiritually wounded friends huddled together in a circle on the floor of their little white house.

"I'll confront my father and see what he has to say," John said. "I'm sure he's not behind this, although I don't know how much he'll support us, either."

"Where do we look for the evil monk?" Edward asked.

John looked at Edward and felt relief that he was with them. Edward was built for battle and was as loyal as any man could be. Big and strong, and with the heart of a lion, Edward was a skilled warrior that was a match for any man.

But Gare wasn't a man, or at least that was the impression everyone got from his grotesque deeds. But John knew better, and he was determined to prove it.

"Gare might be evil, but he's still flesh and blood, like the rest of us. A blade will kill him just as surely as it would kill us. And that's what we keep in mind as we seek him out. Treat him like any other adversary we've faced, and we will conquer him. If we don't, and think him not human, we will lose our heads."

"I shall conquer him," Edward said. "But I have to find him first."

John shook his head. "I honestly do not know where to look for him. For all his evil deeds, he knows how to hide. He seems to vanish into the night like snow melting on the ground, and he only shows himself again when there is more killing to be done."

"If they came for the confessions, then surely they'll be back," Stephen said. "They didn't find them, so Asheborne will probably send him again? He won't rest until they are found."

"Assuming it is Asheborne's son, of course," John said. "But Gare only appears when they want to send a message of fear and hopelessness. They've already done that, so the next time they come, it will be someone with a little more guile if all they want are the confessions."

"Unless Asheborne thinks he can kill us at the same time," Stephen said.

"Perhaps," John said. "But whoever was behind this will keep their heads down for a while now to allow the hatred and disbelief to die down. The nobility, and even the king, will be horrified at what happened here, and the king will make sure that a man like Gare can't run around England dismembering people like he does."

"So, how do we draw them out?" Edward asked.

"I don't know," John shook his head.

"It's in the confessions." Catherine spoke for the first time.

They all stared at her.

"What is?" John asked.

"The answers must be somewhere in the confessions," she repeated. "Why else would whoever sent them have them tear up the place as they did? They might have wanted us dead, but not as much as they wanted the confessions. Find the right confession, and you will find whoever is behind this."

John stared at his wife for a moment and then leaned forward and kissed her on the cheek. "Welcome back, my love. You are the smartest of all of us. Of course, you are correct. Why else would they go to such lengths to find the confessions? The only other possibility is that Asheborne's son wanted revenge, but if that was all he was after, he wouldn't have searched for the confession so heavily."

Silence fell for several minutes while they all thought about what to do next. Finally, John broke the deadlock.

"I have a plan. You might not like it, but it's where we must start." He stared at the faces looking back at him.

"We need to hide out of the way in case Gare comes for us again. We can't be caught unawares twice, and the next time we need to be ready for them. So, we can't stay here, and I don't trust my father enough to ask for his help. We must return to the crypts for our own safety."

"Then what?" Stephen asked.

"We search through the confessions until we find whoever is behind this, unless it really is Asheborne's son just seeking revenge. In the meantime, I will speak to my father and see what he has to say for himself."

"We have a plan," Edward said. "It's not much of one, but it's better than nothing."

"That's not all," John said. "Whoever it was might return here to continue their search. They left the stables untouched, and I don't know why. I suspect they saw us returning and left before we could stop them. If they come back, we need to be ready."

"So, we are staying here?" Stephen asked. "Make your mind up. We either stay or we don't."

"I'm not staying here," Catherine said. John noticed the colour had started to return to her face, and her eyes were not staring into the distance too much.

She was coming back to him.

"No, we're not staying here," John said. "The three of us need to take it in turns hiding in the tree behind the wall at the rear of the house. If they come back, we can follow them and see where they go."

"Do we have to go to the crypts?" Catherine asked. "Isn't there anywhere else we can hide?"

"I don't know of a safer place anywhere in England," John said. "We won't be there for long, and it isn't like last time when everyone in England thought we were murdering criminals. This time the authorities are helping us, so we'll only be there as long as it takes to find Gare and whoever is behind him."

"That's settled then." Edward stood up. "I'll take first watch in the tree."

The subdued group split up into three groups. Stephen and Catherine were tasked with gathering supplies and taking them to the storeroom at the church on Britten Strete, where they were to wait for John to join them later. Their first idea was to take whatever supplies remained in the white house, but nobody wanted to go back to the kitchens where Edmund and Thomas lay slain, so John gave them a bag of coin to use at the markets on Cheppes Syed.

It's like last year repeating itself all over again. John shivered as he threw the bag of coin to Stephen.

"Bring a sack of supplies back here and leave them in the stables," John said. "They will be for whoever is on watch in the tree."

Stephen nodded.

With a last hug and a longing look, John said farewell to his beloved Catherine and watched as she and Stephen exited the gates of the little white house and turned left onto Soperlane.

Whatever happened next, John knew it would never be the same. He turned his head skywards towards the heavens for a moment before closing his eyes and allowing it to flop forward to his chest. He let out an audible sigh and spoke aloud to nobody.

Nobody who was listening anyhow.

"Please give me the strength and courage to keep Catherine safe and do what needs to be done."

"Amen," Edward said.

After a brief silence, John looked up and spoke to his friend. "Stephen will relieve you tomorrow morning, and then the three of us will take it in turns watching to see what happens. It will be brutally cold, but the warm blankets from the house will help if you gather them together."

"I will do what is necessary," Edward said. "Stephen and I will take care of watching the house. We need you to seek your father's help and study the confessions to find the knave who sent Gare. If it's Lord Asheborne's son, we pray thee finds where he's hiding so we can kill him and find the evil one."

John nodded and clasped hands with Edward. "I swear that whoever was responsible for this will pay with their own blood."

Edward gathered the warm blankets from the house and stacked them in the stables. "I'll wait here until after dark. The ground will be frozen, so my footprints won't show in the snow. If anyone comes here, they will not know I'm watching."

John looked over the rear wall towards the large tree on Nederslane, but even though the heavy fog was lifting, he couldn't see far enough ahead to make out Edward's hiding place for the night.

"Are you sure you will see any movement from that far away?" John asked. "I can't even see the tree from here, let alone watch what's happening around it."

"The tree gives good, clear sight into the courtyard on a clear night," Edward answered. "If the clouds are thick, I shall sit in the smaller tree directly behind the wall, and if that doesn't work, I shall be in the stables. Worry not, my friend, for I shall miss no one who dares enter these grounds."

"I never doubted you for a moment," John said, and he meant it.

Leaving Edward to his tasks, John gathered himself and went back inside the house to wait for Sheriff Holley to return for the corpses of the slain men.

He didn't have to wait long.

Edmund and Thomas were to have a proper burial in consecrated ground at John's expense. Willis was to be returned to the Stronde where his father would decide what to do with him.

Once he knew what had happened.

As soon as the house was empty, John pulled the hood of his cloak over his head and locked the gates to the courtyard behind him. Then he headed towards the Stronde and a difficult meeting with his father.

Chapter 14

Curfew wasn't far away as John entered London via Ludgate and cut through the grounds of St Paul's Cathedral. His mind wouldn't stop replaying the gruesome images of Willis, Edmund, and Thomas, and he felt the weight of responsibility as it lay heavily on his shoulders.

All the death and devastation of the previous year was supposed to have ended with the execution of Lord Asheborne, but all death ever did was bring more death, and John had experienced more than any man could take. Most people would be at a breaking point by now, so why wasn't he?

Stop feeling sorry for yourself! You will have plenty of time for self-pity once Gare is dead, and you have avenged Willis and the boys. Until then, you must be strong for Catherine and make sure she is safe from this evil monster.

The voice thundered in John's head as though someone else was speaking to him. He stopped and looked around. *Where am I?*

He was outside the Chapter House of St Paul's, and

when he realised where he was, he fell to his knees in prayer.

If God is speaking to me, then I am listening. Please give me the strength and guidance I so desperately need to see this through. Please don't let me fail my family and friends.

No more words of wisdom came to him, so he thanked the Lord above and got to his feet. He forced the images out of his mind and thought back to his meeting with his father and Sarah earlier that day at the Stronde.

News of the gruesome murders had already reached them by the time John got there, probably because Sheriff Holley had dispatched a constable ahead of John's visit. His father had seemed genuinely upset, especially with the news about Willis, who had been a loyal guard to the Howard family for many years.

Shouts and loud yelling snapped John from his thoughts. The noise grew louder as he rounded the corner of St Paul's gate and approached the cross where the cryers and preachers gave their daily news and views. One such preacher was doing just that to a crowd of several hundred people. It surprised John that so many were out on such a chilly afternoon, especially as curfew was just around the corner.

John Howard comes back to London a pardoned man, and what happens? No sooner is he pardoned and allowed to walk amongst us as a free man than yet more gruesome murders descend on us like a plague from the gates of hell. I tell you, people of London, that no-one will be safe until John Howard and his followers stand before us on the gallows. He claims to have confessions written by Lady Margaret Colte that proved his innocence, and yet it is these very same confessions that are causing all the strife afflicting the great nobility of this country. Howard holds these confessions over their heads like the executioner's axe, so it comes as no surprise when these gruesome murders happen in his own household. No, good people of London, we have to stop John Howard before his evil is the death of us all. Do you want to die at the hands of this disgraced noble?

Roars and shouts told the preacher what he wanted to hear, and John buried his head deep into his hood. He backed away, hoping nobody would recognise him, or he feared they would tear him limb from limb right there in the sacred grounds of St Paul's Cathedral.

John backed away and ran.

Which nobleman gave the preacher such information? John knew it had to have come from someone in the nobility, and he was sure they had given it on purpose, to force John to hand over the confessions.

Well. It won't work.

He got through Aldersgate as dusk settled over the frozen landscape. Curfew was seconds away, and John sighed as he walked past the guards who were preparing to close the gates.

Making sure he wasn't being followed, he turned onto Britten Strete and entered the small church on the left side of the strete. The church was empty, so John found his way to a recess in the rear corner and went down a few steps until a solid door blocked his path.

It was almost dark as John rapped three times on the heavy door. Then twice and then just once. Then he repeated the pattern twice more. It was the signal to those on the other side that everything was good, and they could safely open the door.

John stumbled inside and collapsed on the stone floor of the small storeroom that had given them so much protection and shelter the previous year. It was the safest place he had ever known, and even though he didn't like the nearby crypts—nobody did—there was nowhere safer in the entire country for them than this place.

"John, what happened?" Catherine sat beside him and

took his hand. "We didn't think you were going to make it back here tonight."

John looked at the expectant faces of Catherine and Stephen. "Sorry, the meeting with my father took longer than I expected, and then I got held up at St Paul's when a preacher was telling a large crowd that London will never be safe until we are dead."

"We heard something similar when we were getting provisions earlier," Stephen said. "We had to hurry and get away from Cheppes Syed before anyone recognised us, for I fear they would have torn us apart if they had."

"I felt the same," John agreed. "Did you take some supplies for Edward?"

"Of course," Stephen scoffed. "I left them hidden in the stables. There should be enough to last a few days if we're careful. I'll leave as soon as they lift curfew and relieve Edward. What happened with your father?"

"I believe he is not involved, which is what I thought all along. He was shocked and as upset as we are, especially with poor old Willis, who had served him for many years."

"Did he agree to help us?"

"He demanded that I leave London for Broxley with Sarah in the morn, but even Sarah refused to go until after we bury Willis. Father was angry that I refused, but I think I made him understand when I explained my reasons."

"Is he going to help us?"

"He agreed to provide coin for us to seek Asheborne and Gare, and he agreed to help us find him. But he refused us shelter at the Stronde in fear of reprisals against his guards. Everyone associated with my family is terrified of Gare, and who can blame them?"

"So, what happens next?" Catherine asked.

"We bury our dead, and then we find Asheborne."

John tightened his jaw into a snarl. "Then we force him to tell us where Gare is hiding."

Chapter 15

After the veil of darkness had settled over the frozen city, John made his way by candlelight through the pitch-dark crypts and emerged in the Shambles, which was the area of London where the meat traders slaughtered their animals and sold them to the people of the city.

Except tonight, under a clear sky and a full moon, the frozen stretes were deathly quiet. London was a violent place, especially after dark, when curfew had been called. Only three kinds of people roamed the stretes after curfew—drunkards, the robbers who preyed on them, and the Watch, who were men working for the city who punished anyone who dared to be out after curfew.

John didn't want to run into any of them, so he kept to the shadows while he made the brief journey to the large house near the Old Baker's Hall. He went to the rear and banged on the large wooden door.

He stood back and waited, hoping the old man was home. After a few minutes, the door creaked and swung open, revealing an old man with a long grey beard standing there holding a candle lantern high above his head.

"Who comes here this night?"

"Hello, Gamaliell, it's me, John Howard."

"John, I thought it might be you because nobody else ever comes to my door after curfew. Come on in and get out of the cold."

After a few pleasantries, the conversation turned serious.

"What can I do for you, John? I heard about the murders, and I hear the whispers on the stretes. I don't think the duke's last words helped much either."

"It was Gare." John shivered when he said his name aloud. "He murdered Willis, Edmund, and Thomas in the most evil manner you could ever think of. Only the devil himself could do such a thing."

"Do you know why he did it?"

"Revenge, I assume, for the execution of Lord Asheborne. I'm convinced his son sent Gare after us, but he had other men with him. There were several footsteps in the snow, so we know that for certain. I believe they were trying to find the confessions and kill us at the same time."

"Where were you while all this happened? And I assume they didn't find the confessions?"

John shook his head. "The confessions are safe. We, that is myself, Catherine, Edward, and Stephen, were at the Stronde for the night after visiting my father and sister. If we were home, we could have stopped Gare and ended it that night."

"I hear whispers that the nobles are uneasy about you having the confessions. Be wary, John, because there are powerful people who want them for themselves. They will stop at nothing to get them."

"I'm aware of that, although I don't know what to do

about it. I'll worry about that later. Right now, I have to deal with Gare and Asheborne's son."

"What can I do to help?"

"It's too dangerous for us to go to the markets and get the supplies we need. I fear that if they recognise us, the crowds will tear us limb from limb right there on the stretes. Can we purchase our supplies through you until this is over?"

"Consider it done. And I shall accept no payment from you, so don't even try."

"Thank you, Gamaliell. Once again, you come to our aid."

"What else can I do for you?"

"That's more than enough for now."

"I'll keep you up to date with any whispers I hear," Pye said. "Be careful my young friend, for I fear some powerful men will never stop until both you and your father are dead. Come back here tomorrow night and I shall have your supplies."

"Thank you, Gamaliell. I could not do this without you, and I am once again in your debt."

They shook hands, and John vanished into the night.

After returning Isobel's confessions to their hiding place with the rest of them, John left the crypts and spent a restless night in the storeroom with Catherine and Stephen.

Pye's words burned into his mind as he tossed and turned. *Powerful men will not stop until both myself and my father are dead.* While John knew that was true, did that mean that someone else was behind Gare's attack? If so, then who? John knew his father had many enemies at court. Any noble who had the ear of the king like Robert Howard did was bound to have many jealous enemies.

But how many of them would send a man like Gare

after them? Not very many, that much John knew. It takes a special kind of evil to do that, and while many nobles could be vain and ambitious, very few would go that far.

Still, the question remained. If not Asheborne, then who?

The question haunted John all night long.

The next morning, while Edward and Stephen exchanged places watching over the little white house, John waited in the parlour for word from Sheriff Holley. While he waited, he scrubbed the floors and tables clean of Willis's blood, and he picked up the ransacked belongings that Gare and his men had smashed beyond repair. Once he'd finished, John sank to his knees to pray for his fallen friends.

As he stood up, he noticed a man standing in the doorway watching him. John pulled his sword from his side when a familiar voice spoke up and stopped him.

"Put it away, Master Howard. It is I, Sheriff Holley."

John looked again and relaxed when he saw the long dark hair and friendly brown eyes staring back at him.

"Sheriff Holley, I've been expecting you."

"I bring news regarding the funerals of your men. The priest at the church across the strete called St Mary Aldermary has agreed to inter your two stable boys. I told him you're happy to pay the expenses of their funerals."

John nodded. "That's the least I can do for them. Of course I shall cover the costs."

"Then their funerals shall be the day after tomorrow, after curfew lifts. They will prepare their graves tomorrow."

"And what about Willis?" John asked.

"Your father told me he is to be buried at . . ." Sheriff Holley pulled a folded paper from his pocket. "He is to be buried at St Clement Danes churchyard, which is somewhere close to your family house on the Stronde. He is to be buried the morn after the stable boys."

"Very good," John said. "What else have you learned? Have you discovered the whereabouts of Oswyn Gare?"

"Please," Holley said. "Will you walk with me?" Holley indicated with his head that he wanted to speak with John alone, out of earshot of his men.

They walked out of the rear gates onto Soperlane that was busy with horses and men going about their daily business. They crossed the strete and found solitude in the grounds of St Mary Aldermary church yard.

"I needed to speak to you in private, because although I trust my men, some things are better said between just you and I."

"So, you don't trust them?" John stared deep into Holley's brown eyes. He liked the Sheriff and thought he was trustworthy, but after his experiences over the last year, he knew better than to take anyone at face value. He searched his eyes for any clues, but all he saw was honesty and sincerity.

"Not with information so valuable that powerful men would kill for it. I wouldn't trust anyone with that kind of information."

"Do you have that kind of information?" John asked. "And if so, why do you trust me with it?"

"I trust you because what I have to say involves you. In fact, the information is all about you."

"Go on. I'm listening."

"Several powerful lords have already approached me and offered me coin for information regarding these crimes. They are especially interested in the confessions and whether you have told me where they are hidden. I'm sure that if they have approached me, then they would also approach my men. That is why I needed to speak to you alone."

"I appreciate your honesty, Sheriff." John stared at Holley, even more sure of his assertion that Holley was a trustworthy man. "Who were these men, and what did you tell them?"

"They were told that you never mentioned the confessions. I also told them that even if you did, that I would not divulge what you say to them. They cannot buy me, Master Howard, of that I give you my word."

"I believe you, and I am grateful. Who was it who asked you these things?"

"You would be surprised. At least four so far, and I am sure there will be more in the days ahead."

"One of them wasn't my uncle, was it? Thomas Howard, the duke?"

"I'm afraid it was. He was the first to approach me."

John pulled his face. "I knew he would. Please don't tell him anything."

"Like I said, Master Howard. I cannot be bought."

"Thank you, Sheriff. Do you have any news of Gare and his whereabouts? Or Lord Asheborne's son?"

Sheriff Holley shook his head. "I have my men scouring everywhere, but as of today, they have found nothing. This Gare you speak of is a ghost who has vanished into thin air."

"He is good at that. He did it last year after he attacked us in the Midlands and North Yorkshire."

"I heard about that. The man is a devil who needs to be stopped."

"We've got to find him first," John said.

"Master Howard, we need a person we can trust so we can communicate outside of my normal areas. This is too dangerous, and I fear one of my men will betray you. Do you know anyone we can trust that would act as a go-between for us so we can communicate without fear?"

"Why would we do that, Sheriff? You have your job to do, and I have mine. Yours is to protect London, and mine is to find Gare and Asheborne. Wherever they are, I shall find them and kill them. I doubt you will help with that, Sheriff."

"I'm trying to help, Master Howard. I want to help."

"I'll be in touch, Sheriff. If I need your help, I'll let you know."

John walked away.

Chapter 16

John spread Margaret's confessions out across the floor of the storeroom they once again called home. Daylight from the window gave sufficient light for John to see clearly enough to read.

He shivered when he looked at the papers spread out before him. "These confessions are as dangerous as Margaret's honey was to her son, Mark Colte," he said aloud.

"They are," Edward agreed. "But I fear they would be even more dangerous if they got into the wrong hands."

"The bigger danger is that whoever holds them would use them as leverage over the other nobles and gain even greater power and wealth for himself. I really should destroy them, but if I did, nobody would ever believe me, and we would never be free of them. If I hand them over, then what I just described would become a reality, so I can't do that either. All I know is that these confessions are a curse that we'll never be rid of."

John looked at Catherine.

"As you said, somewhere in here, there must be a clue

as to who is behind the recent attacks, and if there is, I have to find it. I have today and tomorrow to find something, for after Willis's funeral, I want us to have a plan of action. We can't just sit here and wait for the next attack."

"I agree," Edward said. "Gare has many crimes to pay for, but none more so than the death of Sybil and my unborn child. My heart aches for them, and I shall never rest until he is dead. Whatever happens, you must promise me it is I who deals with Gare."

"I promise," John said. "As much as I can promise such a thing. If it is us who finds him, then you have my word that it shall be you who ends his life."

The room fell silent as John got to work studying Margaret's confessions. It would have been much easier with more eyes than just his to help, but neither Edward nor Catherine could read very well, and John didn't trust anyone else to help him.

"You are teaching us to read, and we will gladly help." Edward said.

"You are doing well, but the confessions must be studied closely, and I fear you cannot yet read well enough," John answered without looking up. "Reading is a very important task to master, and it isn't hard once you get the hang of it. Once this is over, we will set aside more time to learn."

"All of us?" Catherine asked.

"All of us," John answered, leaning over and squeezing her hand. "The wife of a future earl needs to be able to read, and I promise you shall."

He fell silent again and got to work reading the confessions.

Many held his interest as he read through them. Margaret's reach and depravity knew no bounds, but John was in a hurry and didn't have time to read those that bore no relevance to his search.

"No wonder the nobles would go to any lengths to get their hands on these confessions." John almost whispered the words. "The depths they went to at Margaret's behest are unbelievable. I'm sure she wrote these not to confess her sins, but to use them as leverage over half the nobles in England."

"She was truly evil," Catherine said.

"Margaret was more than evil," John corrected her. "She was the most scheming person I've ever heard of, man or woman. She used my father to gain a foothold on power, and then spread her poisonous tentacles throughout the nobles of England. If we hadn't stopped her, there's no telling how far she would have gone."

"What was she trying to do?" Edward asked. "She must have had a reason for all of this?"

"You mean other than to gain riches and power over the nobles?" John replied. "Many of the confessions are about the Reformation, and Margaret despised it. She was a staunch follower of Rome and wanted the pope reinstated at the head of the English church. I don't know for certain, but I believe her purpose was to overthrow and witness the execution of Thomas Cromwell, as she seemed to hate him almost as much as she hated me."

"Isn't that treason?" Edward asked.

"Of course it is, and she would have been executed if the king had found out about her. No doubt my father, and indeed my entire family, would have joined her on the scaffold as well. I believe that is why she was gaining leverage over the nobles, so she would stand a chance if she was arrested."

He fell silent again for several hours as he sifted through the many confessions. He used his quill to number them, so they would be in order the next time he needed to go through them.

Isobel was number one. This series of confessions troubled John more than anything else, although he didn't know why.

Why would Margaret kill a young girl who was out for a morning walk? What evil prompted Margaret to even consider such a thing?

John knew he wouldn't rest until he found out the story behind her death all those years ago.

He put Isobel's papers aside. They would have to wait until they had dealt with Gare and whoever controlled him, and that might take a long time if he couldn't find any clues to their whereabouts.

He made a separate pile for the confessions that related to his own family, of which there were plenty. Then he made another pile that mentioned William Asheborne. The rest he scanned through and placed into a fourth pile. They were for another time.

Most of the confessions spoke of nobles John either knew or had heard of. Two of them mentioned a name he had never heard before, and it got his attention. Once he'd finished sorting them into their respective piles, he reached for the two letters he'd put aside. He read them out loud so Edward and Catherine could hear Margaret's words.

When John Howard—Lord how I hate that name—the mere mention of him makes me want to wrench the neck from his sister to force him out of the rat infested stretes where he hides and show himself. When he ran away and became a problem, I needed an escape route if everything collapsed around me. Everything had gone so smoothly until John ran away, and if he'd gone to France and died like he was supposed to, none of what I am about to reveal would have been necessary. His disobedience caused me many sleepless nights as I struggled to come to terms with what he might discover and reveal.

I needed property and coin that was hidden from the usurper's son, so that if my plans were ever to be discovered, he could not confiscate them from me. Robert would lose everything, including his head, but I would watch from a safe distance with all my wealth and power intact. All I needed was a plan, and it was this that kept me awake at night.

As usual, William was the one who had the right idea that would protect both of us should the need arise. William always knew what to do, and he never failed me.

Andrew Griffiths is a northern man whose name is unknown to anyone at court. As nobody knows who he is, he is safe from the greedy clutches of the false king and his greedy half-breed, Thomas Cromwell, whose name I despise almost as much as John Howard's.

I used Griffiths to purchase several properties throughout England, including several in London itself. With careful purchases, I would have an escape route through England to the border with Scotland, where I would be safe, even from Henry Tudor.

Once I had the properties, I passed a significant share of my wealth—or should I say Robert's wealth—to Andrew so he could shield it from the king and his half-breed minister, Cromwell.

I would become Isobel Griffiths, and nobody would ever find me. I could live freely while I went about my duties to my faith. If all else failed, I would take the short step over the border, where I would be safe from retaliation.

Margaret Colte

John looked up at Edward and Catherine. "There's that name again, Isobel. Margaret was obsessed by her, and I am determined to find out why."

"Who is Andrew Griffiths?" Edward asked. "That's a new name to me. I've never heard of him."

John shook his head. "Me neither, but according to the confessions, he is unknown to anyone in the royal court, so he might be hard to find. He's obviously someone of considerable wealth and power, otherwise he wouldn't have been able to do what Margaret says he did, but I don't see how anyone could buy that many properties all over the country without someone knowing who he was."

"How do we find him?" Catherine asked.

"We need to find a property he purchased and find the deeds. That should tell us who Andrew Griffiths is, or was," John said.

He picked up the second confession, which was obviously written much later, at a time closer to Margaret's death at the hands of Catherine.

The wicked boy John Howard tricked me into killing my son, Mark Colte. Howard should have been in that carriage, not Mark, and if he had been, it would be him who now lay dead and not my son.

I should grieve, especially as it was I who gave the order to attack the carriage as it left Henry Colte's home in London that morn. If truth be told, I do not grieve at all. In fact, I feel quite the opposite.

I'm eternally glad that Henry Colte is dead, because he was the only person alive who I feared would discover the truth about me and bring me down. Now he's dead, he is no longer a threat.

I do not grieve for Mark, because if I am to be honest, he was a burden to me and a disappointment. He was weak and not a man at all. At least not a man I could trust. His death was his own fault, for if he hadn't run off with Howard and his sister, he wouldn't have been in the carriage on that morn.

So, his death was not of my doing, and I feel no remorse. If anything, I feel relief, for he is no longer my concern, and I can continue my quest without worrying that my own son will give me away.

After Mark's death, I prayed Howard died with him, but alas, he didn't. Once again, he escaped my vengeance. Now that the earl was dead, along with my son, I knew I needed to act fast.

I made sure Howard took the blame for the attack, but to be certain, I met with Andrew Griffiths and got the list of properties he had purchased on my behalf. I hid them in a safe place, and I shall not reveal their whereabouts in these confessions, for if these are found before my death, I shall need the properties and coin Andrew has so carefully hidden for me so I can escape to safety.

Now that Mark is dead, and the attack is the talk of the entire country, it is time for me to protect myself by readying my escape. Whatever happens next, the end is nearing for either myself or John Howard, so I am making sure I am ready to leave at a moment's notice.

My properties and coin are waiting for me.

Margaret Colte

John threw the letter to the cold floor and looked at Edward and Catherine. "Never has there been an eviler soul than Margaret Colte. She killed her own son and didn't feel a moment's remorse."

"Oswyn Gare," Edward corrected him. "He is more evil than the devil himself."

"Yes, she is more evil than anyone except Oswyn Gare," John corrected himself.

"What do we do?" Catherine asked. "How do we find who this Andrew Griffiths is?"

"I'll ask my father," John said. "If anyone can find Griffiths, it's him. We need to find the list of properties that she hid somewhere. If we find that, we find Griffiths, and we find Gare. Maybe even Asheborne's son, too."

"Where do we find them?" Edward asked. "They could be anywhere in England."

John shook his head.

"I don't know."

Chapter 17

Snow fell softly as the small congregation gathered around two freshly dug graves in the consecrated grounds of St Mary Aldermary church on the corner of Watelyng Strete and Cordewanerstrete.

John looked over at the nearby Gerard's Hall as memories of his close escapes with Isaac flooded through his mind. His eyes dampened as he thought of his great friend, and he wished he was with them this morn.

Stephen was watching the little white house, so it was Edward and Catherine who stood beside John at the gravesides as Edmund and Thomas were laid to rest.

Sheriff Holley was there to pay his respects, and the priest was the only other man present on this freezing wintry morning.

John thought it apt that the snow was falling.

Even the sky is mourning with us today.

"We are gathered here today to pay our respects to the lives of two young men who were taken from us in an act of cruel violence," the priest began his sermon.

John gripped Catherine's hand and held it tight. His chin quivered as images of their mutilated bodies invaded his mind. He shivered at the memories, and the skin on his arms raised like sharp needles. His nostrils flared at the thought of Gare attacking Edmund and Thomas, and as sorrow turned to anger and then back again, John made a quiet vow to their graves that he would never rest until they were avenged.

"Master John," Sheriff Holley nudged him. "Master John, the priest was speaking to you."

"I'm sorry," John said, wiping away a tear. "I was lost in my own thoughts."

"I understand," the priest said. "Would you like to say a few words?"

John nodded and cleared his throat to gather himself together. With a crack in his voice, John spoke.

"Edmund and Thomas, you were good and loyal workers whose only crime was to be in my home when we were so cruelly attacked. Neither of you deserved this, and I am so sorry I wasn't there to protect you. I give you both my solemn vow that I shall never rest until I avenge you, and your souls can rest easy knowing that I will bring your attackers to justice. May God bless you, and I pray you may rest in peace."

"Amen."

"Amen." Everyone echoed his words.

Catherine sobbed quietly, and John wiped away another tear that was falling down his face.

The following morning, John, Catherine, and Stephen gathered around a freshly dug grave outside St Clement Danes church on the Stronde. Sheriff Holley and his father joined them.

Sarah stood beside John and squeezed his hand tightly. Both owed a lot to Willis, who was being laid to rest in the grounds of the magnificent old church that was said to date back to the days of the Vikings.

The Howard family owned a large plot of land in the far west side of the cemetery, and Robert had kindly put a section aside for his most loyal aides at the behest of his son. Willis was to be the first of those aides to be laid to rest there.

Father Kirk stood at the head of the grave and looked at the small group gathered to pay their last respects to a great man.

John looked closely at Father Kirk. Although not very tall, he looked like he knew how to take care of himself. He was slender, with shades of platinum hair falling from beneath his head covering, which was unusual for a man who looked to be in his mid-thirties.

He might be small in stature, but John could see from looking at him he was in great physical shape. And yet he had the kindest eyes that John could ever remember seeing, and even through the cloudy tears that blurred his vision, John felt an affinity to this priest that he couldn't explain.

He was glad Father Kirk was conducting the ceremony on this clear but frozen day.

John stared at the ground, his gaze a distant, empty stare. He felt his chin waver as he remembered all the sacrifices Willis had made for him. Sarah and Catherine clasped his hands, sharing the raw emotion through his touch.

After a short sermon, Father Kirk invited Robert Howard to say a few words.

"Willis was one of the most loyal guards our family ever had the privilege of knowing," he started. Even Robert's voice wavered, and John looked up in shock. His father never showed much emotion in public, and this was a big surprise to John, and no doubt Sarah as well.

"Willis was not always loyal to me," Robert continued. "But his loyalty to the Howard family and what was right never wavered, even when I myself wandered off the path of righteousness. Willis cared deeply for John and Sarah, and I feel it only fitting that the final words should belong to John, as he owes Willis more than he can ever repay."

Robert's voice cracked, and he barely got the words out before he lost the ability to speak at all. He looked down at the ground so nobody could see his tears.

John swallowed hard and fought back the quivering in his throat.

"My father is right: I owe Willis more than I could ever repay. He saved my life more than once, even when doing so got him whipped and caused him severe personal angst. He was present during a battle that almost cost his life, and where he sustained injuries that he never recovered from. And yet he remained loyal to me."

John coughed and spluttered, tears flowing freely down his face. Even though the weather was tortuously freezing, he felt flushed and hot under his cloak. His hands shook as much as his voice, but he gathered himself together enough to continue.

Willis would have been proud of him.

"Even after all his serious injuries, and after Father placed him in the service of Margaret Colte, Willis never faltered in his loyalty to me. It was Willis who showed me the path to the confessions, and it was only with Willis's help that I finally proved my innocence and began rebuilding my relationships with my father and sister."

John closed his eyes and swallowed hard. The next words fell out of his mouth in a jumbled mess, but it was the best he could do.

"And it was Willis who stood alongside my two stable boys and tried to protect them from the evil that was unleashed at my home in London. Willis died as he had lived—loyal to the end and a genuine hero. I owe him more than I can ever repay, but I vow to live my life in a manner that he would approve of. Rest in peace, my most trusted friend. You shall be missed."

John sobbed.

Chapter 18

As the congregation dispersed, John watched through bloodshot eyes as Father Kirk and Sheriff Holley walked together, speaking for all the world as if they'd known each other for years.

Perhaps they had, for all John knew. He shrugged and gave up. *Who cares if they know each other?*

Stephen and Catherine went back to the city so Stephen could get some rest before resuming his watch on the little white house the following day. John went with his father and Sarah to their house on the Stronde to discuss their plans for the coming days.

After the heavy emotion of the funeral, the last thing John wanted was to have a discussion with his father, but he had no choice. His father had practically begged him to return with him to the Stronde to hear what he had to say. John also wanted to ask about Andrew Griffiths, so he'd reluctantly said goodbye to Catherine and Stephen and gone to the house instead of the storeroom.

"Thank you for coming here," his father said as soon as they were gathered around the warm fire in the sitting room. John stood next to Sarah, warming his back and happily allowing the feeling to return to his frozen limbs.

"Please, sit," his father gestured to the large wooden table and chairs against the rear wall. John reluctantly dragged himself away from the warm fire.

"What is so urgent that it has to be said on the day of Willis's funeral?" John asked. "It has been a difficult two days and my mind is not as clear as I would like it to be."

"I understand, and I am genuinely sorry for your loss, but what I have to say cannot wait." Robert Howard looked worried, which wasn't something John was used to seeing. "I don't normally attend the services for my servants, but I made an exception on your account for Willis, so I hope you will now allow me to have my say."

John nodded his head slightly to the ground. Nobles were not in the habit of mourning their servants, and he knew this was probably the first time he'd ever paid any attention to the sufferings of any of them. At least publicly anyway. John hoped his father would learn valuable lessons from today, but he somehow doubted it. The nobles of England didn't think that way.

"Storm clouds are gathering against us in the royal court," Robert began. "Rumours are whispered in dark corners, and they echo off the walls of Greenwich Palace. And they are all directed at me. At us."

"I'm surprised you listen to rumours, father. You know as well as anyone they hardly ever turn out to be the truth."

"Whether or not they are true is irrelevant. What matters is if the king believes them or not, and I fear he is leaning towards that conclusion. Too many nobles are whispering in his ear, and although I do my best to convince him otherwise, once the king decides, he usually acts before he thinks about it too much."

"What are these rumours?" John asked.

Sarah sat silent, listening intently and looking worried.

"The rumours are serious, and they may end up taking all of our lives. The nobles are worried about Margaret's confessions and what they might reveal about them. Some have much they wish to conceal, and they fear for their futures."

"What does that have to do with me?" John asked, knowing full well what was coming next.

"I have many enemies at the court. Anyone who has the close ear of the king does, and the nobles fear I am using my position to bring them down. They believe I have access to the confessions and am plotting to release them to the king."

"But you don't have access to them," John interrupted. "And you never shall, for that very reason."

Robert's face turned deep red, and his voice raised in both tone and volume.

"Remember who you are speaking to, John. I shall not allow that kind of disrespect from you or anyone. Please allow me to finish."

John knew he'd overstepped the line and remained quiet.

"The nobles believe I have the confessions, and they are worried I am about to use them to destroy their reputations and possibly their lives. They whisper to the king that Margaret and I were plotting against the reformists, and that is why I won't hand all the confessions over to him. They say I am withholding many of them that refer to myself and the Howard family. But they say I will reveal the rest of them to remove my enemies."

"Surely the king doesn't believe that after all you've done for him?" John asked.

"I believe he is having his head turned by men he trusts

other than myself. I fear that if I don't hand over the confessions, we shall all be arrested and charged with treason. You know what the penalty for that is."

John bit his lip, deep in thought. "You stated the nobles told the king you would release the confessions that pertain to them, but keep back the ones relating to yourself, so how would me handing them all over help? The king would still believe you were withholding some of them."

"Precisely my dilemma." Robert stood up and paced the room. "I fear we are in grave danger, and I must do all I can to protect my family. Sarah, you shall return to Broxley in the morn. I have loyal staff there who will protect you far better than I can here. John, I would like you to go with her, so I know you're safe."

"You know I can't do that, Father."

John looked at Sarah, who was about to erupt.

"I can see you're unhappy with my decision, Sarah, but it is for your own safety. I was planning a good marriage for you, but that shall not be happening now, at least not until we clear our name and return to our normal lives. Right now, your safety is my biggest concern, so please don't question my decisions. I have decided, and you shall do as I command."

"You're keeping me safe so you can marry me off after you restore your good name? Is that the only reason you want me safe?"

"Enough!" Robert thundered. "It's enough that I have John questioning my every decision. I shall not have you do it as well."

Sarah lowered her head, but John could see she was far from happy.

"There is one more thing." Robert looked at John.

"I'm not handing over the confessions," John said. "And you can command all you want, but I'm not going to

Broxley. My place is here with my wife and friends. I shall find who attacked us, and I shall kill them all."

"Brave words, John. But they will be of no use if you are in the Tower awaiting execution."

"If the king demands it, then I shall have no choice. But even then, he won't get his hands on the confessions. I shall never give them up, not until I find who attacked us."

John's mind flashed to Isobel and the confessions relating to her, but he kept it to himself. He had more than enough to worry about right now.

"Then we are at an impasse," Robert said. "What do you propose we do? I am not saying this lightly, John. If the king has his head turned, which is likely, we shall all perish, and our enemies will have won."

John pondered for a long moment.

"Can't you go to France where you once sent me? Even the king won't be able to reach you there."

"And leave you behind again? I abandoned you once, John, but I shall never do it again. No, whatever we do, we do together."

"What I am doing is not with you," John said, knowing his father would be furious again. "It is too dangerous and unbecoming of a noble."

He tried to soften the blow with his last words. It didn't work.

"You continue to be insolent when I am trying to help you. I'm trying to help all of us. Work with me, son. Please."

"What would you have me do, father? Like you said, if I gave you the confessions today, the nobles still wouldn't believe you were telling the truth. We lose either way."

"That is my greatest fear." Robert bowed his head.

"Actually"—John changed his tone and stood up—"Actually, there might be something you can do to help. We might not prevent the king from arresting us and charging us with treason, but we can find who attacked us and bring them to justice. Who knows, if we do that, then we might have a chance with the king."

"Perhaps, but how do we work together? You already said you won't work with me."

"There is something you can do, Father." John offered his olive branch to his father.

"What is it?" Robert's face looked a little less dour.

"Margaret mentioned a name in two of her confessions. It's a name I've never heard of, but she stated that the man with this name bought a lot of property in London and throughout England in order for her to escape, should her scheming be discovered. She also stated that she transferred a lot of your wealth to this man in readiness for her escape."

"Who is this man?"

"His name is Andrew Griffiths."

"I've never heard the name. Leave it with me and I shall make discreet inquiries."

Robert paused.

"But beware of the wrath of the king."

John nodded before rising. "I shall stay here tonight, so I can have time with Sarah before she leaves in the morn."

As John walked towards the door to the sitting room, the guard outside moved quickly away. Barton had overheard every word, and he was eager to report the news to his master as soon as he got the chance later that day. He was sure his boss would be pleased with him.

Chapter 19

Alexander Carlyle strode into the small house by the side of the George Inn on Lumbardstrete in the centre of London. On this day, he looked nothing like the noble Viscount he was in his other life.

Today, he was Andrew Griffiths.

Eleven guards sat on the filthy, straw-covered floor around a fire that was blazing in the middle of the crowded room to keep them warm. With the exception of the stone fire ring in the centre of the room, it was empty of furniture or anything else that would show that this was a place where a family lived a normal life.

Everyone sat low to the ground because, as in a lot of poorer homes in England, the house had no chimney. They were a luxury for the elite, and this house was definitely not owned by anyone from that side of society.

Except it was.

Thick smoke rose from the fire circle and hung at head height like a dark cloud, choking and blinding anyone who dared to stand up. By sitting and staying low to the ground, the occupants could avoid the asphyxiating void above their heads and keep themselves warm on the decades-old straw covering the floor below.

Andrew Griffiths hated this house. He hated every house like this, but they served a purpose, so he tried hard to hide his displeasure.

The room became even more crowded when the five men who accompanied Carlyle followed him into the house. Well, four plus the frightening beast that was owned by no man.

The eleven guards in the house were the remnants of William Asheborne's most loyal men who now worked for the duke's son, William Asheborne Junior.

Or at least, they thought they did.

As Carlyle and his men gagged for breath until they sat down below the thick black cloud of smoke, one guard foolishly smirked and laughed out loud. He prodded his companion sat beside him and pointed his finger at the stranger who had just entered their house as if he owned the place.

He'd smirked at the unusual physical appearance of this strange man, and he looked up and down the man's body with exaggerated movements of his head.

It didn't go unnoticed.

"We're sorry, sir, but who are you?" the guard who'd sneered at Griffith's appearance asked. "We don't normally allow strangers to just walk into our house, especially ones who don't knock first and introduce themselves."

Silence filled the room as all eyes fell on Andrew Griffiths.

"I don't know this gentleman," another of the guards said, pointing to Griffiths. "But I know that man over there." He swallowed hard and pointed at the man with the cold, lifeless grey eyes and a long scar down the left side of his face. "I was there last year when we cornered John Howard."

"Are you sure that's him?" the guard who'd started the questions asked.

"Very sure. After you've seen him, believe me, you never forget him. This man worked for Master Asheborne." The guard looked at the ground as the frightening man stared back at him.

"Who are you, sir?" the first guard pressed, once again smirking at the unusual physical appearance of their strange guest with his child-sized legs underneath an adult's body, and an oversized head that barely fit onto his shoulders.

"Someone you don't want to cross." Griffiths spat out the words in his high-pitched voice that sounded more like a woman's than a man's.

That was too much for the guard, who laughed openly when he heard Griffiths speak.

Griffiths curled his lips into a snarl. He turned to the fearsome man with the dull grey eyes and nodded his head. In a flash, the man jumped up and grabbed the guard by the back of his hair and dragged him out of the room to a different one.

One guard went to go after them, but another placed his hand on him and shook his head. It was the one who'd said he knew who the man was.

Screams pierced the silence, and Griffiths smiled at the pale-faced men staring at him, wondering what on earth was happening to their fellow guard.

They didn't have long to wait for the answer. More screams, followed by the sounds of the guard begging for mercy.

"Please, No! Please, in the name of God, no!"

His words were to no avail. More screams and then silence.

The remaining ten guards sat in stunned silence as the frightening man returned to his place next to the doorway. His clothing was soaked in the guard's blood, but the killer didn't seem to care.

"This is what happens if you dare to mock me. Learn your lessons well and carry out your duties as ordered by Lord Asheborne's son, who sent me here this morn, and you will be left alone. Mock me again, or refuse to carry out my orders, and you now know what fate awaits you."

Stunned silence.

What the men didn't know was that William Asheborne Junior hadn't ordered this meeting. In fact, he knew nothing about it.

Griffiths pulled a piece of parchment from under his cloak. "Here are your lordship's orders," he said in his high-pitched croak. He rolled his eyes as the ten remaining men stared back at him with a mixture of fear and loathing.

"I need eight of you to volunteer for a very important task," Griffiths gave his orders. "You will protect my man here, but you must not interfere with what he does, for if you do, he will kill you. Do I make myself clear?" Griffiths indicated with his head that the men were to assist the murdering aberration with the lifeless eyes sitting in the doorway.

Nobody volunteered.

"I don't have time to wait for you to decide," Griffiths said, pulling his large, rounded face into a snarl. "I give you one last chance, and then I'll decide who goes with him."

A knock on the door interrupted the tension in the room. Griffiths threw his hand in the air at the disruption and looked at the man sat by the door.

"See who it is and get rid of them."

The man with the cold grey eyes stood up and opened the door, revealing a man with a long, pointed nose that was dripping in the frosty morning's chill.

"What do you want?"

"Sir, my name is Barton, and I'm a guard for Lord Howard at the Stronde. I bring news to whoever is in charge here."

"Let him in," Griffiths shouted.

The man stood aside, and Barton entered the smoke-filled room. Asheborne's guards shuffled around to make space for him in front of the fire.

"What news do you bring?" Griffiths asked.

"It's good to see you again, Lord Griffiths," Barton said.

"I don't have time for small talk, so tell me your news."

"Yes, sir. I'm sorry. John Howard attended the funeral of a guard who was recently killed at his house near St Paul's. He was with his father, Lord Howard, and his sister, Lady Sarah Howard."

"I knew about the funeral. What news do you bring?"

Barton revealed everything John and his father had spoken about earlier that morning after the funeral. After he'd finished, Griffiths reached into his pocket and tossed a shilling at Barton.

"You're too generous, sir." Barton scooped up the coin and hid it from the envious eyes sat around him.

"Seeing as you know John Howard and his followers, I might have another task for you," Griffiths said to Barton. "Wait outside until I'm finished here, and I shall tell you what to do."

"Yes, sir, thank you." Barton got up and hurried out of the house. Griffiths smiled to himself as he watched Barton give as wide a berth as he could to the scary man at the door, who was saturated in blood.

"That changes my plans." Griffiths turned to face the ten men staring at him around the fire. "Now I only need five of you to go with my man. The rest of you have another task."

Griffiths gave his orders, and when he'd finished, he rose and headed for the door. "You know what to do, and I don't expect you to fail me, so see that you don't."

He turned to the man at the door. "Gare, I have a task for you that I think you're going to enjoy. I'll explain on the way out of this horrible place that's only fit for knaves and mumpers. Now, where's that man I sent outside?"

Oswyn Gare smiled and followed Griffiths out of the door.

Chapter 20

Damp, heavy fog hung over London, and the driving sleet-soaked John to the skin the moment he stepped out of the warm comfort of the Howard residence on the Stronde.

He shivered and buried himself as far as he could under his cloak, but no matter what he did, the wind driven sleet was so strong that no gap in his clothing went unpunished.

He thought about Stephen having to sit in the tree watching their home in this weather all day. Then he realised that with the visibility down to little more than a man's body length, Stephen would probably spend the day either inside the house itself or, at worst, in the stables. Stephen would probably be warmer and more comfortable than the rest of them this day.

Especially himself, who at this very moment was wishing he was huddled around the fireplace with Sarah, who he was going to miss terribly.

After a tearful goodbye, John decided he wanted to search the white house again, just in case Margaret had hidden the missing confessions regarding Griffiths and the properties he'd purchased somewhere there. It was a long shot, especially as the house had been searched so many times already, but he was willing to give it another go.

He'd searched a little the previous evening at the Stronde, but not much because he didn't want his father to know what he was doing. He wanted to go back when his father wasn't in residence, but he doubted Margaret would have been so foolish as to hide such damning evidence in the house where Robert lived, but then again, John knew she would have taken great pleasure in knowing something so dangerous was sitting right under Robert's nose.

It was worth a try. John didn't have a clue where she'd hidden them, and in all honesty, they could be anywhere in the country.

But he had to start somewhere.

The visibility was so bad that he almost missed the turning for Watelyng Strete as he walked through the grounds of the magnificent St Paul's Cathedral. He stopped to make sure he was on the right road.

A man walking close behind bumped into him, taking him by surprise and almost knocking him over.

"I'm so sorry," the man said from deep under his cloak. "Please forgive me. The weather is so poor that I never saw you stopping."

"Everything is good." John was about to say something else when five more men appeared out of the thick fog and surrounded him.

He knew the bump hadn't been accidental.

John stepped forward to get out of their way, but the men blocked his path. A fist crashed into his face, knocking the senses out of him, and as he fell backwards, he felt a sharp pull on the back of his cloak that yanked him to the ground even harder.

Feet smashed into him from all angles, and John lost his senses.

Is this it? Do I perish in a blizzard for a robbery over a few coins?

As consciousness faded in and out, John thought he was being robbed of whatever coin he was carrying. He expected to be stripped of his thick, warm cloak and left to freeze to death on the empty stretes of London. He thought of Isaac and how he'd soon be joining him in heaven.

Then he heard his name and knew it was more than a robbery.

"Are you sure this is Howard?" a breathless voice shouted through the sheets of sleet and fog. "If it isn't, we'll be dead men."

John kicked himself for not paying attention to his surroundings. He was getting lazy and too comfortable. He didn't think anyone would want to harm him on a day like this.

I have to do better, and I pray I will get another chance to do so.

"It's Howard, alright. I've kept close to him from the minute he left his big fancy 'ouse."

I recognise that voice!

John's senses reached out from the fog that had enveloped his brain. He strained to keep his focus on the man's voice, which was difficult when feet were crashing into him from all directions.

"That's enough, boys," the familiar voice said. "We've softened 'im up enough. Let's take 'im to the boss."

Memories flooded back from his early days on the stretes of London when John had been beaten and dragged across the river to meet a different boss. Images of Ren Walden, the vicious Strete Master and leader of the strete gang, filled John's mind. He remembered Walden's rancid breath when he'd got too close during the terrible beatings he'd been forced to endure. And the feelings of hopelessness and despair when he'd realised that innocent boys were dying in his name for nothing more than the possibility that they might be the missing noble, John Howard.

John shuddered. *Not again, please, not again. I can't take going through that again.*

The familiar voice spoke again. *Where do I know that voice from?* Then it hit him. The guard! He was the guard with the long runny nose from his father's house on the Stronde! There had been something about him that John's senses had picked up on when they'd first met, but he'd ignored them.

Now he wished he hadn't.

What was his name? Barton, that's it. John made a mental note to end Barton's existence if he ever got out of this alive.

A fist crashed into his stomach as hands dragged him to his feet. John gasped for breath as they knocked all the air out of his body. Blood ran down his face and into his mouth, leaving the all too familiar salty taste in his throat.

Then everything went dark.

Chapter 21

Margery Davenport rocked from side to side like a drunken sailor during a wild ocean storm. Anyone who saw her from the rear would have been forgiven for thinking she was quite mad, but on closer inspection, they would have seen that she was doing her best to quieten and soothe the restless ten-month-old baby boy feeding from his wet nurse.

Arthur Shipley, as his father, Robert Howard, insisted he be known, was the son supposedly born from the union of Margaret Colte and her husband, Robert Howard, in April, 1536. Margaret's confessions discovered after her death revealed that Robert was not, in fact, Arthur's father. Instead, it was the deposed Duke of Berkshire, William Asheborne, who Margaret claimed to be his father.

After the celebrations of Arthur's birth, Robert Howard, the Earl of Coventry, had publicly disowned his older son from his first marriage, the outlawed and disgraced John Howard, who at the time was the most wanted man in England. In his place as the heir to Robert's titles and wealth, the earl named Arthur Howard, and everything seemed set for Arthur and his mother to look forward to a life of luxury and privilege.

When the truth came out, Robert acted quickly to distance himself from the child. John Howard was proclaimed innocent, so after a somewhat strained family reunion, Robert reinstated John as the heir to his fortunes. And he sent Arthur away to be raised as the bastard child that he was.

Robert kept the whereabouts of Arthur a secret from his family, partly because at the time it happened, he still didn't trust that John was completely innocent, but also because of the shame he felt from Margaret's deceit.

Robert Howard, the influential Earl and leader of Henry VIII's Privy Council, felt embarrassed, and because of this, he'd arranged for young Arthur to be raised by a family friend whose wife was barren. They kept Arthur close, but at a far enough distance that he wouldn't bring further shame on the Howard family.

It was against this backdrop that seventeen-year-old Margery Davenport had been hired by Charles and Mary Packwood as the wet nurse to young Arthur after losing her own son to sickness a few months earlier. Small and slightly plump, Margery wasn't blessed with the good looks of some of the other girls her age, but she had a heart of gold and would help anyone, even to the point of going without herself if it meant a stranger had a good meal and a warm bed for the night. Her husband had adored her, and as far as Margery was concerned, she had had the perfect marriage, which wasn't the case for most of the women she knew.

Charles Packwood was the fourth son of Richard Packwood, the wealthy Earl of Bedford. At just twenty-two-years old, Charles had married the love of his life against the wishes of his father, who then banished him to the wilderness for his disobedience.

Chessett House was in Waltham Abbey close to London, but to Margery Davenport and the baby at her breast, it might as well have been an ocean away. Robert paid for Arthur's upbringing, but other than that, had no involvement in his life, which was part of the agreement between him and Charles Packwood.

Not that Margery knew much about it. She was just another servant in the household whose sole job was to raise the infant boy until her services were no longer required, although she harboured hopes of remaining as his nursemaid after her milk dried up.

Margery Davenport liked the Packwood family. Master Charles was good to her, and Lady Mary was as kind as a lady could be. After the death of her own child and husband, Margery had landed on her feet, and she would not let this go.

Master Charles and Lady Mary were having a good old time this evening in the great hall. They had friends staying with them from London, and plenty of wine and ale were being consumed. This was a cheerful house, and Margery was loving every moment of her time there.

Arthur was suffering this evening with his stomach, so he cried late into the night. Margery was exhausted, but she sat patiently in her favourite chair, rocking the baby and trying her best to comfort him and soothe his upset tummy.

Margery didn't hear the loud knock on the front door late into the night. Neither did she hear the shattering of glass as someone broke into the house through the rear door that was reserved for the servants.

Margery heard nothing over the cries of the sick baby.

The steady sound of the master and his guests having a good time drifted up the stairs to the nursery, but Margery was too busy to hear them. She was worried that Arthur was ailing with something that was beyond her skills, and she knew he needed a physician urgently. Arthur was screaming in agony, and no matter what she tried, he threw everything back up and all over Margery as she tried to comfort him.

He couldn't even keep her milk down, and in the dim candlelight, Margery was sure he was throwing up blood along with the milk. She placed the ailing baby in his crib and went to find the Steward, Upworthy, who would know what to do.

Upworthy had been with Master Charles and his family for decades. Now in his late forties, Upworthy, or Unworthy to his detractors, of whom he had plenty due to his caustic tone with the other servants, had nonetheless been a good and faithful servant to the Packwood family ever since he was a young boy. He'd followed his own father and his grandfather before him into service for the Packwood family.

Margery ran down the rear stairs the servants used, and for the first time she noticed the loud laughter and frivolity that had been coming from the great hall had fallen silent.

Margery shrugged her shoulders. *They must be having a serious conversation, or maybe some prayer time*. Whatever it was, it didn't concern the likes of her. She had other, more important, things to worry about.

At the bottom of the stairs, she turned to her left and approached the kitchens, where she would ask one of the servants who was serving the Master and his guests to fetch Upworthy so she could tell him about Arthur. As she got there, she stopped dead in her tracks and placed her hand over her mouth to stifle a scream.

All four servants and the five kitchen staff lay on the ground, with blood oozing from beneath their still bodies.

They're dead! Somebody has killed them!

Margery froze to the spot in a frightened daze. She stood there for what she thought was an age, but it was in fact only a few seconds. Thoughts of Arthur alone and crying brought her back to her senses. She forced herself to look away from the terrible sight and ran for the stairs.

Screams rang out from the great hall. Margery heard Master Charles shouting angrily, but most of all, she heard the blood-curdling screams from Lady Mary, and what she heard made her own blood churn inside her body.

What on earth is going on? Is somebody attacking us? Margery was stunned and didn't know what to do.

Master Charles screamed so loudly that the shock caused her to lose her footing on the stairs. She slipped down several of the steps, gripping onto the handrails as hard as she could. What she was hearing didn't belong in this happy household. It didn't even belong in this world. It belonged to the devil and his followers.

"No! For the love of God, please stop!" Master Charles pleaded. "I'll do anything you ask. I'll get you whatever you want, but please leave my wife alone."

Margery shivered as she heard the shouts and screams from the great hall. She slowly and carefully made her way back up the stairs to Arthur, who was now quiet and still. It was as though he, too, was listening to the carnage going on below them.

Margery grabbed the baby and scooped him into her arms. Arthur stirred and cried again, but this time, his cries were weak and pitiful. Margery knew she had to ack quickly or she would lose him just as she had lost her own son not so long ago.

She heard footsteps running up the stairs, so she tried

hiding behind the curtains. Arthur cried a little and then fell silent again. The door burst open, and Margery held her breath, hoping that little Arthur would remain quiet long enough for them not to be discovered.

But whoever the men were, they were no fools. They ripped apart the curtains, revealing the most frightening man Margery had ever seen. He had lifeless, grey eyes that seemed to violate her very soul, and a long scar down the left side of his face.

Margery screamed.

The man smiled and pulled a bloody knife from under his cloak. He plunged it into Margery's neck and grabbed the baby from her arms. One of the men who had entered the room alongside Margery's attacker grabbed Arthur from him and stepped back.

"We're not killing a child, Gare. It's bad enough that you're murdering women, but you are not touching this child."

The evil man reached forward and sliced the baby's protector's throat. The man's eyes grew wide with shock and fear, as in disbelief at what was happening to him. He fell to the floor.

The man he'd called Gare grabbed Arthur and laid him on the bed.

As the life drained from her body, Margery watched in horror as the man set about his unholy work.

Chapter 22

Dawn was breaking over the frozen landscape as Edward Johnson slipped out of the rear doorway of the house on the corner of Watelyng Strete and Soperlane. He shivered and pulled his cloak tightly around his body as the wintry morning air penetrated his senses and made him regret his decision to leave the relative warmth of the house.

He'd spent the night inside the house as there was no benefit to be gained from freezing to death sitting in the tree on Nederslane, from which he wasn't able to see anything through the darkness. If anyone was coming to the house during the night, Edward was going to make sure he was there to greet them.

Now that dawn was breaking, he moved outside to the vantage point in the tree on nearby Nederslane. Once there, he'd wait until curfew lifted and Stephen came to relieve him.

Edward settled into the tree at the point where he could see over the wall at the rear of the house and into the courtyard. If anyone was coming to search for the confessions, this was the way they would come, as nobody would be foolish enough to enter from Watelyng Strete, where they would be seen by the city dwellers going about their daily business.

The morning was clear and cold. Freezing cold. Edward huddled under his cloak and cursed the weather. The only time he'd ever felt colder in his entire life was a few months earlier, when they'd jumped into a river during a snow blizzard in Malton, North Yorkshire. Compared to that, this day was like a warm summer's afternoon.

Loud bells rang out, disturbing the morning peace and signalling that curfew was over. London would shortly come to life, with traders setting up their stalls all over the crowded, stinking city. Edward would go back to the storeroom and the crypts via Gamaliell Pye's slaughterhouses, where he'd pick up whatever supplies Pye had gathered for them.

It was unsafe for them to be seen around the markets as the cryers were busy whipping up the angry crowds, telling everyone that John Howard and his followers were to blame for the recent murders at the white house where they had lived.

Edward's thoughts turned to John. Two nights prior, he'd gone to spend the night with his father and sister at the Stronde, where John was trying to discover who the mysterious Andrew Griffiths was. He should have arrived back at the crypts yesterday, but as Edward had left after curfew to relieve Stephen, it had forced him to wait until this morn to discover what John had found out.

Movement in the courtyard caught his eye, and Edward's mind immediately focused on the scene unfolding ahead of him.

A shadowy figure jumped over the wall at the side of the stables, and for a few minutes went out of Edward's view as he no doubt crouched low to make sure anyone that might be inside the house hadn't seen him. After several minutes, the figure emerged back into view as he crossed the courtyard towards the house.

Edward kicked himself because he'd left the door unlocked for Stephen, who'd no doubt take refuge in there because it was too cold to sit in the tree for very long. Any man would freeze to death if he just sat without movement in this weather.

The shadowy figure tried the door and slipped inside the house. Edward climbed down from the tree and walked over the frozen ground, keeping close to the houses that lined Soperlane and the shadows they provided. He climbed the small tree and slid over the wall, stopping as the intruder had done to make sure he hadn't been seen. Any noise he might have made was drowned out by the sounds of horses clattering along the cobblestones and the traders shouting and yelling to each other as they passed on the narrow stretes.

Satisfied, Edward ran around to the front of the stables and hid inside the doorway, watching and listening for any signs that he'd been seen. A few minutes later, he ran over the exposed courtyard, keeping to the sides and away from the windows as much as he could.

Edward ducked under the windows and pushed the rear door open so he could squeeze through. With his knife at the ready, he slipped inside and closed the door behind him.

Edward didn't know what to expect once he was inside. Either the intruder was alone, in which case he would capture him and force him to explain why he was there, or he'd opened the front door to allow others to enter after him. Edward was prepared for both scenarios.

He heard a loud crack from upstairs. Edward had memorised every step inside the house, both upstairs and down, and he knew where to step to avoid any creaking or groaning from the wooden steps or floorboards.

He slowly made his way up the stairs and stopped at the top, listening for signs of movement from the intruder and any others he might have let in from the front.

The sound of floorboards being ripped up came from the room at the far end of the corridor, so Edward tiptoed towards it. The door was ajar, and Edward peered through to see what he was up against.

A man facing away from the door was on his knees, pulling on the floorboards, trying to rip them up. Edward noticed his full attention was on what he was doing, and he paid no mind to anything else around him. The man was alone, and he must have been sure that John and the rest were not there.

Edward sprang into action.

He pushed through the door and grabbed the man from behind, catching him off guard and completely vulnerable to attack. Edward's powerful arms did the rest.

"What are you doing here?" Edward asked, choking the man just enough so the intruder knew he meant business, but not enough so the man couldn't speak.

"I . . . I . . . I left my knife here a few weeks ago, and I'm trying to find it."

Edward smashed the man over the head with the handle of his knife before placing the blade at his throat.

"One more lie, and it will be the last words you ever utter."

"I . . . I'm searching for something, and I can't tell you what it is because the master will kill me if I do."

"I'll kill you if you don't," Edward said.

He dragged the man away from the hole in the floorboards he'd made in the corner near the window and threw him against the wall. Edward hit the man hard on the side of his face, causing him to let out a high-pitched yelp as he fell to the floor. Edward placed his knee on the man's chest and searched him for any weapons, and after he'd removed three knives, he once again hit the man roughly on the jaw and sat him up.

Edward noticed the long, runny nose that was now bleeding from the blows he'd received. "I know you from somewhere. Who are you?"

"My name is Frederick, and I'm just trying to find shelter and warmth," the man said, staring at the knife in Edward's large hand.

Edward slammed the handle into the man's temple, no doubt causing him to see stars through the pain he'd be feeling. "One more lie, and you're done. This is your last chance. I know who you are. You are the guard who works for Lord Howard at the Stronde, aren't you?"

The man nodded slowly.

"What's your name? And don't lie to me."

"Barton, My name's Barton."

"Why are you here, Barton?" Edward pushed the point of his knife into Barton's side and felt warm blood flow down his fingers as it pierced his skin through his torn clothing.

Barton screamed in pain.

"Scream all you want, but you're going to tell me why you are here and what you are doing."

"The master will kill me." Barton looked pale and scared.

"You are as close to death right now as you've ever been, so if I were you, I wouldn't want to be any closer. Last chance."

"Alright, but promise you won't kill me."

"I won't if you tell me the truth."

As Barton opened his mouth to speak, a loud crack

came from the hallway outside the room. Edward smashed his large hand into Barton's head, rendering him unconscious, and ran to the doorway, ready for whoever was on the other side.

The door opened with a crash, and a man in a hood raced in. Edward grabbed him from behind in a bear-like grip and held his hand to his throat. He dragged him to the side of the door in case there was anyone else behind him.

"Who are you?" Edward growled.

"Edward, it's me, Stephen. Let go."

Edward relaxed his grip and let go. "Stephen, I'm sorry. I didn't know it was you."

"I realise that," Stephen said, rubbing his neck tenderly. "You've got a grip like a bear. Who's this?" Stephen pointed at Barton.

"This is Barton, the guard with the big nose from the Stronde. I caught him in here, tearing up the floorboards. He was about to tell me what he's doing here when you came along."

"Well, he can tell both of us then, can't he?" Stephen kicked the stirring Barton. "Wake up."

Barton opened his eyes and looked at the two determined men staring down at him. Edward noticed him staring at Stephen's scar glistening down the side of his face, and he watched as the man shuddered at the frightening appearance Stephen made to anyone who crossed him.

"Tell us what you are doing here." Stephen kicked Barton's legs. "And don't lie."

"I'm trying to run away from Lord Howard. He hates me, and I need somewhere to sleep until I find other work."

Stephen lashed out with his fist, catching Barton square

in the jaw. Blood trickled down Barton's mouth, and Edward watched as the guard's eyes grew wide when Stephen placed the tip of his blade at his throat.

"I don't have time for your lies. John never returned to us yesterday after spending the night at the Stronde. He never does this unless we know about it first, and we're all worried about him. What do you know about that?"

"Nothing." Barton shook his head. "I saw John Howard with his Lordship and Lady Sarah, but I don't know nothing about him not leaving yesterday morning. Honest, I don't."

"I don't believe you." Stephen pushed the knife deeper into Barton's exposed neck. "John is never this late, and we're worried something has happened to him. It's strange that you're here the day after he disappeared. Tell me where he is, or it's going to get very painful for you, and if I catch you lying, I'm going to really hurt you. I'm worried about my friend, so don't think I'm not serious."

The look Stephen gave Barton must have convinced him he wasn't bluffing, because he started speaking at a rapid rate.

"If I tell you, the master will kill me. He'll set that evil monster on me. I'm more scared of him than I am of you."

Edward leaned forward. "The evil monster?"

Barton nodded. "The one with the scar like he's got." He pointed at Stephen. "But he's scarier than this one. He's scarier than any man I've ever seen."

"Does this man have grey eyes that stare right through you?" Edward pressed.

"Yes." Barton nodded. "That's him. The man with the dead eyes, as we all called him."

Edward looked at Stephen. "Gare."

"That's him," Barton shouted. "That's what the master called him."

"What happened to John?" Edward asked, turning to Stephen. "I'd assumed he'd returned to you yesterday."

"He never showed up, and I think this mumper knows where he is." Stephen pushed his face closer to the terrified Barton.

"I'm only going to ask you one more time. What happened to John Howard?"

Barton stared at the two powerful men, and he must have known there was no escaping.

"And we want to know who your master is, and where he's staying with Gare." Edward's mouth was etched into a snarl.

"What about me?" Barton asked. "If I tell you what I know, the master will kill me. If I don't, you will kill me. I don't fancy my chances either way."

"We promise we'll help you, if you'll help us," Edward said. "For a start, we won't kill you if you tell us all you know. Then we'll keep you safe until we find John and kill Gare."

"You promise?"

"You have our word."

Chapter 23

Barton sighed, and Edward could see that he had no choice other than to tell them what he knew.

"Promise you won't kill me for what I'm about to tell you," Barton said. "I was just carrying out me orders, and I meant no harm to John Howard or any of you."

"What did you do to him?" Stephen's knife pushed deeper into Barton's throat.

"I'm here because the master thinks the confessions left behind by the Colte woman might be hidden here. He knows John Howard has them, and he thinks he hid them here."

"Why does your master want the confessions?" Edward asked.

"Because some of them are about him, and he wants them destroyed. If you ask me, he wants the rest of them so he can bribe whoever is in them for his own good, but that's just my opinion."

"Who is your master?" Edward asked.

"Andrew Griffiths is his name. He's cruel and ruthless."

Edward and Stephen looked at each other. John had

mentioned that name only a few days ago and told them the confessions relating to him were missing.

"Isn't he the one who bought all the properties for Margaret?" Stephen asked.

Edward nodded. "I'm sure that's him. Carry on, Barton. Tell us about this Andrew Griffiths."

"And tell us where John is, and he'd better not be hurt," Stephen added.

"You can't mistake Griffiths. He's a funny-looking man, that's for sure. He has a man's body on a boy's legs, so he's small, you see, and he looks strange. But he's cruel. One of Asheborne's men laughed at him when he walked in on them a few days ago, and the next thing, he set this Gare on him. He dragged him into another room and carried out the devil's work on him. He cut him open and"—Barton stopped for a moment—"The man is evil, that's all I've got to say about him. I never want to see him again."

"I do." Edward gave Barton an intense, fevered stare of pure hatred.

Barton shivered. "Lord Asheborne used to be my master, but before he died, Lord Griffiths came for me. He sent me to work for Lord Howard, so I could spy on him. I didn't want to, but what could I do about it? I was just following me orders. Griffiths told me stay close to Howard and find out all I could about the confessions, and where John Howard hid them. His Lordship told me to wait until he came to London for further orders."

"And? You obviously saw him."

"What was left of Lord Asheborne's loyal guards were staying at a house he'd got for us. I went around there every few days to report what I knew about Howard. Two days ago, Griffiths was already sitting there when I arrived. The boys told me what his man had done to poor old Fitz."

Barton looked around the room and then settled his gaze on Stephen's scar. He shuddered.

"I stood outside the door while Lord Howard and John spoke. I heard them talk about Griffiths. John asked his father who he was. He didn't know, but he promised to find out. Lord Howard wanted the confessions, but John wouldn't give them to him." Barton paused and looked at Stephen's scar again.

"I told all this to Griffiths. As I knew what John looked like, he sent me with five of the others yesterday morning to ambush him on his way back to you. It was foggy. Very foggy, which was perfect. We took him by surprise and roughed him up a bit."

"Is he hurt?" Edward asked.

"Not too much, but he was unconscious." Barton winced as Stephen's knife dug deeper. "We took him to the house, and that's all I know. I promise. Griffiths was coming back to talk to him, but he sent me here to find the confessions, so whatever happened to him had nothing to do with me."

Stephen smacked Barton around the head with the handle of his knife. "Where is this house?"

"Next to the George Inn on Lumbardstrete. You can't miss it. A church is on one side of it and the Inn is on the other. Whatever happened to John Howard had nothing to do with me. I didn't lay a finger on him."

Edward grabbed Barton by the neck, almost squeezing the life out of him. "You had nothing to do with it? If it wasn't for you, he would be here this morn with us, so don't tell me you had nothing to do with it. It's all your fault he's where he is now."

"What you going to do to me?" Barton asked.

"You're staying here until we get back, and you'd better

hope nothing happened to John, or the same thing will happen to you." Edward spat the words out.

"But I can't stay here," Barton protested. "What if Griffiths sends someone else? They'll find me and kill me."

"You'd better hope they don't then," Stephen said. "You're staying here until we find John and then we'll be back for you."

Edward ran out to the stables and came back with a length of rope. He bound Barton's arms and legs so he couldn't go anywhere and threw him over his shoulders. He carried him down the stairs to the great hall, where he tied him to the legs of the heavy table.

Edward and Stephen walked out of the little white house.

Chapter 24

John Howard's eyes flickered open, and he immediately regretted waking up. Pain wracked his body from head to toe, but especially from his face. He could barely see out of his right eye, and his left eye was completely closed.

White hot spasms of misery shot down his face when he tried wiggling his jaw, and he couldn't feel his hands from the rope that bound them tightly behind his back. His shoulders ached, and John knew he was in serious trouble.

He took a moment to see where he was, and slowly his vision came into focus. They'd sat him propped against a wall in the corner of a small, filthy room that was covered in old straw. A stone fire ring was burning wood in the middle of the room, and five men were sitting around it, laughing and joking. The exit door was on the opposite wall from where he was sitting, but it was a straight line to freedom if he could make it.

John's arms may have been bound, but his legs were free. He thought about trying to stand up and making a run for it, but he knew he was in no shape to do that. The men would be on him before he got to his feet, so he made the wise choice to remain where he was. His body couldn't take any more abuse.

"How long have I been here?" John almost didn't recognise his own voice. His jaw felt like it was on fire, so he knew he wouldn't be speaking much.

"He's awake," one of the guards announced. "The famous John Howard speaks to us."

"It's Lord John Howard now," another corrected him.

The guards laughed.

"Give him some ale," another said. "The boss said we've got to take good care of him."

"We'll take good care of him," yet another said. "Just like he took good care of Lord Asheborne."

They all laughed again.

One of them walked over with a jug of ale and forced John's mouth open, pouring most of it down the front of his clothes. John's mouth exploded in agony, and he longed for the relief of unconsciousness.

The guard sneered. "It looks like Lord Howard doesn't want to enjoy our hospitality, boys." He threw his head back and laughed.

"We need to be careful," another guard said. "Griffiths gave orders that he was to be able to hold a conversation. Look at him. Right now, he can't even hold his head up, never mind have a talk with the boss."

A moment's silence. Then roars of laughter.

"You've been here since yesterday morning," the guard holding the jug of ale said, crouching down in front of John. "The boss wanted a little talk with you, so we brought you 'ere after your visit with your father and sister."

"Are they alright?" John croaked. Every word seemed like shards of glass were exploding in every corner of his mouth.

"Of course, Lord Howard is alright. Who do you think we are? It's you the boss wanted."

John had heard this before with Ren Walden, and for a moment, he wondered if he was having a nightmare. Then the door to the house opened, and he knew that whatever was happening, it was all too real.

John watched as a man with an oversized body on child-sized legs strode into the room. Whoever this strange man was, he carried himself with an air of authority that John had only seen in the noblemen.

The man walked over to John and kicked his feet. "Is this him?" he asked in a high-pitched voice that John could have taken for a girl. "Is this the infamous John Howard?"

"The one and only, sir. He's a bit roughed up because he put up a bit of a struggle, but he can talk alright if he wants to."

The strange man grabbed a chair from a different room and sat down in front of John.

"John Howard. I have heard so much about your famous exploits, and to be frank, I'm a little disappointed. I thought you would be ten feet tall and have muscles the size of a bear."

The guards sat around the fireplace roared with laughter.

John thought about responding, but his mouth and body hurt too much. He didn't need to encourage any further beatings than the ones he knew were inevitably coming. He would bide his time and try to survive, and if he did, this strange little man would see the real John Howard on his terms.

"You probably don't know me, but we can't all be as famous as John Howard. Allow me to introduce myself. My name is Andrew Griffiths."

The hackles on John's arms went up. Andrew Griffiths!

He studied the man's features as best he could through his impaired vision, but the man was so strange looking that he knew he would have no problems recognising him if he ever saw him again.

His accent gave further clues about where he came from. Griffiths spoke in the same manner he'd heard the previous year in Yorkshire, so now he knew where to look when he escaped from here.

If he escaped from here.

"You're going to tell me where you hid Margaret Colte's confessions," Griffiths continued. "Especially the ones pertaining to me and your father, Robert Howard. The rest you can keep. If you tell me where they are, my men will let you go without further harm, but if you don't, well, let's just say that you will regret it. So, make it easy on yourself and tell me where they are."

"I destroyed them," John croaked.

"All of them?"

"All of them."

"I don't believe you." Griffiths leant forward and grabbed John's jaw, sending jolts of pain shooting through his body. Daylight faded and everything went dark.

He awoke to the sensation of being soaked. He opened his eyes to see the guards throwing a bucket of piss all over him to wake him up. The stench was terrible, and John heaved, causing even more pain.

"As I was saying before you fell asleep on me," Griffiths continued. "Tell me where the confessions are, and I promise my men will take it easy on you."

"I told you, I destroyed them." John could barely speak, but he felt a deep rumbling in his stomach that was bursting into the open. He would go to his grave before he told this obnoxious, poisoned man anything about the crypts or the confessions.

Griffiths kicked John hard in the groin, forcing him into a tight ball on the ground.

"I dislike these sorts of rough tactics," Griffiths said, rising to his feet. "I have to be somewhere else, but you are not going anywhere, and you shall tell me where the confessions are."

He leant forward again. "I believe you have met my friend, Oswyn Gare," Griffiths sneered, enjoying the look of disgust etched on John's battered and bruised face. "You have seen how he carries out his work, which is a little extreme, I must admit. But he's effective. Right now, he is taking care of another task for me, but when he's done, he'll be back here to persuade you to tell me where the confessions are. If I were you, I'd consider telling my guards here before he arrives, or he'll get it from you in a manner that only he can."

Griffiths pulled away from John and kicked him hard one last time. "I doubt we will meet again, John Howard. The next time I hear your name, it will be news about your sad passing. Please don't say I didn't give you a chance."

Griffiths turned to the guards stood behind him. "Don't hurt him any further. I want him to be fully aware when Gare gets here in the next few days. Keep him fed and give him ale. Whatever you do, do not let him escape, because if he does, it will be you who Gare drags into the back room. Do you understand?"

"Yes, Master Griffiths, we understand completely. Howard won't escape. He can't escape. We'll get the information you want, or if we don't, we're sure Gare will."

Griffiths smiled. "Oh, I know he will. Gare has a way of getting people to talk."

He turned and left the house.

John sat in a ball, praying that his body would be strong enough to endure the coming days. If he was still here when Gare arrived, he knew what was coming, and no matter how strong his resolve would be to resist, he knew no man could withstand the brand of torture Gare specialised in.

John knew that either he had to escape, or he would die in this house. Right now, his chances looked extremely slender.

Chapter 25

Robert Howard sat slumped behind his desk in his study. He chewed on his fingernails and continually shifted positions in his chair as he relived the events from the previous day over and over in his mind. No matter how he tried, his thoughts led him to the same dark places his mind didn't want to go.

He'd known for a while that other powerful nobles were plotting against him, but Robert had always believed he was above all that. He was the leader of the elite privy council, and above all else, he had the ear of Henry VIII. As long as he had that, he could stave off any plots the other jealous nobles could ever devise against him.

But things were different now. Yesterday, for the first time in his entire life, the king had refused to see him, even when they had urgent business to discuss. Instead, the king had summoned that weosule, Barkley Stephenson, the Marquess of Dover, to his chambers and barred Robert's entry. Stephenson was rich and powerful, but above all else, he was ambitious. Along with a few others, he'd eyed Robert's position with envy for a long time.

Robert was well aware of what happened when a noble fell out of favour with the king. As with Lord Asheborne, Henry would accuse the noble of treason and use an Act of Attainder to remove their lands and titles. Finally, after a quick trial, Henry VIII removed their heads, as had been brutally demonstrated with William Asheborne.

Robert Howard didn't want to be next.

A firm knock on the door pulled Robert from his dark thoughts. "Enter," he yelled.

His trusty steward, Evans, entered the study, and Robert could tell from the look on his face that he wasn't bringing good news.

"What is it, Evans?"

"Sir, Lord Stephenson is here along with Sheriff Holley. They claim to bring urgent news for your Lordship."

Robert Howard rubbed his bloodshot eyes that ached from a sleepless night. He sighed and allowed his head to sink into his hands.

At least Sarah got out of here before it was too late. Robert was grateful for his insistence on Sarah going back to Broxley two days prior.

"Show them in." Robert stood up to his full height. Stephenson might be his senior in the English system of nobility, but Robert was every bit as wealthy and powerful as the snake-eyed marquess. More so, because Robert was still the leader of the privy council. Or at least he had been until yesterday.

"Lord Howard, it's good to see you again." Barkley Stephenson strode into the study like he owned the place. Robert watched as his eyes scanned the study like a hawk studied its prey from upon high.

Robert fought the urge to slap him.

Instead, he grabbed the offered hand and studied

Stephenson's thin and pale features for any clues about what news they brought this day.

Barkley Stephenson was in his mid-thirties and had short brown hair that was so thin that it reminded Robert of a bunch of straw sticking out from under his oversized hat. Robert knew that underneath that hat, the Marquess was almost bald except for the few hairs that grew down the sides of his head.

Tall and painfully thin, Robert thought Stephenson would look better if he got a good meal inside him, but whatever his physical appearance, Robert knew that Stephenson had a sharp mind. He had to be careful with the man known in the court as Snake Eyes.

"Please, sit." Robert gestured to the chairs at the other side of his desk. "What brings you here this morn?"

Robert looked at Sheriff Holley, who reminded him of an older version of his son, John Howard. His long black hair sprung out from under his hat in all different directions, and Robert would have smiled at the similarities if the sheriff hadn't looked so serious and miserable.

Holley glanced around the room, his eyes not settling on any one thing for long. Robert felt his unease but put it down to the fact that he was in the presence of a powerful lord. It was nothing unusual.

"I'm afraid we don't bring good news, Robert," Barkley Stephenson said as he sat down. "The Sheriff here has to report some rather ghastly news to you, and then I'm going to make your day even worse."

Stephenson tried to look serious, but Robert could see the pleasure he was taking from the glee in his eyes. Once again, Robert resisted the urge to punch the marquess in the mouth.

"What news do you bring, Sheriff?" Robert fixed his

gaze on Sheriff Holley, so he didn't have to look at the smug face of Lord Stephenson.

"Lord Howard, as you know, I am leading the investigation into the murders of your men at the white house on Watelyng Strete where your son, John Howard, lives." Holley looked up with a pained look on his face.

"Yes, Sheriff, I'm well aware of your investigation. Have you caught the men responsible for this vile act?"

"No, Lord Howard. I'm sorry, for I wish I had better news for you this morn."

"What is it then?" Robert watched Stephenson from the corner of his eye as he sat feigning sympathy. Robert knew he was enjoying every moment. He suppressed his rising anger once again and settled his gaze on Sheriff Holley.

"Sir, I know you are aware of a place called Chessett House that is located close to Waltham Abbey just outside of London in Essex?" Holley's words tumbled out of his mouth at a rapid pace.

Robert felt his heart race. "Chessett House? Yes, of course I know it. It's owned by the Packwood family, the Earl of Bedford. What about it?" Robert's pulse raced. He didn't like where this was going.

"Lord Howard, do you know the infant that Charles Packwood and his wife"—Holley looked at his notes—"Mary Packwood were raising?"

"Should I?" Robert felt his face flush deep red.

"Sir, pardon me for my bluntness, but we don't have time for any mind games. A serious crime has been committed and I am here to inform you of the details. Lord Stephenson will take it from there."

"Tell me what happened."

"Someone—or more likely a group of people—broke into Chessett House a few days ago and murdered everyone in the household." Holley sighed and looked at Robert Howard. "Sir, the level of brutality was astounding, and no-one was spared. Not even the infant boy called Arthur Shipley, who we know is your son."

The blood drained from Robert's face. "They killed Arthur?"

"Yes, sir. Tortured him, to be more precise. We have reason to believe it was the same man who murdered your guard, Willis, at the house on Watelyng Strete because, well, because of the manner of the crime committed."

Robert sat in silence, staring at Sheriff Holley. His knees shook, and he dropped the quill that he was holding in his hand. "Why?" he said after a long pause. "Why would anyone want to hurt an innocent baby?"

"We're not sure, my Lord, but it's possible that it was done to hurt you and your family."

Robert stared at Holley, unable to speak.

"Why would murdering Packwood's baby hurt you?" Stephenson asked, feigning innocence. Holley looked at the floor.

"Stop the pretence, Stephenson. You know damned well why it hurts me." Robert stood up. "Arthur might not have been my son, but he was being raised as a noble and would have had a good life." Tears fell from his eyes, and he wiped them away quickly, hoping Stephenson hadn't seen them.

"The same man committed similar crimes last year, and we believe it was under the orders of Lord Asheborne," Holley continued. "So, for now at least, we believe that whoever this man is—and we believe his name is Oswyn Gare—he is following the orders of Lord Asheborne's son, William Asheborne Junior, after a hat in his colours was left at the scene."

"Do you know where he is?" Robert was struggling to

keep control of himself. He was shaking from head to foot, and he felt as though he was about to throw up. "What kind of man would do such a thing to a small baby?"

"A man that will go to any lengths to hurt you and your family. Lord Howard, I'm very sorry to bring such bad news to you on this day. I assure you we are doing everything in our power to apprehend this inhuman man and bring him to justice."

"Who exactly are the 'we' you keep referring to?" Robert shouted, his nostrils flaring. "I want this man's head, do you hear?"

"After the crimes he's committed, losing his head is the least of his problems," Holley said. "The 'we' I refer to are myself and my colleagues, both here in London and those in Essex. Together, we shall not rest until this man, and anyone associated with him, are captured and put to death. I assure you, Lord Howard, that we will catch him."

"Does John know about this?"

Holley shook his head. "Not yet, sir. I'm going to find him after I leave here and tell him. He has already met Gare first hand, and he knows what he looks like. John will be an important witness when we eventually capture Gare but keeping your son safe is proving to be an arduous task."

"John is single-minded and determined, I'll give you that," Robert said. "But he's persistent, and if you allow him to help you, I believe you will find him to be an excellent asset to your investigation, especially as he already knows what this Gare looks like. When you see him, please tell him to come here after he hears the news."

Holley looked at Stephenson, and Robert felt the tension rising once again. As if it wasn't high enough already after learning that Arthur had been brutally slain.

"What is it?" Robert demanded. "Is there something else?"

Stephenson looked at Robert and Robert was sure he smiled as he opened his mouth to speak. It took everything Robert had to stop himself from jumping over the desk and beating him to death right in front of the Sheriff.

"You must have been aware yesterday that the king is displeased with you," Stephenson said, smoothing down the wrinkles on his cloak. "You have my sympathy for the death of your bastard, and it is unfortunate that news of this comes at the same time I was sent here, but I follow the orders of Lord Cromwell and the king, and you know well that nothing, not even the murder of your bastard, impedes orders from the king."

"Stephenson, if you refer to Arthur as the bastard one more time, I swear the sheriff will arrest me for murder. Do you hear? I shall not tolerate your thoughtlessness for another moment."

"Please forgive my directness, Robert. Of course I have compassion for the murder of your son, but I am here on the orders of Thomas Cromwell, and I have in my possession a warrant for your arrest."

Stunned silence.

Robert threw his hands forward. "A warrant for my arrest? On what grounds? What made-up charges am I accused of? Isn't it enough that I suffer the loss of my son in such a brutal way?"

"As I said, I am sorry for the loss of your child, but this has no bearing on the matters of the court. You know this as well as any man does."

Barkley Stephenson stood up to his full height. "You are accused of treason against the king and are ordered to be imprisoned in the Tower until your trial date, which is yet to be fixed. Do not resist, for I have men outside that are more than willing to arrest you either dead or alive."

Robert gave Stephenson an intense, fevered stare. "What lies have you made up about me, Stephenson? What lies have you whispered into the king's ears that convinced him to agree to this injustice? Don't think I don't know about your treachery in the court. The whispers reached my ears some time ago, so don't play the innocent messenger with me. I shall have my vengeance, and when I do, you will regret your actions here this day."

"Your threats have been duly noted, Lord Howard. However, I have some good news for you, if you are prepared to listen. The king is sympathetic to your cause, but he is tired of the drama surrounding your son and the danger the confessions pose to the court. He generously offered you a way out of this if you choose to take it."

"What is it?"

"You have until March to hand over to Lord Cromwell every one of Margaret Colte's confessions. Further, William Asheborne and the man known as Gare must be captured and executed. The king demands that the whole sorry tale of Margaret Colte and her confessions be ended once and for all. If you agree to this, then you shall be released from the Tower and allowed to go free. If not, a trial shall decide your fate."

Robert sighed and slumped into his chair. "You mean I either hand them over so Cromwell can use them against his enemies, or I am executed? You realise I do not have Margaret's confessions, don't you? John has them, and he refuses to give them up for any reason. He is the one you should go after, not me."

"You are the one who had the king's ear, not your son, and it is through you that any danger to the king shall transpire. It falls upon you to convince John to hand over the confessions. If he cares about you at all—and that is debatable after the way you treated him last year—if he has any feelings left for you, then he will hand over the confessions. If he doesn't, you will lose your titles, your lands, and also your head. It's up to you, Robert. You have one month to comply."

If looks could kill, Barkley Stephenson would have been stone cold after the glare Robert gave him.

"Guards!" Stephenson barked his orders.

Chapter 26

John Howard moved his aching jaw from side to side and instantly regretted it. His teeth ached from the beatings he'd received, and he knew he wouldn't be holding down any long conversations for a while.

His eyes matted, and he could barely make out the shapes of the guards as they sat around the stone fire ring drinking ale and laughing at crude jokes, many of them at his expense. He tried forcing himself to look harder so he would recognise them after he'd escaped, but as hard as he tried, he wasn't able to focus his vision with any accuracy. He would have to rely on the sounds of their voices and hope that he'd recognise them by their sounds.

Escape! Who am I kidding? I'm not going anywhere, and if I don't find a way out by the time Gare gets here, it's all over. For all of us, including Catherine and Sarah. I have to escape before that animal gets here.

John groped around in the straw where he was sitting, hoping to find something - anything that could be used as a weapon. But he found nothing. He clenched his fists behind his back through the rope that bound them together and came up with a plan.

I'm going to die anyway, but I will not die at the hands of Gare, giving up my secrets so he can kill everyone I care for after he's done me in. No, I shall die on my own terms here this day. I'm going to run for the door and force the guards to kill me here and now. At least that way I can die knowing Catherine and Sarah are safe. I need not worry about Edward and Stephen, for they are powerful warriors who will avenge my death. Of that I am sure, for I have never met more worthy friends and warriors in my entire life.

John moved his legs around to get the circulation going, and he clenched his fists together, steeling himself for what was about to happen. He began forcing himself to his knees.

He stopped. *What was that?* A firm knocking at the door made John's blood go cold. He sank to the floor in defeat.

I'm too late. Griffiths is back with Gare!

The guards fell quiet, and John could sense the tension in the air. Nobody wanted to be around Gare, not even the men who supposedly worked with him.

"Are we expecting anyone?" a guard asked.

"Not that I know of," another answered.

Maybe it isn't Gare after all. John readied himself to bolt for the door as soon as they opened it.

Two of the guards rose and went to the door. When they opened it, the sound of a woman's voice drifted through the room.

"I'm sorry to disturb you, gentlemen, but I'm trying to find my husband. He was in the tavern next door, but they said he fell out as drunk as could be. I was wondering if any of you had seen him?"

John's heart stopped beating. He shook from head to foot, and he forced his battered eyes to open as far as they could.

It was Catherine! He would recognise that heavenly voice anywhere.

"This pretty lady is tryin to find 'er husband," the guard at the door turned to the other four, who were getting to their feet. "He staggered out of the George as drunk as you like. Isn't that the one we took in so he could sober up before going home?"

"I believe it is," another guard said. "Come on in, lady, and we'll show you where he is." The men smiled at each other.

John struggled to stand up. He kept quiet because he knew Catherine would never go to a place like this alone, so Stephen and Edward would be somewhere close, but he couldn't help himself when it came to Catherine.

"What's yer name, Miss?" the guard asked as he closed the door behind Catherine as she entered the house.

"Isobel." Catherine gave John a hard look, and even through the hazy mist of his impaired vision, John could see the look of concern on her beautiful face.

"Who's that?" she asked, pointing at John.

"Oh, don't mind him. He's one of us we caught stealing. He got a bit violent, so we taught him a lesson and tied him up until he calmed down a bit."

Catherine smiled at John and melted his heart. He stood up, swaying at the effort to stay upright. But he was ready for when Catherine gave the signal. He didn't know what it was, but he knew it was coming.

"He's back here sleeping it off, Miss. Come with me and I'll show you where he is." The men lined up behind Catherine, smiling at each other, leaving John alone with his thoughts.

He struggled and fought the ropes that bound his wrists, but they were too tight, and the rope cut into his flesh the more he struggled. He tried yelling, but all that came out was a guttural scream that seemed to come from the depths of his soul.

Where are Edward and Stephen?

He was about to run after the guards when he heard a loud crash. Shouts and screams of men in agony sounded like music to John's ears. He staggered towards the melee until Catherine ran up to him and pushed him against a wall.

"Turn around," she ordered. John did as she commanded and felt the rope binding his wrists relax and fall away as she cut them open.

"Are you alright?" Catherine pressed a knife into his hands. "We have to get out of here."

She kissed him softly on his cheek and pulled away.

John never said a word through the entire ordeal. He stared at his wife as though he'd never seen her before. And in this manner, he hadn't. He'd never seen Catherine so calm and brave before, and whatever love he'd felt before was suddenly amplified a thousand times.

Catherine was a warrior!

"You bitch!" One of the guards ran towards John and Catherine at speed. He never even gave John a second glance as he fixed his stare on Catherine. He raised his knife in the air as he approached, but John thrust his knife into the man's stomach as he got close.

The man fell to the ground in a heap, clutching his midriff. Summoning his last vestiges of strength and comprehension, John fell to his knees beside the fallen guard and pressed his knife to the man's neck.

Bloodcurdling screams came from the room at the back of the house, and John could hear a man's voice begging for mercy, which was something the guards gathered in this house today would not receive.

"Where are Griffiths and Gare?" John demanded. His

jaw screamed at him as he formed the words, but he ignored the pain. "Where are they?" John pressed harder and felt warm blood flowing down his fingers.

The guard screamed.

"Tell me where they are, and I'll let you live." John pressed even harder.

"I . . . I . . . I don't know," the guard stammered. "Griffiths comes and goes without telling us anything. We'd never seen him before. He came here a few days ago."

"What about Gare?"

"Griffiths sent five of our boys with him days ago. He never told us where they were going. That's all I know, honestly. That's all any of us know."

"What were your orders?"

"Griffiths told us he's working for Lord Asheborne's son, Master William, and we were to carry out his orders as though Master William gave them, because he had."

"What did Griffiths order you to do?" White hot pain scorched John's mouth and face, but he forced himself to concentrate on the guard and ignored the intense agony the men had inflicted on him.

"He ordered us to grab you and keep you here until Gare comes back from wherever he is to speak to you. We saw what he did to one of our boys, so we all felt a bit sorry for you."

"Not enough to stop you from beating me half to death." John pressed harder with his knife, gaining some satisfaction from hearing the man scream.

Catherine remained on her feet in front of John and the guard, watching the space around them for any of the other guards that had followed her to the room at the rear of the house. John looked up, part in admiration and part in shock.

Where had this side of Catherine come from? Then it

dawned on him. He'd seen it once before, on that unforgettable night when Margaret had been about to kill him. Catherine had got in the middle and killed Margaret. There was more to his wife than met the eye. John shook his head and concentrated on the guard laying before him.

Before he could speak, another bloodcurdling scream rang out and a man almost flew into the centre of the room, holding his side. He tripped over the stone fire ring and fell into the glowing embers. He screamed again as Edward's sword pierced his throat, and John watched as his blood drained into the fireplace and spread over the embers, making them spit and glow an even deeper red.

Edward and Stephen, covered in blood and guts, joined John and Catherine around the last remaining guard.

"You alright?" Stephen asked.

"Perfectly fine," John lied. "Just trying to get some answers from this one."

"Speak," Stephen barked. "Or I'll slit yer throat." Stephen's scar glistened in the half light of the glowing embers, and even John shuddered at the frightening spectacle.

The guard shivered and made a strange sound from his throat. "I'm telling him everything I know. I promise."

"What did Griffiths order you to do?" John repeated his earlier question.

"He ordered us to keep you here until Gare came back."

"Did he order you to beat him to death?" Edward asked.

The guard shook his head.

"I didn't think so." Edward wiped his blade on the man's cloak.

"Where are they?" Edward asked. "Where is Gare?"

"I don't know. I don't know where Griffiths sent him."

"What about Asheborne?" John asked. "Where is he?"

"I don't kn . . ." John sliced down on the man's neck, causing blood to splatter over his hand and arms. "One more lie, and I'll end your life."

"Please, don't kill me. I've got a wife and a child."

"Should have thought about that before you brought John here," Stephen said. "Answer his question."

"I honestly know nothing about Griffiths. I've never seen him before. He came here a few days ago. Same with Gare. Until he came here with Griffiths and killed one of our boys for just smiling at Griffiths, I'd never seen him before."

Stephen raised his blade.

"But I have been to see Master William." The guard rushed his words. "I know where he is."

"Tell me." John pressed the knife harder still.

"If I tell you, promise to let me go."

"If you don't, I promise I'll kill you right now." Stephen's scar glistened with sweat and blood.

The guard sighed. "He's in Yorkshire, in an old house. It's built like a square and it's got lots of windows. From what I heard, it's very old, like ancient. You can't miss it because there's nothing else like it anywhere around."

"Where in Yorkshire?" John asked.

"I only remember the name of the place because it's small and we couldn't find it. We were getting our orders after the Master first went there, and it's the only time I saw it. He sent us back here and told us to wait for his orders."

"Where is he?"

"It's a village called Burton something or other. Agnes, that's it. Burton Agnes. I only know because we had to keep asking the locals where it was."

"Where do we find this place?" Stephen asked.

"Don't ask me, because I couldn't find it. It's somewhere in Yorkshire. That's all I know."

John pressed the knife deeper into the man's throat. "That's not good enough."

"All I know is that after we stopped in York, we were told to ride out on the road to Bretlinton. We rode for two days and that's when we found the village, but we had to ask the locals in another town because we couldn't find it. When the young master said he was going to hide in a place where he wouldn't be found, he meant it."

John made a mental note of what the guard said and pulled his knife away from his throat. Edward reached down to help him to his feet.

"You need a physician"

John nodded. "I know where to find one. Let's get out of here before the other five guards return."

Stephen walked behind the guard and then suddenly sprung forward and thrust his blade into the man's throat. The guard's eyes opened wide as the shock of what was happening reached his brain. Blood spurted in all directions as the man gargled his final breaths.

The guard fell silent and still. He was dead.

"What did you do that for?" Catherine asked. "He told us everything he knew."

"He'd have told them we were coming as soon as we left here," Stephen said. "If we're going to find Gare and Asheborne, we need to surprise them. Look what they did to John. He deserved to die for doing that."

"Let's go." John held onto Edward.

They staggered out of the house onto Lumbardstrete and gathered on the frozen strete.

"Where are we going?" Edward asked. "You need a physician, so it's no use going to the crypts."

"The white house," John said. "I'll wait there while you get word to my father."

"The white house it is." Edward gripped John and stepped away from the house with Asheborne's five dead guards inside.

Chapter 27

Oswyn Gare let out a deep, gratified sigh and stared straight ahead at nothing in particular. His lips curled into a distant, unfocused smile. His soul was satiated.

For now.

Andrew Griffiths had been insistent on ordering Gare back to London immediately after his latest mission had been accomplished, but Gare took orders from no man. He had other, more pressing things to do that he'd put off for far too long, so Griffiths and the Howard boy would have to wait.

After a soul soothing, which was the name he'd given to his ritualistic murders, Gare needed to be alone. He needed time to reflect and replay what he'd done, and he needed time to adjust himself back into a normal life.

Gare laughed out loud. *A normal life! Who am I fooling?*

Four of the five men Griffiths had sent north with Gare stood outside Chessett House, shivering in the predawn darkness. The other lay dead inside the house.

Three of them had run to the bushes and vomited, their guts unable to withstand the waves of nausea from witnessing the frightening monk with the cold grey eyes at work. They wanted nothing more than to get as far away from this place as possible.

"Gare, hurry up. We have to get as far away from here as we can before dawn breaks. Lord Griffiths wants us back in London as soon as possible, and none of us wants to be here."

Gare ignored the men outside. They were weak, just like every other man he'd ever met.

No, not every man. He rubbed the scar that throbbed in the freezing cold on the left side of his face. *The man who did this wasn't weak, and I look forward to our next meeting. Edward Johnson is a worthy adversary that I shall enjoy killing.*

The image of the tall young man with large hands, and a grip as strong as a bear, was burned into Gare's brain. A day rarely went by that he didn't think of their meeting at Burningtown Manor in the Midlands the previous year, and the fight they'd had with each other. Gare smiled in satisfaction as he remembered the fear on the face of Johnson's wife, who had been heavy with child when he'd killed her. He knew that Edward Johnson would never rest until they met again in a fight to the death, and Gare couldn't wait.

He desired it. He dreamed of it. It was his destiny to finally kill a man worthy of his skills.

But Johnson would have to wait. He had another task that demanded his attention, and he'd put it off for way too long. It was time.

Drenched in the blood of his victims, Oswyn Gare walked outside into the freezing night. As soon as the four men waiting saw him, they ran like little girls to the bushes and threw up. Gare looked at them in disgust.

He changed into the familiar robes of a monk while the men regained control of themselves and mounted their horses. Gare could feel the hatred and fear as they stared at him, and he turned to face them in the pale moonlight.

"Why did you have to kill the baby?" one guard asked. "I understand the others, but why the baby?"

Gare stared at the man who dared question his methods. He pulled his bloodied knife from his blood-stained clothes and walked towards the brave guard.

"Do you question my methods?" Gare hissed. "Do you wish to join your friend who questioned me in there?"

The man pulled on the reins of his horse and backed away from the devil approaching him. Gare's lifeless eyes stared after him, but the man refused to meet them with his own.

Gare flexed his muscles under his cloak. Although small in stature, Gare knew that his strength was a match for any man, even the bear-like strength of Edward Johnson. None of these cowards stood a chance, and they knew it.

"No, of course not," the guard relented. "But tell us, why did you have to kill the child? That's not what any of us agreed when we came out here with you."

"Griffiths ordered you to help me break in and to take care of whoever was in here. The child was the target Griffiths sent me here to kill. That's why I killed him."

Silence.

"Griffiths sent us here to kill a baby?" the guard was becoming animated. "We didn't know that, or we would have refused to come here with you. And even then, why did you torture them and gut them like a fish? Even the woman? What kind of devil are you?"

Gare's nostrils flared. He reached up and with one hand pulled the guard off his horse and threw him on the ground. The man stared at him, his eyes wide open in fear.

"One more word and I'll kill you right here." Gare's

dead eyes stared into the man's frozen soul. "You're lucky that I can't kill you and leave you here because your worthless corpse would leave a trail back to Griffiths. But be warned, if I ever see you again, you are a dead man. I'll gut you just like I gutted those people in there."

Gare saw the terror etched on the man's face and he knew his words had made their desired effect. If he hadn't already satiated his soul with the killings inside the house, no number of orders from Griffiths or anyone else would have saved this man's life this night.

The guard stood up and mounted his horse, his face noticeably pale, even in the moonlight. The guard went back to the relative safety of his comrades and never said another word.

"We have to go," another guard said.

"I'm not going with you," Gare said. "I have other matters to attend too. Tell Griffiths I'll be there as soon as I can."

"Weren't our orders to do this and then get back to London as fast as possible?"

"Recover your friend's body and bury him somewhere far from here. And then get lost."

Gare stared at the guard, waiting for a response. There wasn't one. Instead, the guard dismounted and went back inside the killing house to retrieve his fallen comrade. With the help of the other three, they threw him over his own horse and tied him down. After he remounted, the guard shrugged and kicked his horse. The four men galloped off as fast as their horses could get them away.

Gare was glad. What he craved right now was solitude and quiet. He wouldn't speak to another person for several days. He mounted his horse and set off on the five-day journey to his next destination.

Chapter 28

The town of Hereford loomed large in the distance. The cathedral that had stood since before the time of the Vikings stood tall, even from this distance, and the sight of it made Oswyn Gare smile.

Hereford was the town where his life had finally taken some meaning, and he'd been looking forward to revisiting his old killing grounds on the way to Brecon and his date with destiny.

Gare's mind wandered as he stared at the cathedral far ahead of him. He figured it would take another hour or two before he reached it, and by that time, darkness wouldn't be far away. He'd stay the night and take some time the next morning to visit some of the places that stood out in his mind. Looking back, his time in Hereford had been the happiest times of his life.

Oswyn Gare settled back in his saddle and allowed the memories of his childhood to consume his thoughts. He needed this time to put his past to rest, and once this was over, he would never allow another thought of it to waste a moment of his life.

What would have become of me if I had been born into a different family? That is the question I have asked myself over and over, or at least I used to do until I came to terms with who I am. No, even though my father and brother were to blame for my younger years, the path I have chosen is all down to the person I am deep down in my soul. I was born to do the things I do, and no matter my origins, I would still be the same person I am today. Of that, I am certain.

GARE'S THOUGHTS drifted back to his childhood in Brecon, Wales, and the cruel manner in which he was raised. Born to a gentle mother and a violent and abusive father some twenty-eight years earlier, young Oswyn had endured a tough start in life.

Not that he could remember much about it, but he was a sickly child who had suffered from a severe bout of the sweating sickness as a young boy. Even though he survived, young Oswyn always seemed to be behind his peers in his physical development.

This angered his father constantly, who often complained that his first-born son was lazy and weak, and was either unwilling or unable to help with the back-breaking work in the fields. Beatings often accompanied his father's wrath, and Oswyn would find sanctuary hiding in the thick bushes around the River Usk. He would take comfort listening to his father, and later his younger brother as they thrashed around shouting his name and yelling at him for shirking his work.

The severe beatings with a horse whip were worth it.

Young Oswyn always knew he was different. As far back as his earliest memories, he always took out his frustrations on the local wildlife. One time he'd gone missing for two days after his father had beaten him half to death in a drunken rage. Oswyn took out his frustrations on a toad he'd found hopping around the riverbank. Using his knife, he'd dismembered the toad, and he remembered how he'd revelled in the feelings of euphoria for a long time afterwards.

This was the start on a long, slippery road that ultimately led to where he was today. Oswyn moved around in his saddle to find a more comfortable riding position and then allowed his thoughts to drift back in time, once again.

Gerwyn, his younger brother, was the apple of his father's eye. He was everything that Oswyn wasn't. Tall and physically strong, by the time he was ten years old, he towered over his twelve-year-old brother. Gerwyn was the workhorse that his father had always wanted.

But Gerwyn hated his brother. He blamed him for not taking up his share of the family workload on the farm, and he enjoyed helping his father beat him with the horsewhip several times a week.

Oswyn retaliated on the small animals around the riverbank. Eventually the frogs and toads weren't enough to satiate Oswyn, and he searched for bigger prey. His father raised pigs, which he used to not only sell for coin, but also for meat to feed his family. Not that Oswyn ever saw much of it.

Because of his laziness, his father made sure that he got what he deserved, which wasn't much. He always reserved the bigger portions for Gerwyn, who never gave up an opportunity to rub it in to his older brother.

Sometimes, his mother would save some of her food and give it to Oswyn when his father and brother weren't around.

His mother was the only human being Oswyn Gare had ever loved.

One day, after a particularly severe beating, Oswyn

snapped. The anger he'd kept in reserve for all those years exploded in a fit of rage that both frightened and excited the young boy. He waited until everyone was asleep before creeping out of their tiny home to the pigpen. Once there, he went to work on the Sow and gutted her like a fish from the river. Covered from head to toe in blood, Oswyn ran to the river in the middle of the night and threw himself in to cleanse himself of his sins.

For weeks after, Oswyn relived what he'd done over and over. At first, he was disgusted and terrified of himself, but as time went on, he enjoyed the memory more and more. He wanted more. He needed more. Oswyn felt the power he wielded, and he loved it. He was in control of something for the first time in his life.

He was someone.

The repercussions were severe. His father never suspected his own son would commit such a terrible crime, so he blamed another farmer who he'd had a dispute with for years. With no evidence other than his father's accusations, the ruling Lord, Earl Watkins, who had never liked Gare's neighbour, had him arrested and executed.

Oswyn never batted an eyelid over the death of his neighbour. Instead, he relished the fact that he'd got away with it.

AS HE RODE towards Hereford and reflected on his past, Oswyn realised that the weeks following the execution of his neighbour were the happiest times he could ever remember from his miserable childhood.

EARL WATKINS GRANTED Oswyn's father access to some of the dead farmers' lands and animals, so the extra workload meant that Oswyn barely saw his father or brother. Oswyn kept to himself and avoided the regular whippings.

For a while, at least.

Expanding the farm meant extra food for the family. Everyone that was except Oswyn, who did everything he could to avoid being around his father and brother, and in return, his father made sure that Oswyn didn't share in the extra food he brought to the table.

One night after a severe storm, his father and brother came home late. Soaked to the skin and frustrated at the amount of extra work they had taken on, his father grabbed the sleeping Oswyn, and with the aid of his younger son, he beat Oswyn to a bloody pulp. He was so enraged at Oswyn's lack of effort that he forced his head into a barrel that he used to collect rainwater outside their small cottage.

Oswyn was sure he was going to die that night, and if it wasn't for his mother, he would have. He was convinced that his father and brother were intent on killing him. His mother pulled them off and saved her son's life, but even that was not without consequence.

Shivering and whimpering in the corner, Oswyn sat and watched as his father taught his wife a harsh lesson with the horsewhip for interfering with his decisions. His mother's screams still haunt him to this very day, and he wakes up at night with the sounds of her pleading for mercy ringing in his ears.

"This is all your fault, Oswyn," his father yelled at him. "If you weren't so lazy and helped more, none of this would have happened. It's your fault that your mother gets beaten. If you were a man like your brother Gerwyn, you would help more in the fields. You'd better be

ready for a hard day tomorrow, or I swear your mother won't be able to stop me from killing you."

But Oswyn didn't put in a hard day. Instead, he hid by the river, and when a stray dog from the village drank from the water's edge, Oswyn grabbed it and gutted it as he'd done to the sow several weeks earlier.

This time, though, he took his time and enjoyed himself much more. Every slice of his knife was dedicated to his father, and every cut was for his brother. If he couldn't stand up to them physically, he'd do it this way.

PASSING riders dragged Oswyn from his thoughts and brought him back to his present surroundings. He was so entrenched in his daydreams that he'd almost missed the two people riding past him, and his horse passed too close.

The riders were a man and what looked like his son, and they bade a pleasant, good day as they passed. Annoyed at having his memories disturbed, Oswyn Gare shot them a look that must have scared them to death, and they galloped away from the frightening man as fast as their horses could take them.

GARE SCOWLED and returned to his memories. He was enjoying this.

SUMMER TURNED INTO WINTER, and that winter was a bad one. His father needed all the help he could get, and for once, Oswyn stepped up and worked as hard as he'd ever worked in his life. A sense of peace and tranquillity had fallen over him, and this gave him the drive and the purpose he needed to be productive in the family's daily activities.

Now he looked back, Oswyn realised this period was where he had finally learned who he was, and what he needed to do to find peace in his world.

What had brought about this sudden change? Oswyn smiled to himself as he remembered.

Every few weeks, he would sneak out of his house after dark and find one of the many dogs, cats, or livestock that ran around the village and the fields. One by one, he would take his time and carve them open and revel in the power he wielded over them. He either buried their remains after he'd finished with them, or when the ground was frozen, he'd break the ice on the river and throw them in the water, hoping the currents would carry them away downstream.

Eventually, the villagers began complaining that their animals were disappearing, and it forced Oswyn to slow down and even stop the killings. But not for long.

By now, Oswyn wasn't getting the same levels of satisfaction from killing the animals that he was before. He needed more, but he was afraid to take the next, ultimate step.

Until fate stepped in.

He needed a push to cross that line, and the one event that changed the course of his life was about to happen. Late at night, when he was supposed to be asleep, Oswyn slipped outside to find an animal to kill. After failing to find a suitable victim, he returned home frustrated and enraged.

As he approached the small cottage, Oswyn heard noises in the pig barn. As he got closer, the voices turned into shouts and screams, and when he got close enough to see what was happening in the dim candlelight, he became enraged even further.

His father was drunk. Very drunk. And he was beating his mother with the horsewhip. Although this was nothing unusual, Oswyn noted that this time, his father wasn't slowing down.

"I'm going to kill you, woman. When I say I'm giving away that useless boy, I mean it, and I don't need any lectures from you. The Clayton's need a boy to help in the fields after their son died, and Oswyn is no use to us here. The two pigs I get for handing him over will keep us fed for the winter."

"You're not giving my son away for two pigs!"

Her husband struck her with his fists and feet as she lay on the ground.

"I'm not giving him away, Bethan. I'm just loaning him for the winter so he can help them out."

"It's the same thing, and I shall not allow it."

"You have no choice. I've already told them they can have him tomorrow morn."

"No. I shall not allow it."

Oswyn watched as his father beat his mother over and over. A red mist descended, and Oswyn grabbed a plank of wood that was propped up against the side of the barn. Running towards his father, he hit him over the head with it as hard as he could.

His father groaned and fell to the ground.

After a few more moans, his father fell silent. Oswyn stared at what he had done, because it was the first time he'd ever stood up to his father's bullying, and he felt empowered.

"Mother, are you alright?" Oswyn helped his bruised and battered mother to her feet.

"Why is your father so still?" she asked. "What did you hit him with?"

"A plank that was propped against the barn."

Oswyn reached down to remove the plank and help his father to his feet.

When he reached down, he felt a warm, thick, sticky fluid on his fingers, and Oswyn knew immediately what it was.

Blood!

He reached down further and felt around in the half light. The plank was stuck to his father's head, and Oswyn realised what had happened. A large nail that protruded out of the plank had buried itself in his father's temple.

"He's dead." Oswyn said after a long silence. A rising excitement that was coursing throughout his body had replaced the panic. "There must have been a nail sticking out of the plank."

His mother screamed.

Chapter 29

As soon as dawn broke, Oswyn was forced to go to Lord Watkins's manor, along with his battered and bruised mother. A visibly stunned Gerwyn went too. There, she broke down in tears and told the story of how her husband had met his end.

Oswyn would never forget the words as she told the Earl what had happened to his father.

"Your Lordship, I am here to report the death of my husband last night. He'd been drinking heavily, and during the night he went to the barn for reasons unknown to me. He must have tripped and fallen, because this morn I found him lying on the floor on a plank of wood with a big nail in it. The nail is buried in the side of his head, and he's as cold as the ground he lies upon. I'm sorry, my lord, but I throw myself at your mercy. If you allow it, my sons will take over the farm and carry out the work my husband did for you."

"I'm sorry to hear that, Mrs Gare. And what happened to you? Did the plank hit you several times before it collided with your husband's head?"

"No, my lord. I foolishly fell earlier and banged my head on the stone floor."

"Really?" Lord Watkins looked at her with raised eyebrows. "Why do I find that so hard to believe? However, I accept your explanation. Allow me to consider your proposal and I shall get back to you in a few days."

After several days of tension and uncertainty, Lord Watkins allowed his mother to stay on the land as long as Gerwyn continued the work his father had done before him. Bethan Gare readily agreed and thanked his lordship for his graciousness.

Gerwyn never believed his mother, and eyed Oswyn with hatred and contempt. Two days later, Oswyn was gone.

"Gerwyn," Bethan said before he left for the fields. "Your brother and I are going to Hereford to get some supplies. We'll be back in a few days."

"I don't care," Gerwyn spat back. "You murdered my father, so I don't care if you never come back."

Bethan hurried Oswyn out of the farm and away from the village as fast as she could. Oswyn remained silent and calm, reliving what he'd done over and over in his mind. Whatever happened from here, he was changed, and he knew it.

He wanted it.

When they arrived in Hereford, Bethan took Oswyn straight to St Guthlac's Priory and produced a letter from Lord Watkins. Oswyn had not spoken a word since he killed his father, and he showed not a sign of emotion or resistance as they accepted him into the brotherhood of silence. He knew his actions had finished him in Brecon, and the silence of the monastery was perfect for his soothed soul.

"I'm so sorry, Oswyn, but I fear Gerwyn will kill you if you remain in Brecon. At least here I know you are safe and alive."

Oswyn bowed his head and turned away. He was done with that life, and a new one beckoned.

Oswyn Gare quickly settled into life in the priory. Although the conditions were sparse and harsh, they suited him to the ground. The silence seemed to calm his troubled soul, and for the first time in his life, he fitted in.

He belonged.

Oswyn learned how to read and write, and the more he learned, the more he wanted. He read everything he could get his hands on, and he quickly became more learned than he'd ever dreamed.

But the dark spectre of his needs reared its ugly head, and the voices got louder and louder. At first, just reliving the murder of his father was enough to appease him, but as time went on, he craved more. Finally, he snapped.

One night, he crept out of the priory and hid close to the cathedral to watch and see what he could get away with. He noticed there were several people that appeared to be homeless. Either that or they were drunkards that didn't want to go home.

He followed one dishevelled man to the riverbank and watched as he relieved himself into the waters of the River Wye. When he was at his most vulnerable, Oswyn attacked him from the rear, and a messy, noisy fight ensued. Oswyn finally overcame the man when he grabbed a rock and beat him over the head.

After he'd cut him open and enjoyed himself, Oswyn threw his victim into the river. After a few minutes, he jumped into the water to cleanse himself up before heading back to the priory.

With his soul soothed, Oswyn Gare reflected on his experiences. He knew he wasn't physically strong enough to overcome his victims, especially ones who were bigger than himself. So, he set about building his strength and endurance. Every spare moment he got, he spent getting stronger and stronger until he felt and looked as strong as any man in Wales.

He was ready.

By now, his soul was screaming loudly for another victim, and he obliged in much the same manner as before. He waited by the cathedral until he spotted a man by himself in the darkness of night.

Then he pounced.

His newfound strength worked, and he quickly overpowered the much bigger man in seconds. It was quick and silent, which gave him more time and space to do what he needed to do.

Gare dragged the man to the riverbank and set about mutilating him in the way only he could. Then he threw the body into the river as before and went back to his life as a peaceful monk. The silence was the one thing he craved other than the soul soothing's, especially after carrying out a brutal killing. The life of a monk suited him perfectly.

He continued in this pattern, killing a new victim every few months. Eventually, the killings got the attention of the cryers, and it forced Gare to hold off for a while.

He stopped for as long as he could, but eventually the voices screamed so loud he couldn't ignore them anymore. He snuck out at night and waited for a new victim.

During the night, a man wandered into view by the cathedral. He was alone, and he presented the perfect target. Gare attacked.

After doing what he needed to do, Gare threw his victim into the river and jumped in to cleanse his body. After he hauled himself onto the banking, he lay there for a few minutes to reflect and enjoy the moment.

"Finally, we meet." A cultured nobleman's voice rang out of the darkness, taking Gare by surprise. He bolted upright.

"Please, do not worry," the voice said. "I have been searching for you for a long time, and I am here to help if you would spare me a moment?"

"Without killing me, that is." The voice added.

"Who are you?" Gare said after composing himself. He got up and approached the nobleman who dared disturb his sacred rituals. "And what do you want with me?"

"Who I am is unimportant. It is what I can do for you that matters. Your activities are famous throughout the land, and many people want you dead. You're fortunate that it was I who found you and not the sheriff, or you would be hung, drawn, and quartered without mercy."

Gare got a closer look at the man stood before him in the pale light of the half moon. He looked to be somewhere in his thirties, but other than that, it was hard to see much else. The man was covered from head to toe in a thick cloak, making it impossible for Gare to see his features. His voice gave away the fact that he was from the noble classes, but other than that, Oswyn didn't have a clue who he was.

Gare knew the man's words were true. Talk of his murders was on everyone's lips, and the cryers in the town shouted out his deeds almost every time Gare crossed their path on his walks about Hereford.

He'd never considered the possibility that other towns and cities would have any interest in his activities, but the words of this nobleman seemed to confirm his worst fears. Maybe it was time to leave Hereford and start again somewhere new, where they knew nothing about him.

"What do you want with me?" he asked again.

"I'm here to help you, if you give me a chance to explain myself. Just so you know, I am not alone, and I have my most loyal men

hidden in the trees with their bows aimed at you as we speak. If you make any moves towards me, they will kill you without a moment's hesitation. I may look vulnerable, but I assure you I am no fool, Oswyn Gare."

"You know my name?" Gare felt the veins standing out in his neck. He wanted to feel the blood of this intruder on his hands.

"I know everything about you. I know you come from Brecon, and that you probably killed your own father before you came to Hereford. You have a special talent for causing ungodly trauma to fellow humans that makes you unique. And I also know that unless you accept my offer, you shall be arrested, and will die as you no doubt deserve, with a large crowd cheering as you suffer your final moments. You know that virtually the entire country wants to see you dead."

"How do you know all this?"

"I am a man of resources, Gare, and I do my homework before I agree to partner with anyone, especially a man as dangerous as you."

Gare looked around in the trees, trying to see if the man was telling the truth. The man waved his hand, and Gare watched as the branches in three different trees parted to reveal men with bows aimed right at him.

The man was not bluffing.

"I'm listening."

"I am in need of a man with your talents. I guarantee that if you agree to come with me today, you shall have plenty of victims to satiate yourself with. Never again shall you feel the need to seek innocent drunkards to satisfy your cravings. I have many enemies, and I have an almost endless supply of people that you can remove for me."

Gare pondered for a moment. "You said I had to go with you? Where would I be going?"

"I know you enjoy the sanctity and quiet of the priory, and I would not take that away from you. It also makes a perfect hiding place until your services are required again. So, I have arranged for you to stay in a priory in London, where you shall be safe and free of the noise of daily life."

"How can you arrange such a thing when you don't even know me?"

"Like I said, I have many resources and I do my homework before I act. I have already arranged matters on your behalf, and the abbot at the priory in London knows you are coming. Naturally, he doesn't know your true purpose, and I hope he never does, but he is being well compensated for his troubles, so you will have no issues settling in there."

"And if I refuse?"

The nobleman sighed. "If you refuse, then you leave me no choice other than to arrest you for murder right here and now. You shall be handed over to the sheriff, and a few days hence you shall be hung, drawn, and quartered, which is no more than you deserve after all the lives you have taken. And if you resist, my men will kill you. So here is your choice, Oswyn Gare. Either live the life you crave working for me, or die. It's up to you."

Gare felt trapped, but he knew he had no choice. "You leave me with no choice. I shall go with you, but before I do, tell me what you would have me do?"

"I want you to be the major weapon in my fight against my enemies. I shall keep your identity a closely guarded secret, and you shall have more than enough victims to satiate your thirst. All I ask is that you work only for me and that you never reveal my name to anyone."

Gare nodded. "I agree."

A week later, Gare settled into his new home at the Charterhouse Priory in London, and began his long association with William Asheborne, Duke of Berkshire.

In the years leading up to Asheborne's arrest and subsequent execution, life had been good for Oswyn Gare. Asheborne had lived up to his promise that he'd keep his identity a secret and provide him with a steady number of unwilling victims. Gare especially liked the fact that he got to carry out his work on several noblemen, who in his opinion were the weakest minded of them all. One glance at Gare's deadpan eyes was all it took for them to piss themselves and plead for their lives.

He enjoyed that.

Around the time of Asheborne's arrest, Gare didn't know what his future held. He'd long since lost the fear of being captured and executed, for even he knew that what he was doing was as unholy as it gets. He knew that one day he would have to answer for all that he had done, and if that moment was nigh, then so be it.

As instructed, he waited for orders from Asheborne's son, and as time passed, the voices in Gare's head grew louder and louder. He knew he would have to find a new victim soon or he would go mad. It was right around then that the small nobleman from the north, with the large head on a child's legs, approached and told him he was there on behalf of William Asheborne Junior.

Andrew Griffiths, as he was to be known, gave Gare several new victims to work on, and when he told him that Asheborne Junior was weak and not to be trusted, Gare believed him. Griffiths became his new master, and Gare's life carried on as it had under Asheborne Senior.

There were only two adversaries he'd ever met that Gare would consider it an honour to kill, and both of them had escaped his grasp. The first was John Howard, the young noble who was accused of so many killings that even Gare couldn't keep up with it. When they'd met at Burningtown the previous autumn, Howard had shown no fear, which was highly unusual for anyone who came across the grim reaper that was Oswyn Gare.

Howard had put up a good fight, and Gare was looking forward to finishing the job on him when he got back to London a week or so hence. But there was one who stood out even above Howard, and that was the man who was with him that day in Burningtown.

Edward Johnson.

Ever since their altercation, Johnson had consumed Gare's thoughts. It was Johnson who'd given him the scar that ran down the side of his face, and it was Johnson who had matched his strength in their hand-to-hand combat. No man had managed that for many years, and the thought of renewing their battle kept Gare awake at night. Johnson had extra motivation, because Gare had murdered his wife who was heavy with child, along with his master and his wife.

Once he'd dealt with Howard, Gare planned on seeking out Edward Johnson, and he salivated at the thought of what he would do to him once he had overcome his physical strength.

HEREFORD CATHEDRAL CAME into view once more. He had arrived. The hustle and bustle of men and women buying and selling in the busy market stalls dragged Gare back to his senses. His time of reminiscing was over, and now it was time to focus all his attention on the present and the future. From now on, he would not allow any thoughts of the past to enter his mind. He was on a mission, and he knew what he had to do.

Gare exchanged his horse for a fresh one at the horse fair. He found a room at the inn closest to the cathedral and settled in for the night.

It has been too long, and now it is time to right the many wrongs of my childhood.

After a restless night, Gare left the following morn for the long days trek ahead of him. His next stop was Brecon.

Chapter 30

Gare cracked his knuckles as the rage inside him grew. The small cottage that had caused all his childhood misery came into view, and all at once, the memories that Gare had vowed to banish forever flooded back into his mind.

Except for his mother, not a one of them was a good memory.

Nothing had changed. In all the years since he'd left, virtually nothing was different. Everything was in the same place it had been when he was a child. It was as though time had stood still in Brecon, Wales. Or, at least, at this tiny cottage on the outskirts of the town.

Gare dismounted and secured his horse. When he turned around, he saw what he had come for. His younger brother, a lot bigger than Oswyn, lumbered up towards him. His physique bore the tell-tale signs of hard physical labour, and he looked as strong as a horse.

"What do you want here?"

Oswyn felt his hackles rising. His brother looked and sounded so much like his father that he felt like he was talking to a ghost.

A ghost he hated.

Oswyn turned to face his brother and pulled down the hood of his cloak, revealing his identity. His brother took one look at the scar running down the side of his face and stepped backwards. He swallowed hard several times and tugged at his right ear.

Oswyn knew his revelation had had the desired effect.

"Hello, Gerwyn. Don't you recognise your own brother?"

"Wha . . . Wha . . . What? Oswyn, is that you?" Gerwyn Gare stepped back a few more steps.

"Aren't you happy to see me?" Oswyn stepped forward. He was enjoying this. Fire raged inside his body, and he could barely contain himself.

"What are you doing here?" Gerwyn regained some of his composure.

"I'm here to see you." Oswyn stared at his brother with his cold, dead eyes. "And mother."

"Mother died years ago. It's just me now."

"You don't have a wife and children?" Oswyn was fishing to see who was at the cottage with his brother. He stepped forward again.

"I had a wife, but she died of the sickness three years back. We didn't have any children."

Oswyn stepped even closer, forcing his brother back towards the cottage.

"What do you want?" Gerwyn asked, his voice getting higher in pitch with each passing word.

"I've merely come to visit my brother and see my old home."

"You are not welcome here." Gerwyn Gare was regaining his confidence as he looked down at his older, smaller brother. "Mother told me on her deathbed what you did. You killed our father, and I vowed that if I ever saw you again, I would avenge him. I don't want you here, so get lost before I hurt you."

"You would hurt me?" Oswyn smiled, his cold eyes shining. "Please try." He stepped closer.

"Oswyn, I'm warning you."

Oswyn Gare attacked his brother.

Chapter 31

George Mallory rode the six miles to Bretlinton to pick up supplies for his master, William Asheborne, the son of the duke. Tall, strong, and with the kind of features that made the girls of any town swoon after him, George was looking forward to spending the night in one of the local inns and finding himself a good woman to keep him company.

Even though Master William had told him to get back to the old manor house that day, George would find a good reason why he couldn't make it. He hated the old house. It was so isolated, and there was nothing to do all day except to train with his weapons and sleep.

George wanted more. He wanted excitement and adventure. After all, that is why he'd signed up with the duke in the first place, and while the old man was alive, he'd certainly seen plenty of action.

His mentor had been the captain, and George had adored him. The captain had taught George everything he knew about the art of war and how to command men. He had been grooming George to one day become the leader of Lord Asheborne's men, and perhaps even be a captain himself.

He had been inconsolable when he learned that John Howard and his men had killed his beloved boss, and he had vowed over the captain's grave that he would one day avenge him.

As one of Lord Asheborne's most loyal men, young William had chosen Mallory to escort him to Yorkshire after the duke's arrest. While Mallory was grateful to have been recognised, he yearned for action. Master William was safe where he was. Indeed, the manor house was so secluded half the locals didn't even know it existed.

So, for today at least, George Mallory was going to enjoy himself in this small seaside town and forget the old house and its boring occupants for a night. He'd take the wrath of the master tomorrow when he returned.

He settled his horse into the stables and took a room at the nearby inn. Before settling down to enjoy the local ale, Mallory went about the tasks for which William Asheborne had sent him. He purchased the supplies that master William had asked for, and which were to be kept secret from Andrew Griffiths' men at the house.

George didn't yet know what William was up to, but he knew something was afoot. Master William was as bored there as he himself was, and he'd hinted that they would soon be on the move. Whatever he wanted the rope for, George was glad he was going to be a part of it.

He stepped into the strete.

Men and women were running towards the sound of a raised voice in the centre of the busy strete. George followed to hear what the town cryer had to say. It had been a while since he'd heard any news.

Oh yeah, oh yeah, oh yeah, the cryer yelled. *Gruesome murders near London. Baby boy brutally murdered in his crib. Hear me, good people of Bretlinton. Charles Packwood, son of Lord Packwood, the Earl of Bedford, brutally attacked and murdered along with his wife, Lady Mary Packwood, in their home in Waltham Abbey, along with the baby boy they were raising as their own.*

The baby is said to be Arthur Howard, son of Lord Robert Howard, the Earl of Coventry, who is the father of the infamous John Howard, and it is thought the baby was the target of the gruesome murders. From items found at the scene, it appears the attack was carried out on the orders of William Asheborne, son of the disgraced Duke of Berkshire, Sir William Asheborne, who was executed by the king at the Tower of London.

Lord Asheborne blamed John Howard and his family for his execution, and before the axe fell, he vowed revenge on the Howard family. This is the act of revenge William Asheborne carried out—the brutal slaying of an innocent child.

The whereabouts of William Asheborne are unknown, and Lord Howard has offered a reward of five pounds for any information leading to his whereabouts.

Oh yeah, oh yeah, oh yeah, brutal murder of a baby in his crib . . .

George Mallory ran to the stables and grabbed his horse. They covered the six miles back to Burton Agnes as fast as the horse could gallop, the cryer's words banishing any thoughts of staying for the night to the back of George's mind.

Chapter 32

William Asheborne stared longingly at the open countryside surrounding the ancient Erikson Hall. From the windows of the great hall, the frozen landscape looked barren and yet somehow inviting, as if it were taunting him for staying in his makeshift prison while the world carried on outside without him.

Soon. Soon, I shall re-join you.

Motion in the distance caught his eye, and he watched as the tiny speck took shape as it got closer. A rider approached at great speed, and as he approached, William knew who it was.

He listened as footsteps echoed on the ancient spiral stairway. Mallory was in a hurry, and William's heart raced as he waited to hear what news he brought from the seaside town close by.

By the time the door to the great hall burst open, William was sitting at the head of the table, in readiness to receive his hurried messenger.

"Master William, please forgive my intrusion," Mallory

gasped for air. "But I bring important news for your ears that cannot wait."

William gestured for the steward and the two guards to leave the room. Once they were alone, William Asheborne turned to Mallory.

"For goodness sake, man, sit down before you fall over. What is so important that you race in here like a madman?"

"Master William, I was getting the supplies in Bretlinton that you sent me for when people gathered around the town cryer to hear the latest news. I followed to hear what he was saying, and as soon as I heard his words, I raced back here as fast as I could."

"Did you get the rope?"

Mallory nodded.

William sat back and placed his fingertips together. "Tell me what you heard."

"Sir, the baby boy, Arthur Howard, has been murdered, and they have blamed it on you. The cryer said there was an item of some sort left behind that showed you were behind it. Further, the murder was said to have been especially brutal, and I know of only one person who could do such a thing. I came here as fast as I could, because you are in danger, my lord. I fear Lord Griffiths has double-crossed us."

William shot to his feet. "You're sure the cryer said Arthur Howard?"

"Yes, sir. He said they also murdered Charles Packwood and his wife in the same brutal manner in their home in Waltham Abbey. I know this place because you sent me there to spy on the child after Lord Howard gave him to the Packwood's to raise as their own. I saw the baby with my own eyes that day, so I know the cryer was telling the truth."

"Who blamed me for it? What was the item that was left behind? Tell me exactly what the cryer said."

"He said the murders were carried out on your orders, and that Lord Howard has offered a reward of five pounds for information leading to your capture. He didn't say what the item was. They don't know where you are, sir, so that's a relief at least."

"Who blamed me for it?" Asheborne's neck turned red as he raised his voice.

"The cryer didn't say, but he gave information that very few people knew about. The Howards knew, but they wouldn't send someone to kill Arthur, and they wouldn't know where to find that evil creature you call Gare." George Mallory shivered at the mention of Gare's name. "Only one other person knows who Gare is, although I didn't know that he was aware of Arthur Howard, or Arthur Shipley, as he was to be known."

"What are you saying, Mallory?" William knew exactly what Mallory was saying, but he wanted to hear him spell it out.

"Sir, I'm not trying to cause trouble or anything, but I've never trusted Andrew Griffiths. He is the only other person who knows about Gare other than us."

"But how would he know about Arthur?" William asked.

"I don't know, sir, but how did he know about Gare? He was your father's most closely guarded secret."

William slammed his fist on the heavy table. "I shall gather my men and kill the traitor myself. You are right, it has to be Carlyle who's behind this."

"Carlyle, sir?"

"He goes by Andrew Griffiths, but his real name is Alexander Carlyle."

"What do you wish of me? I can gather our men and

lead an attack on Carlyle, if that's what your Lordship commands?"

"How many men do we have at our disposal?"

"Thirty in total. Eleven are in London, and there are nineteen here in Yorkshire, including myself."

"Good. Carlyle is coming here in the morn, so get the men in position before he gets here. I want to give Carlyle a chance to explain himself, and I don't want him to suspect I know anything, so keep them out of sight until I give the command. I want you by my side when he arrives, but you are to remain quiet at all times, no matter what you hear."

"As you command, my Lord."

ALEXANDER CARLYLE WAS LATE. Midday came and went and still he wasn't here. William Asheborne paced around the great hall like a wolf stalking its prey, and he kept looking out of the windows every few minutes to search for signs of his arrival.

"He's here, Master William." George Mallory pointed at the procession of horses approaching the house along the frozen lane.

"Not before time."

Asheborne sat and poured himself some ale from the abundant refreshments laid out on the large old table. His shaking hands caught the jug of ale and knocked the contents all over the floor. He sat back and stared at Mallory sitting next to him. He took a deep breath and rubbed his fingers down the sides of his legs.

"Calm down, Master William. The men are ready to act on your command, and they know what to do. Lord Carlyle doesn't stand a chance."

Asheborne nodded and paced around the room again.

"You'll wear a hole in the floor if you keep pacing around like that." The familiar high-pitched female sound of Alexander Carlyle's voice broke the awkward silence as he entered the room. "Please accept my apologies for my lateness, but other urgent matters required my attention this morn."

Asheborne and Mallory watched the strange-looking man with the child-sized legs stride into the great hall and inspect the banquet laid out on the table in his honour.

Carlyle grabbed a tankard of ale and warmed his body by the roaring fire. He turned and faced the painting of himself in full armour and the Yorkist regalia hanging on the wall opposite the fireplace. Asheborne was sure he saw him silently speaking to it, but he pulled a face and put it down to pre-discussion nerves, because Carlyle must be as nervous as he was, or he wasn't human.

William felt his chest tightening. It was all he could do to stop himself from running his sword through this back-stabbing dwarf right here and now, but he forced himself to smile and pretend that everything was rosy.

"We need to speak," Carlyle said, his friendly tone turning suddenly sharp. He stared at Mallory. "Alone."

"Mallory stays." William gestured for Mallory to sit in the seat next to the one he would be taking.

"As you wish." Carlyle frowned. He took his seat and waited for William Asheborne to sit opposite.

"What news do you bring?" William forced himself to remain calm and friendly. "It is driving me quite mad waiting here with no news."

"My plan is working, although there was one slight change I was forced to make. My men went to the house where John Howard was living with his wife and friends. Their orders were to kill them all."

"Was Gare with them?" William cut in, staring into the eyes of his dishonest ally.

"Yes, he was to deal with Howard, and as you know, he has a personal vendetta against Howard's guard, the one they call Edward Johnson."

"What happened?"

"Howard and his friends weren't there. All they found was an old guard and two stable boys, so I had to change my plans a little."

William stared at Carlyle but said nothing.

"I have a spy in Robert's household on the Stronde, and he reported to my men that John and his friends were there during the attack. John stayed overnight while his friends left. This meant that John would return to them alone the next day, and it gave me the opportunity I required to capture him. My men waited for him in the heavy mist and captured him before he entered the city gates."

"Is he alive?"

"I promised you his head, and I shall deliver on that promise. He is a captive at the house in London where your men are staying. They roughed Howard up a little, but he is alive. I sent Gare on another mission that required his skills, but he should be back in London by now, and he will enjoy removing Howard's head in the manner in which only he is able."

"Yes, quite." William shivered at the thought of Gare going about his work.

"As for Lord Howard, steps are in motion to take care of him. In fact, that is why I am late for this meeting with you. I was waiting for a rider to arrive from London with the news that my plan was working, and I am happy to report that he brought good news. Robert Howard has been arrested and taken to the Tower. He has until the first of March to hand over all the confessions, or they will try him for treason. The only person who knows the location of the confessions is John Howard, and as you shall have his head, his father can never hand them over to Cromwell. As a result, they will execute him, just as they did to your father."

Carlyle sat back in his chair with a smug look on his face. "I told you I would deliver the head of John Howard and bring down his father, and I have delivered my promise to you. We should drink to our glorious victory."

Carlyle raised his glass and waited for William to do likewise.

He didn't.

Instead, William Asheborne leaned forward and stared into the smaller man's eyes. "You have indeed delivered on your promise, and for that I am grateful. However, there is much you have done that you haven't told me about, so perhaps now is the time to reveal the information you have withheld."

Carlyle blinked rapidly and gave a nervous smile. "I don't know what you mean, William. We have won! Victory is in our grasp. We should celebrate this great moment and enjoy what we have accomplished together."

"What happens to all the confessions after both the Howards are dead?" William asked, ignoring Carlyle's attempts to steer the conversation away from topics he didn't want to discuss.

"With John dead, the location of the confessions dies with him, so they'll never be found."

"You said Gare is going to kill John Howard. Are you also telling me you didn't instruct Gare to find the location of the confessions while he is torturing him? Please don't play me for a fool, Alexander. We both know that nobody can withstand Gare's torture, and you wouldn't miss the opportunity to get your hands on the confessions for yourself. And who could blame you?"

Carlyle sighed. "You seek to drive a wedge between us, young William. I did indeed instruct Gare to encourage John Howard to reveal the whereabouts of the confessions, and when I have them, I shall use them to my advantage in the court. I was going to destroy any that mentioned your family, so there is no need for you to worry about them."

"And yet you deemed it not important enough to tell me?"

"I have done more for you than anyone else in England ever has, including your useless father." Carlyle jumped to his feet, his face a deep red. "How dare you question me and accuse me of withholding anything from you? You should kiss my arse after all I've done for you."

"And I am grateful, but I am also curious why you would place yourself at such a risk for me. You told me a good story about how Robert Howard mocked you and took your rightful position in the court, but you also lied to me and used me as a scapegoat for your own ambitions. Tell me, Alexander, where did Gare go after he killed the guard and the stable boys in London?"

Carlyle stared at William Asheborne. He clenched his fists and raised his shoulders in the same juvenile manner that he'd done the last time he'd thrown a tantrum in front of William in this same room several weeks earlier.

"What are you accusing me of?" Carlyle stared at Asheborne, his face and neck deep shades of purple and red.

"Where did you send Gare after he killed Howard's guard? It's a simple question."

Carlyle turned to leave the room.

"You sent him to kill my half-brother, Arthur Howard, who was the only family I had left in this world. Then you planted evidence to show that it was I who killed him, and even as we speak, the town cryers all over the country are shouting my name as the man who butchered his own brother in his crib. That's what you're not telling me, isn't it, Carlyle?"

William gestured Mallory to stand up. It was time.

Carlyle stopped and turned to face Asheborne, slowly and deliberately. "You think I did any of this out of the goodness of my heart?" Spittle flew from his bared teeth. "You think that I actually care for you?"

Carlyle shook his fists once more. "You are correct. I used you to carry out my own plans. Not only that, I also gladly received all the gold and coin you sent to me before your father's execution. It was all gratefully received in my coffers, and it will ensure my wealth and status until the day I die."

Now it was Asheborne's turn to recoil from Carlyle's words. He tried to speak, but the words wouldn't come out of his parched throat. Instead, he just stared at Carlyle.

"You have been penniless since the day you got here, and you were too stupid to even know it. You haven't paid your men for months, and yet they are still here, seemingly loyal to you. Why do you think that is? Do you think they stay out of loyalty to you and your family? No, Master William, they stayed because I paid them handsomely. How else do you think I knew of your plot to kill my men and hold me prisoner today with the rope you sent your fool here to purchase yesterday in Bretlinton? I knew about it all along."

William Asheborne let out a guttural cry from deep within his throat. "Carlyle, you traitor. You shall die for this." He pulled his sword out and ran at Carlyle, who was now by the doorway.

Carlyle stepped aside and opened the door. Several

guards charged towards Asheborne and Mallory, who were retreating towards the back wall of the great hall. Men dressed in Asheborne's colours ran behind them with their swords raised. Carlyle watched the ensuing carnage with amusement and indifference.

Asheborne broke out in a cold sweat. In an instant, he knew it was over. He'd been played completely, and he'd fallen for it. He was madder at himself than he was at Carlyle.

That was all he had time to ponder, because a moment later, he was swarmed by his own men. He felt the sharp pain of a blade piercing his side, and the furious yelling of men who were once loyal to him. The last thing he felt was a pair of hands wrapping themselves around his neck. He got a glimpse of Mallory charging his own men and falling beneath an onslaught of blades and feet before everything went dark.

"Don't kill him. I need him alive so he can stand trial for killing his brother." Carlyle's words filtered through to William's brain before he fell to the floor in total darkness.

"Kill the other one."

Chapter 33

The gates to the courtyard of the little white house were unlocked and partially open, as Edward and Stephen helped John struggle through the frozen stretes to the place they used to call home.

"Wait here," Edward spoke softly to John and Catherine.

Edward and Stephen entered the rear courtyard to make sure it was safe, and that they weren't walking into a trap. They returned a few minutes later, looking relaxed and at ease.

"Sheriff Holley is here," Stephen said. "That's why the gates are open. He seeks an urgent meeting with you."

"Let's not keep him waiting, then." John hobbled into the courtyard.

Sheriff Holley was waiting for him in the same room where Gare had so brutally murdered Willis, and John winced at the memory as he entered. What had once been a safe and joyous haven was now a viper's nest of tragedy and heartache.

John forced the memories from his mind and turned

his attentions to the sheriff who was sat at the large table. The fireplace that had once roared and kept them warm lay still and silent, allowing the cold tentacles of the never-ending winter to penetrate the room, making the atmosphere as cold and doom-ridden as the feelings racing around John's tortured mind.

He shook his aching head to rid himself of the unease and tried focusing on Holley's words.

"You look like you have had quite a battle." Holley's deep voice boomed throughout the cold room. "Please, tell me what happened."

John tried to smile through his aching jaw, but the sharp pain stopped him. The cold air numbed the bruising around his matted eyes, and he could see Sheriff Holley clearly. "Men loyal to Asheborne attacked me on the way back from the Stronde a few days ago. They beat the living senses out of me."

"Why did they capture you? They beat you good and proper."

"They beat me and dragged me to a house on Lumbardstrete next to the George Inn. Once there, they beat me a lot more and demanded I hand over the confessions. Andrew Griffiths himself made an appearance and tried forcing me to reveal their whereabouts. When I refused, he warned me that Gare was on the way to London to torture me and get me to reveal where I hid them. Then he left. The next thing I remember was Catherine knocking at the door, pretending to be looking for her drunken husband and distracting the men, while Stephen and Edward took care of them. We came here to seek a physician with my father's help."

Holley sighed and shot John a glance that told him much had happened since his capture.

"What happened to the men at the house?"

"We killed them," Stephen said. "All five of them. It was them or us, and after what they'd done to John, they deserved it."

Holley nodded. "Did you at least find out why they took John before you killed them?"

"We did," John said. "One of the guards told us everything, and we were going to let him go, but as we were leaving, he lunged at Stephen with a knife, so we had no choice other than to kill him." He looked long and hard at Stephen, who stared back in defiance.

"And?"

"He told us where Asheborne is hiding. He's in Yorkshire somewhere. From the sound of Griffiths' voice, he's from that area too, and he's the one doing the dirty work for Asheborne while he hides like a coward in Yorkshire."

"Did he tell you where Gare is?"

"He didn't know, but he said that Gare left London with five of Asheborne's men to carry out a task for Asheborne before returning to London to take care of me. He's due back any day now."

"Good, we'll watch out for him then. What about Andrew Griffiths? Would you be able to recognise him again?"

"Easily. He's the most unusual looking man I've ever met. He speaks in a high-pitched voice like a girl, and he has a long body on legs no taller than a young boy's. Once you've seen him you can't ever forget him."

"That's good. I'll ask around if anyone knows where he is."

"Why are you here, Sheriff?" John asked. "Are you going to arrest us for killing the men who captured and beat me?"

"Not at all." Sheriff Holley shook his head. "Leave them to me. "I'll make sure they're removed and buried somewhere. No, I'm here for a completely different reason, but before I get to it, what were you thinking when you tied up one of your father's servants in this room?"

"I was going to ask what you'd done with him?" Stephen said. "Is that what he told you, that he was a loyal servant to Lord Howard?"

"He did." Holley nodded. "He said he'd come here to warn you that John was in danger, but you beat and threatened him before tying him up and leaving him here. He feared for his life when you returned."

"So he should," Edward spoke up. "That's all lies, Sheriff. We found him upstairs tearing up the floorboards, trying to find the confessions the Colte woman wrote about Griffiths. They're still missing, and nobody knows where they are. It was he who told us where John was being held captive, so we tied him up and left him here. What did you do to him?"

"Much has happened since we last met, and I didn't believe him. After the events at the Stronde yesterday, I thought it best to keep Barton, as he called himself, close. He's in Newgate gaol for his own safety."

"Good. Let him rot there," Stephen said.

"What happened at the Stronde?" John asked. "Is my sister safe? And my father?"

Sheriff Holley leaned forward. "I'm sorry to tell you this, John, but your entire family is in danger."

John's heart beat fast in his chest, and he felt his blood pumping as fast as a horse's as it raced through the woods. "What happened?"

"Your sister is safe. Your father sent her back to your home in Warwickshire." Holley hesitated before continuing in a more soothing tone. "I know where Gare went when he left London. He went to Chessett House in Waltham Abbey. Does that mean anything to you?"

"I know of it." John nodded. "But what does that have to do with my family? We don't own it or have anything to do with it."

"Apparently that's where your father sent your half-brother, Arthur, so he could be raised by the young nobles that lived there. Were you aware of that?"

John shook his head. "No. Father kept the whereabouts of Arthur a secret from all of us for his own safety. Wait. Are you telling me that Gare went after Arthur?"

Holley sighed and closed his eyes before looking John in his bruised and matted eyes. "I'm afraid he did. He killed your brother and the entire family in the way only he can."

"No!" John leant forward and closed his eyes. Catherine immediately went to him and caressed his shoulders. Even Stephen and Edward closed their eyes in shock and disgust.

"That's what he was doing before he came back to kill me, then," John said through clenched teeth. "At least we know where he's going next, and when he gets here, we'll be waiting for him."

"Leave Gare to me," Sheriff Holley ordered. "You have other issues to address. Unfortunately, that is not the only thing that happened."

"What could have happened that is worse than that?' John placed his head in his hands and rubbed his temples.

"When I told your father the news of Arthur, Lord Stephenson accompanied me. I assume you know him?"

"Stephenson?" John looked up. "I know of him, but I know nothing about him. Should I?"

"It seems he and your father have issues, and Lord Stephenson appeared to revel in your family's misery. He was with me because he had in his possession a signed warrant from Thomas Cromwell for the arrest of your father. They have taken him to the Tower, and he has until March to either hand over all the confessions or face a trial for treason. We all know how those trials end. If found guilty, they will execute him, and the king will confiscate all his lands and titles under the Act of Attainder he issued along with the arrest warrant. Your family is in deep trouble, John, and you are the only one that can save it."

John stared at Sheriff Holley for a long moment. His chin trembled, and he fought to retain control of himself. "Why?" he asked in a monotone voice. "Ever since mother died, I have suffered nothing but heartache and misery. If it wasn't for the people with me today, and those we lost along the way, I wouldn't have been able to face the dawning of a new day. I'm defeated, Sheriff, and I have nothing more to offer." He slumped forward into Catherine's arms and buried his aching head in her cloak.

Everyone in the room looked down at the ground. Nobody had ever seen John this broken and defeated. The silence was deafening.

After a few minutes, John composed himself and looked at Holley. "I apologise, Sheriff, and I know I have to stand strong. I had a moment of weakness, and for that I am sorry."

"Good Lord, man. You have nothing to apologise for. What I just told you would break any man, and God alone knows how much you've suffered over the last year." Holley patted John's knees and sat back in silence.

Another period of silence passed before John spoke again. "I don't have all the confessions. The ones pertaining to Andrew Griffiths are still missing, and I don't know where they are. Please inform Lord Cromwell that I shall gladly hand over the ones I have. All they bring is death and misery. That's all that woman ever brought to this world."

"You know Cromwell will use them to destroy his own enemies, don't you?" Edward said. "Handing them to him does not differ from handing them to Griffiths or Asheborne, or even your own father."

"I fear you are right, my friend," John said. "But what other choice do I have? If I don't, he will execute my father, and I would have to carry that guilt for the rest of my life."

"He'll probably execute him anyway," Stephen said. "That's how you people work, isn't it?"

John's eyes closed to a frown. "Maybe so, but at least I would have done all I could to save him."

"There is another way," Sheriff Holley said softly.

Silence. Again.

"What would that be?" John asked finally.

"This might sound outrageous, but it is the truth as far as I see it. Your father is safer in the Tower than he is out here with Gare and Griffiths running around, not to mention Asheborne's men, who will no doubt attack as soon as they get back to London. You have a month before you have to turn over the confessions, and while I strongly suggest that you do so, I also say that you have the time to find Asheborne and expose the truth. That way, your family may be exonerated, and your brother shall be avenged. What say you?"

John looked at Edward and Stephen, who both nodded back at him.

"Sheriff Holley, you are a man I am proud to say I'm associated with. Am I able to see my father before we leave? I would like to explain my plans to him, so he knows I haven't abandoned him like he abandoned me."

"I'm afraid not. He isn't allowed to see anyone other than Lord Stephenson or myself. You won't get anywhere near him."

John pursed his lips. "In that case, I would be grateful if you would tell him what we plan to do. Otherwise, you are exactly right, and we shall leave for Yorkshire at first light in the morn."

"I shall appraise Lord Howard of your plans," Sheriff Holley said.

"I do have one more request though, if you can manage it," John asked.

"What would that be?"

"When Gare is executed, please arrange for the executioner to be Edward. He is more than proficient with an axe, and he, above all others, deserves to deliver the fatal blow to the back of that madman's neck."

"I shall do my best."

John stood to his feet.

Chapter 34

The ride to York took just five days. John, Edward, Stephen, and Catherine rode as fast as their horses could take them, and they exchanged them often, so they would always have fresh horses to serve them on their long journey. John's body ached, but his bruises had now turned a deep purple and weren't as sore as they looked. At least he could see clearly out of both eyes again now.

They rode from before dawn until long after dusk, and the further north they went, the colder it got. The freezing winter had a firm grip on the northern part of England, and all of them were glad of the thick cloaks John had provided.

"I'm just glad we're not going to Malton," Stephen said as they exchanged their horses for the final leg of their journey.

"Aye, so am I," Edward agreed.

"I'm more pleased that we aren't being hunted every step of the way, and this time we have the coin to get where we're going as fast as we can," John said. "We're cutting it fine if we are to get back by the end of February with the evidence we need to prove my father's innocence."

"How long do we have?" Edward asked. "What date is it today?"

"It's the eighth day of February, young sir," the owner of the horse fair said. "May I ask where you are heading in this terrible winter?"

"Have you ever heard of a place called Burton Agnes?" John asked. "We have business there if we can ever find it."

"I do indeed, sir. I am from Bretlinton, which is a town by the sea a few miles past Burton Agnes. In fact, I would suggest you go there to get fresh horses if you plan on riding hard. It's only around five or six miles from Bretlinton to Burton Agnes, and if you follow the road to Bretlinton, you can't miss it. What business do you have in such a godforsaken place as Burton Agnes? There is nothing there other than an ancient old house that's empty as far as I remember, although it's been a long time since I was there."

"Thank you, you have been most helpful." John tossed him an extra coin and ignored his questions. "Bretlinton it is then."

They left the old city with the ancient Roman walls still intact long before dawn and rode through the frozen wastelands of Yorkshire as fast as they dared over the ice-covered hills and dales. That night, they huddled together around a makeshift fire, and shivered in the sub-zero temperatures.

"Sometimes I question my sanity," Catherine said, pushing herself as close to the fire as she dared.

"Who can blame you?" John asked. "I wouldn't blame any of you if you turned around and waited for me in York, where there is a warm fire and a soft pallet waiting for you. I can do this on my own, and I'll meet you in York when it's over."

"You think we're leaving you to face Asheborne and who knows how many of his men because we're cold?" Edward asked, holding his hands dangerously close to the fire. "You know us much better than that, John Howard."

"Don't even think about it," Stephen joined in. "We live and die together, even if it means we freeze to death out here in the middle of Yorkshire. It isn't the first time."

"I don't deserve such great friends, and I'm very grateful you stay with me. I can't do this without you, that's for sure."

"You weren't saying that a minute ago," Catherine said. "Make your mind up."

"I was just giving you a reason to stay safe and warm."

"Shut up and put more wood on the fire," Stephen ended the conversation.

CATHERINE WAITED with the horses while John, Edward, and Stephen crept over the hill in the dead of night towards the ancient house known locally as Erikson Hall. The night was clear, and the light from the moon reflected off the snow and ice so that everything looked as clear as a colourless day.

Steam poured out of John's mouth and nose as he breathed, and his hands and feet were frozen blocks of unfeeling ice. He huddled as deep into his thick cloak as he could and pushed the thoughts of a warm fire to the back of his mind.

Erikson Hall loomed in front of them in all its glory. All John knew about it was what he'd learned from Asheborne's guard in London, and he didn't know how accurate his recollections were. The building was almost square and had three floors. According to the guard, Asheborne lived on the first floor, and the other two were empty. The lower floor was the undercroft, and the living areas were the two floors above it.

It remained to be seen if he had been telling the truth.

The three boys watched as a single guard walked around the house several times. The guard stopped frequently to rub his hands and blow into them. He then stamped his feet several times, presumably to get the circulation going before continuing his walks around the perimeter of the house.

"He's not worried about anyone attacking," Edward whispered. "He thinks they're safe out here in the middle of nowhere."

They watched for a while to make sure there were no other guards, and when they were satisfied it was just the one, Edward sprang into action. He moved forward to get into a better range and readied his longbow.

When the guard came around the side of the building, he stopped to rub his hands and blew on them. It was the last thing he ever did. Edward's arrow struck straight and true, and the guard fell in a heap on the ground.

John quickly led the way to him, and together they dragged him into the trees off to the side of the house. John checked him for any papers, but he was clean.

And dead.

The three boys entered the ancient undercroft and took a moment to get their bearings. Silence prevailed, and John saw a narrow spiral staircase in the pale moonlight streaming through the empty window frames. He pointed in the direction they should go.

Edward led the way, and the three of them silently climbed the spiral stairs to the floor above.

The sound of footsteps clattering on a stone floor stopped them in their tracks. They fell to their knees and listened, trying to make out where it came from.

The sound of men whispering got closer. However many there were, they were getting too close. John, Edward, and Stephen drew their blades and waited.

Two men padded down the narrow stone corridor to their right. They came out of a room off to the left at the far end of the house and headed for the steps leading down to the undercroft. John signalled they should retreat down the steps, so they had a better chance of remaining unseen.

They crept down the steps and waited, making sure their shadows didn't alert the guards coming towards them.

"Jack should have been back by now. Where is that lazy mumper?" one of the men whispered loudly enough that John and the rest could hear him.

"Who knows with him?" the other man replied. "I'm frozen already, so let's get this over with."

They never reached the doorway. Stephen and Edward closed in behind them and held their mouths while their knives slit their throats. They pulled the two dead men out of sight and re-joined John.

"If there's two of them, there must be another one outside somewhere," Stephen whispered.

"If there was, we'd have seen him," John whispered back. "I don't know why, but the guard was out there alone."

"I agree," Edward said. "If there was another, we would have seen him. Let's find Asheborne and get out of here."

The three of them crept back up the steps and made their way to the room two guards had emerged from.at the left end of the corridor. As they neared it, they heard men snoring inside.

With knives at the ready, John led the way. Moonlight streaming in from the windows showed them four more men sleeping on the hard floor.

The three boys quickly took care of the sleeping men, and soon the snoring stopped.

"They're all wearing Asheborne's colours," John noted. "So he must be here somewhere."

They didn't have to look far. The next room they checked was what must have been the great hall, and at the side of the glowing embers of the fireplace was a man sitting against the wall, staring right at them.

"You make a lot of sound for someone who's trying to be quiet." The man spoke loudly, startling John and making him jump backwards.

"I've been waiting for you to come and finish me, so I'm surprised that you took so long."

"William Asheborne," John said, regaining his composure. Edward and Stephen spread out, looking for more guards who might be hiding in the shadows.

"You're wasting your time," Asheborne said, before leaning forward and coughing loudly. "You killed them all. At least all those who were still here. I suppose you wanted the men wearing my colours dead, so you could prove to the sheriff how loyal your master is to the king." Asheborne spat on the ground. "Kill me if you must, but your master is a traitor and a snake. Tell him that from me."

"I don't know who you think we are, but we're not here to kill you," John said. He watched Asheborne as his head cocked from side to side, trying to work out who his attackers were.

Edward and Stephen returned to the great hall. "It's clear. We killed all the guards who were here."

"If you are not Carlyle's men, then who are you?" Asheborne demanded, before leaning forward in an uncontrolled coughing fit again.

"I'm surprised you don't recognise me. After all, you and your father spent most of your time trying to frame me for murders I didn't commit."

"John Howard? Is that you?" Asheborne rubbed his eyes for a long moment. "How could it be?"

"You sound surprised to see me, Asheborne. You think that after murdering my brother and some of my closest friends, as well as having my father arrested, that I wouldn't come after you? I thought you would have known by now that I don't suffer attacks on my family without gaining revenge."

Asheborne spluttered and then burst into wild laughter.

"I don't see what you find so humorous." John jumped forward and grabbed Asheborne by the hair and pressed his knife against his throat. "You sent Gare to murder an innocent baby, you murdering knave, and you are going to pay for your crimes."

"Who is Carlyle?" Edward asked.

William Asheborne laughed again. "You really don't know, do you? You think I sent Gare after Arthur? He was my half-brother as well as yours. You don't even know who Carlyle is, do you? I'm disappointed, John Howard. Your reality is far less impressive than your reputation, although I must ask, how did you know I was here?"

John dragged him to his feet by the hair. "You shall answer to Sheriff Holley in London, and they will execute you for the murders of Arthur and my other friends." John shoved Asheborne forward after checking him for any hidden weapons.

"Move."

Chapter 35

William Asheborne lurched forward and fell towards the heavy oak table that was the centrepiece of the great hall. He struggled into the nearest chair and sat down, grabbing at his side and coughing up what looked like blood.

"You're injured," John said. "What happened here?"

"I never thought you'd ask," Asheborne said sarcastically. "You obviously came here for me because you think I killed Arthur and your friends, but you couldn't be further from the truth. Don't misunderstand me, Howard, I'd just as soon see you dead as be here talking to you, but I am as innocent of killing them as you were of the crimes my father and Margaret Colte accused you of."

"And yet you still pursued me, even after your father's execution. If you knew me to be innocent, then you should have admitted it and left me alone."

"You destroyed my family. The king has taken all our wealth, and I was to be left with nothing. What else was I supposed to do?"

"Your father brought it on himself by his own actions," John spat the words out. "And now you continue his evil deeds just so you can get your hands on the confessions. Well, let me tell you, you shall never see them. Not as long as you live, which won't be very long once we get you back to London."

"You don't believe me, do you?" Asheborne said, between coughing fits. "Do you think I would stay here like this if I had a choice? My own men turned on me because of another man's treachery. He played me perfectly, just as he's playing you, and even the king. If we don't work together to stop him, he wins."

"Who are you talking about?" John asked. "Andrew Griffiths?"

Asheborne laughed. "You might know him as Griffiths, but I assure you that is not his real name. His name is Alexander Carlyle."

"I'm confused, Asheborne, and even though I don't believe you, I need you to tell me what's going on here."

"Isn't it obvious? Carlyle's treachery and cunning betrayed me. He stole my wealth and used it to buy my men's loyalty. They turned on me and are keeping me here against my will."

"Are you hurt?"

"Yes, one of my men stabbed me with his knife, and I fear I have little time left. Whatever I may have done before pales in comparison to what Carlyle is doing with Gare. You must help me stop them before it's too late."

William Asheborne lurched forward, grasping his side and groaning in pain. He coughed up more fresh blood, and John knew he wasn't faking his injuries.

"Andrew Griffiths is Alexander Carlyle?"

"You might know him as Andrew Griffiths, as he goes by that name when it suits him, but his true identity is Alexander Carlyle. If you've met him, then you know he has an unforgettable physical appearance. He's got a long body on small boy's legs, and he speaks with a high pitch, like a girl. If you met him, then you will know exactly what I am talking about."

"I have indeed met the man you speak of." John nodded his head. "He paid me a visit when your men were beating the life out of me in a house your father purchased for Margaret in London. He told me that Gare would be along in a day or so to end my life."

"I had nothing to do with any of that. I didn't even know he was in London. Carlyle lied to me and set me up to take the blame for everything he is doing to you and your father. He somehow found Gare, who is now doing his bidding, and he's let him loose on anyone that gets in his way. I swear, John Howard, that as much as I hated your family, and I admit I wanted to see you fall, I had nothing to do with any of this. And I would never harm an innocent child. I knew nothing about it until the only man who'd remained loyal to me heard the cryer in Bretlinton yelling it all over the town."

Asheborne steadied himself as he suffered another coughing fit.

"I'd already decided to leave here, as I knew I was being held more as a prisoner than a guest. Mallory rode to Bretlinton to purchase ropes, candles, and knives so we could escape. I planned on tying up Carlyle's guards and leaving with my own men, who I still considered loyal."

"What happened?" John asked.

Stephen and Edward stood close to the doorway with one ear on the dark corridors outside in case of attack, but they were both listening intently to Asheborne's words as he spoke.

"Mallory told me what Gare had done to Arthur, and we decided there and then that we would use the rope to secure Carlyle and take him to London to pay for his crimes, especially as I realised the only reason he was keeping me here was so I would take the blame, and he would look like the hero who stopped me."

"So why didn't you?"

"Carlyle stole my gold and paid my men to turn against me. When I confronted him, he set them upon us, and they killed poor old Mallory. I was injured, and they've kept me under guard ever since."

"Where is Carlyle now?"

"From what I heard, he's riding to London. He has to be stopped before he meets with Cromwell and blames me for everything he's done. He told me about your father's arrest, and he is probably behind that, too. I fear he intends to step into the position your father holds with the king, and he is using both of us to get there."

"What about Gare? Where is he?"

"I don't know. All I know is that he killed Arthur. After that, I don't know. He probably sneaked back into his hiding place, where he thinks he's safe until the next time he's needed."

"You know where he hides?"

"Of course I do. How else would my father have known where to find him when he's needed?"

"Where?" John leant forward. This was important.

"I'll tell you if you promise to help me out of here and get me back to London safely. Now I know how you must have felt all those days when you stood accused of poisoning your other brother, as well as of all those murders my father and Margaret committed in your name."

"You have no clue how I felt. Tell me where Gare hides and where I can find Carlyle, and I promise that my friends and I will take you back to London with us, unharmed and without further injury."

William Asheborne sighed. "Alright. As much as I dislike you, I hate Carlyle more. I shall tell you what I know, and trust that you will not betray me as he did."

"I am a man of my word, Asheborne, which is more than I can say about you, your father, and anyone else you associate with."

"I believe you, John Howard. As much as it pains me, I believe you. I never thought I would end up working alongside you with a common goal."

"Let me be clear, Asheborne. We are not working together. I don't like you, and I don't trust you. If you are telling the truth, then we have a common purpose, although our paths shall divide again when it comes to saving my family from suffering the same fate that befell yours. We stop Gare and bring Carlyle to justice. Then we are done, and you shall never see the confessions. Are we both clear on this?"

"Perfectly."

"Tell me about Gare."

"He hides in the Charterhouse Priory, close to Smithfield Market outside the city walls. My father set him up there and paid the Abbott handsomely to allow him to stay."

"Gare is a monk?" Edward cut in. "I always thought he was using the monk's robes to disguise himself."

"He's a monk. My father found him murdering people in Hereford when he lived in the priory there, and he brought him to London where he would be closer, and where my father could keep him safe."

"We head for the Charterhouse Priory, then," John said, looking at Edward and Stephen.

"He has a brother in Wales. In Brecon, to be exact. He hasn't been there since his childhood, but he might be there if he has nowhere else to go."

"We'll find him. Let's go before more men arrive here."

Edward and Stephen helped the struggling Asheborne to his feet. Stephen gave John a long stare that told him he didn't think Asheborne would survive the long journey to London.

John agreed with his assessment.

As they were about to leave, John looked at the strange painting hung on the wall opposite the fireplace. "That's him, isn't it?"

Asheborne nodded. "In all his glory. He had it painted to show he was a loyal Yorkist, and to demonstrate his claim to the crown. He's very proud of that painting."

John reached up and pulled hard on the heavy frame. It crashed to the ground with a loud thud and broke into several pieces on the stone floor. He rolled up the painting and placed it under his cloak.

"I think the king will find this interesting when we show it to him. This alone is reason to execute Carlyle, so it's coming with us."

Asheborne chuckled. "I like your thinking, Howard. Carlyle will be furious when he discovers his painting has been stolen. By you, of all people."

John waited in the undercroft with the injured Asheborne, while Edward and Stephen took a horse from the stables belonging to one of the dead guards. They helped Asheborne onto it and led him to where Catherine waited with their horses.

WILLIAM Asheborne's former loyal guard watched from the safety of the trees at the side of Erikson Hall. He'd been patrolling with Jack earlier, when he'd gone into the cover of the trees to allow the urge of nature to take its course.

The soft thud of an arrow caught his attention, and he crouched deep into a thick bush and watched as Jack fell under the onslaught. He remained hidden as three men entered the house, and he listened as the shouts and screams of his fellow guards were silenced one by one.

Now he watched from the safety of his hiding place as the three men helped his former master onto his horse, and he watched as they vanished into the frozen darkness and away from Erikson Hall.

Once the danger had gone, the guard quickly checked to make sure all the guards inside were dead, and when he was done, he ran to his horse and galloped off as fast as he could.

His new master needed to know what had happened at Erikson Hall.

Chapter 36

Gare hurried back to London as fast as he could. He knew he was several days late, but nobody would question where he'd been.

Nobody dared. Not even Griffiths.

The events of the last few days filled Gare's dark soul with the same euphoric feelings he always had after one of his soul-soothing events. This one was especially pleasing, and he felt as relaxed as he'd felt in a long time. All the tensions that had built up over years and years were gone, and now Gare could sit back and enjoy the memories as he hurried back to the big city.

His younger brother had always haunted his dreams, and for the last few nights since he'd killed him, Oswyn had slept better than he could ever remember.

Oswyn Gare was content, and although he knew it wouldn't last long, he was determined to enjoy the time he had before the voices inside his head rose again and told him it was time to find another victim.

But no victim would ever give him the satisfaction that Gerwyn Gare had.

GARE JOINED the small crowd hurrying about their business on Lumbardstrete. Most of them were heading to and from the busy markets on Cheppes Syed, so Gare allowed himself to be shoved and harried as they attempted to avoid the horses and carriages racing along the busy strete.

Is this how normal people live their lives? Gare watched a woman struggle with a heavy sack she was carrying back from the markets. Every few steps, she stopped to put the sack down so she could blow on her hands, trying to hold off the frozen numbness in her fingers. *Is this what it's like to have no other worries or desires?* Gare stared at the woman until she vanished out of sight down one of the narrow side stretes. For a moment, he wondered what it would be like if he were different. *What would I have been if I didn't have my urges?* He shrugged and looked away. *I am who I am.*

If the biggest concern people had was staying warm, then they led pointless, meaningless lives, and Gare knew he would never be happy living a life like that.

But he was cold, which proved that he had feelings just like normal people.

London was still deep in the clutches of the never-ending winter, and even Gare, who often wondered if he possessed any normal human feelings, wished it would hurry and end.

Steam rose from fresh horse droppings that were seemingly everywhere in the filthy strete, and Gare took amusement as he watched another woman fall headfirst into one of the larger piles of shit after an impatient man had shoved her out of the way. The woman shook her fist at him, but the man ignored her. Wherever he was going, he was obviously in a hurry.

Gare watched him as he disappeared into the George Inn.

Getting closer to his target, Oswyn Gare experienced the familiar feelings of excitement rising inside him. Sensing his pulse rate rising, he felt like his entire insides were vibrating, and he stood for a moment to allow the feelings to wash over his body, encompassing his mind and his emotions like nothing else ever could.

Taking a deep breath, Gare stepped forward. He was ready.

It was time to put an end to John Howard's life. He hoped Griffiths' men hadn't roughed him up too much, because he looked forward to seeing the all too familiar fear in his eyes before he killed him. Griffiths had made it clear that he wanted Howard to reveal the whereabouts of the confessions left behind by the Colte woman. After that, Howard was his to do with as he pleased, and after the events at Burningtown the previous year, this was something Gare had looked forward to for a long time. He especially wanted to know the whereabouts of Edward Johnson, and these were the last words Howard would ever utter in this life.

Rather than bang on the front door, as Griffiths had done the last time they were here, Gare walked past the house and turned up the strete at the side of the church. He'd taken a good look as he walked past, but he had seen nothing, which was exactly as it should be.

Gare didn't trust anyone, especially Andrew Griffiths. This was the reason they had never caught him, because no matter who gave the orders, unless he could do it his own way, Gare wouldn't do it. If the person who wanted the killing complained too much, Gare would kill them instead. It had worked for him so far, and he saw no reason to change now.

Especially for Andrew Griffiths. There was something about him that signalled dishonesty. It wasn't his physical appearance, as strange as that might be. No, it was the sneer on his face and the way he avoided eye contact that spoke truer than his words. Gare knew Griffiths would betray him the instant he was no longer useful, and whilst he'd provided Gare with many opportunities to satiate his desires over the previous years, he knew that their time together was nearing the end.

Gare was going to kill Griffiths once he'd got Howard and Johnson out of the way. Then he would leave the priory and start a new life somewhere else.

Oswyn Gare crept along the rear side of the church and made sure nobody was watching him. The narrow strete was much quieter than Lumbardstrete, and the small number of people using it were in too much of a hurry to notice the monk sneaking along the rear walls of the church.

At the end of the church, Gare took a knee and watched the rear of the house. Seeing it was clear, he ran to the wall at the edge of the house and waited, listening for signs of movement. Or at least, he tried to listen over the beating of his heart in his chest.

Satisfied, he made his move. He had been going to force the door, but when he pushed on it, it flew open. Someone had already been here.

With his senses heightened, Gare entered the back of the house. He was expecting to at least see the four guards who had survived the attack in Waltham Abbey, as well as the others that had stayed behind to guard Howard and keep him alive until he got there.

In short, Gare had expected the house to be busy.

It wasn't.

He'd expected to be greeted by a roaring fire and the

sounds of almost a dozen men shouting and laughing. Instead, the house was cold and silent.

Voices from the main room where the fire ring was located drifted to Gare's ears. He drew his knife and crept forward. Peering around the corner, he saw three men stood together deep in conversation. None were wearing Asheborne's colours, and he didn't recognise any of them.

One of them spotted Gare in the doorway. "Hey, who are you?"

Hiding his knife behind his back, Gare stepped forward. "Forgive me, sir, for I am cold and seeking warmth for a few moments before I journey back to the priory."

"It's a monk," one of the men said.

"It's *the* monk," another said. "Sheriff Holley told us to watch out for a monk."

The man went to draw his sword, but his hand never reached the hilt. Gare's knife flashed across the room and struck him deep in his throat. The man fell instantly.

Another knife appeared in the monk's other hand, and Gare took advantage of the confusion in the faces of the two remaining men.

He leapt forward and buried his knife through the eye of the man closest to him, and after a loud, bloodcurdling scream, the man fell to the ground.

The last man alive ran for the door, but Gare was quicker. He wrapped a strong arm around his neck and pulled him backwards, forcing him to the ground.

'I'm going to have fun with you," he said.

The man screamed, but Gare stifled him with a powerful forearm.

"Who are you, and why are you here? And I warn you that if you scream again, I shall cut your eyes out."

The man nodded, his eyes wide with fear. Gare released his forearm.

"Sheriff Holley sent us here to guard the house. That's all he told us, honestly, sir."

"Where are the men that were here before? And where is John Howard?"

"His friends rescued him, and together they killed the men that were here. Sheriff Holley arrested another group several days ago that rode into town from the north. We were guarding it in case anyone else came here. We were to arrest them and inform the sheriff. That's all we were supposed to do."

"Where are Howard and his friends now?"

"I don't know, sir, honestly. All I know is that they rescued him and they're not here."

Muffled screams rang out as Gare did what only he could.

Gare left the way he'd entered. He had swapped his blood-soaked cloak with the thickest one he could find from the dead men and headed for the safety of the priory. The authorities were getting too close, and it was almost time to leave. But not before he'd seen Griffiths one last time.

Daylight was fading by the time he reached the small room set aside for him at the Charterhouse Priory. Other monks filed past him in silence, and Oswyn Gare felt at peace within himself.

The priory was the only place that could ever soothe him, and he looked around his humble abode with sadness, because he knew his time there was at an end.

A pallet rested in the corner, and a small desk and chair occupied the wall to the right of the doorway. The stone floor was swept and clean, and along with a solitary candle that was allowed for reading and writing, these amounted to Gare's total worldly possessions.

It was all he needed.

A sealed envelope sat propped up on the desk, and Gare lit the candle so he could read the contents.

Gare,

J.H escaped from London and tortured my guards to reveal the whereabouts of W.A. They killed my men and left along with W.A. They are now on their way back to London, where they will reveal everything they know.

You are no longer safe in the priory, as W.A. will betray you. Wait for me at the big house where I have a plan to end this.

A.G.

The letter was in code, but Gare knew exactly what it meant. He checked for dates, but found none. The letter could have been there for days for all he knew, and he had to get out of the priory immediately.

He threw the letter across the room. He felt his blood boil, and he cursed the day he ever agreed to listen to Andrew Griffiths. Once this was over, he had a special surprise for him.

Gare gathered his meagre belongings and, with one last long look at the place that had been his sanctuary, he turned and left. He hid in the small chapel near the gatehouse until first light.

After curfew, Oswyn Gare headed into London and away from the priory for the very last time.

Chapter 37

Four horses occupied the first half of the stables in the courtyard of the little white house on Watelyng Strete. John had half expected someone to be there, so it didn't surprise him when he saw them.

John, Catherine, and Edward took the remaining three stable places, and Stephen and Edward tied the final two horses outside at the side of the building. The eighth and final stable slot was full of manure and wasn't available.

It also held a secret that only John and his close friends knew about, and he intended keeping it that way.

John and Stephen carefully lifted down their wounded captive and carried him to the side of the house, where they laid him down. William Asheborne moaned and grabbed his side. "Are we here?" he croaked.

John nodded. "Yes. Wait there until we know it's safe, and we'll be back for you."

Asheborne didn't complain.

Edward drew his sword, just in case. John and Stephen followed suit, and together they entered the rear door of the house. A man stood facing them with his blade drawn as well, and for a moment there was a tense standoff.

Recognition dawned quickly on all of them, and John led the way, sheathing his sword. The man was one of Sheriff Holley's closest constables, and if he was here, then so was Holley.

"Is he here?" John asked.

"I'm here." The familiar voice of Sheriff Holley came from the largest room in the house, down the corridor to John's right.

"You made good time," Holley said, greeting them at the door. "But you are cutting it fine if you are to save your father. What news do you bring from Yorkshire? Did you find William Asheborne?"

"We did, and we have him here with us. He is injured and needs a physician but it wasn't by our hand. I'll let him tell you himself what happened."

Holley cleared the large table to make room for Asheborne, as John, Edward, and Stephen helped him into the house.

Sheriff Holley sent one of his men for a physician while Asheborne took a long swig of ale and lay on the table, holding his side.

"We have little time," Holley said. "So, tell me what happened to you. If you want my help, I need to know everything, including the whereabouts of Alexander Carlyle and Oswyn Gare."

"You know about Carlyle?" John gasped. "How? That was the secret we discovered from Asheborne in Yorkshire."

"When I described Griffiths to your father in the Tower, he knew immediately who it was. I approached Lord Cromwell for an arrest warrant, but he refused until we have more evidence. I'm hoping Master Asheborne here can provide it for us."

The room fell silent while Asheborne told Sheriff Holley everything he knew about Alexander Carlyle, along with everything that had happened to him since he left London after his father's arrest.

"Your story sounds believable," Sheriff Holley gave Asheborne a stern look. "But there's something important that you're leaving out."

"What is that, Sheriff?" Asheborne asked. "I thought I'd told you everything."

Holley sighed. "There's no doubt that it was Gare who killed Arthur and the Packwood's, but he wasn't alone. My men and I arrested four of your men returning from the north, and when questioned, they told us everything. You sent them to assist Gare. What they insist they didn't know was that a child was involved, and that Gare was going to commit such unholy acts upon him."

Asheborne's neck bulged, and John could see the rage behind his eyes. "Those were my men, and they believed they were carrying out my orders, but I didn't know Carlyle was even in London, much less ordering Gare to send my men to kill my own half-brother. My men were set up just as much as I was, Sheriff, and I hope you will show them leniency."

"They played a part in the murder of an entire family," Holley said. "They are in Newgate gaol awaiting trial, and they shall get what they deserve. That's all I can promise you."

"Carlyle did this." Asheborne clenched his fists and shook them in the air. "He played us all, and if my men and I should die for his sins, he would have played you, too."

"Going back to your original story, are you telling me

that Carlyle manipulated the king's court to have Lord Howard arrested and removed from the Privy Council?" Holley asked. "And then, not content with that, he punished the Howard family even more by sending that madman Gare to kill an innocent baby that was Lord Howard's illegitimate son and John's half-brother?"

"That's about the gist of it, Sheriff." Asheborne said, sitting propped up on a chair while he waited for the physician to arrive.

"And he set you up to take the blame for killing baby Arthur, so you would take the fall and he would enjoy the spoils of his victory?"

"Carlyle is a cunning, thoughtless creature, much like his hired killer, Oswyn Gare. They are a perfect fit because neither has a compassionate bone in their bodies." Asheborne swigged more ale.

"What was the point of all his treachery? Obviously, he'd been planning this for a long time if he went to all the trouble of setting you up first. What does he hope to get out of all this? Revenge? It's a lot of effort just so he can gain some kind of revenge on the Howard family."

"As I said, Carlyle is very cunning. He's also vindictive and forgives no one who dares cross him. The Howard family crossed him a long time ago, but Carlyle never forgot. He says he wants the position which Robert Howard currently holds, as it was promised to him years ago. But I don't think that's what he wants at all. The king mocked him, and I'd wager he wants to get close to the king so he can kill him."

Sheriff Holley leapt to his feet. "Are you accusing Carlyle of conspiring to kill the king?"

"I am."

"Do you realise what you are accusing him of? If that is true, it is the most serious crime in England."

"Then you'd better find him and arrest him." Asheborne held Holley's gaze. "For I am deadly serious, Sheriff. Alexander Carlyle intends to murder our great king, and you are the only person who can stop him."

"I shall go to Lord Cromwell at once and get an arrest warrant."

"Perhaps this will help." John reached into his cloak and pulled out a large sack that was rolled into a long, thin container. He pulled out a rolled-up painting, and when it revealed itself on the table, Holley and his men gasped.

"Sheriff Holley, I give you the proof you require to arrest Carlyle for treason." John pointed at the painting of Alexander Carlyle sat on his magnificent white stallion wearing the full regalia of a Yorkist knight. "That should be enough to convince Cromwell to act."

"It will indeed," Holley agreed. He rolled up the painting and stored it safely inside his cloak. "John, may we have a word in private?"

John followed Holley into the kitchens at the opposite end of the house, which was another part of the building John had no desire to be in after Gare's attack.

"What is it, Sheriff?"

"John, you only have three days before you have to hand over the confessions to Lord Cromwell. If you don't, you know what will happen to your father."

"I'm well aware, Sheriff, and I stand by my promise to hand them over. I was planning on doing it today if that works for you."

"I haven't told you this, but Cromwell has an arrest warrant ready for you. If you haven't handed them over by noon three days hence, I am to arrest you and charge you with treason, and you shall be tried alongside your father. We both know what will happen after that. You must get them to Cromwell before that time, or I shall have no other choice than to carry out his orders."

"I understand. I already said that I would get them for you. Today, if you will allow it."

"Hold off at least for one more day, as I have more to tell you. If we can find Carlyle before the warrant has to be executed, we can end this before you and your father go to trial. I fear there are many powerful lords who desire to see your family fall from grace, but if we can find Carlyle, we can stop this madness before it gets that far."

"How? What further news do you have?"

"I had my men search day and night through the records for properties purchased by Andrew Griffiths in London over the last three years, presumably for Lord Asheborne and Margaret Colte. We found plenty, including this house and the one where they held you captive. My men have searched most of them, and they are all empty. I'm also presuming Griffiths, or Carlyle, purchased them with your father's coin, because Margaret Colte is named on the deeds of all of them."

"I'm not shocked by anything that woman did. If we can find the deeds, then I shall take possession of them and turn them into homes for the poor."

"That's very noble of you, but it doesn't help our situation right now. My men also found several properties that were bought by people using names nobody has ever heard of. This isn't unusual, because many times the nobles want a property for a mistress, or for some other business that they'd rather no one know about. But one stood out to me, and I think you might find it of interest."

"What is it?"

"Do you know who owns the large home in the Stronde that's next to your father's house?"

"No. Come to think of it, none of us ever knew who

built it. Even Sarah and my father never knew who it was, and they said they never saw anyone there either. It was built and left empty. Did Griffiths build it?"

"I don't know. All the records say is that someone called Henry Devaux built the house. Nobody has ever heard of him. Normally, I would dismiss it as a noble who didn't want to be known, but it's strange that it's right next to your house, don't you think? It might be worth a look, even if nothing comes of it."

John sighed. "You have done excellent work, Sheriff. We shall stay at the Stronde this evening, and after dark, we will pay the house a visit."

"Keep me informed. I've temporarily moved my office here, so I can be close to the action. I hope you don't mind. No matter what you find there, be sure to hand over the confessions in time, or I won't be able to help you."

"I understand, and I shall be back tomorrow."

As John was about to leave, a commotion broke the silence. A runner burst into the rear of the house, panting and out of breath. He shouted for the sheriff.

"Sheriff Holley," he panted. "Where are you?"

One of his men pointed towards the kitchens, and the runner, who looked like he was another of Holley's men, skidded into the kitchen and almost knocked John over as he crashed into him.

"What is it?" Holley asked.

"Sir, I bring bad news." The man looked at John before turning his gaze to Sheriff Holley.

"He's good," Holley said. "He can hear what you have to say."

The man nodded. "Sheriff, I have just returned from the house you had us watching on Lumbardstrete. They're dead. They're all dead."

The man collapsed onto a chair and threw his head into his arms.

"All three of them?" Holley squeezed his eyes together.

"Yes, and Driffield . . ."

"What about Driffield?"

"Sheriff, he was cut open, mutilated, just like the ones here were. It's him, Sheriff. He's back."

"Seal it off and I'll be right there. Then we're going to the priory. It's time we had a talk with the Abbott. If Gare's there, he's coming with us, either dead or alive."

Holley turned to John with that distant, dull stare that John had seen too many times. "Go, John, and I hope you find what we are looking for. I'll have some men over there this evening to assist you."

John placed his hand on the Sheriff's arm. "No need, Sheriff. You have enough to keep you and your men busy. We can take care of ourselves, and we work better alone. We'll report back to you with our findings tomorrow, and I promise to bring what we discussed."

"What about Asheborne?" John asked as Holley headed for the door. "What do you want me to do with him? We need to keep him alive and safe from Gare."

"I'll take care of him. He'll be safe, I promise. Once he's seen a physician, I'll send him to a safe place where he will be guarded around the clock. Gare won't be able to get to him."

"Thank you, Sheriff."

Holley bowed his head and was gone.

Chapter 38

The Howard residence alongside the banks of the Thames in the Stronde sat empty and quiet. Four men guarded the front gates, but once they were inside the large grounds, John and his small group were alone.

Evans, the steward, and even Harris, the master of the stables, were not present. They were all in Broxley with Sarah.

After helping themselves to food from the massive kitchens, John gathered everyone together to tell them his plans.

"We wait until after dark, and then myself, Edward, and Stephen shall go around the banking of the Thames and find a way inside the house. I don't know what we'll find, and we don't know if it's empty or not, so we assume the worst and deal with whatever we find. Our aim is to find something—anything that links Carlyle with that house."

"What do I do while you're all gone? Can't I come with you?" Catherine asked.

John shook his head. "No, I don't want to put you in

any danger. We don't know what we're facing, and while I'm expecting it to be empty, we just don't know. I want you to remain here and wait for our return."

"But John, I . . ."

"Please, Catherine, I know how brave you are, and you have saved my life more than once, but I want to keep you safe. Please stay here and wait for us to return."

Catherine scowled, but as no help was forthcoming from either Edward or Stephen, she relented and agreed.

After darkness fell, John gave the sulky Catherine one last kiss and lead the way out of the rear entrance into the frozen night.

Catherine was alone.

She shivered and set about making a pallet for herself on the ground in a room off from the kitchens. She made sure she had plenty of candles and laid down to sleep, knowing full well that she wouldn't be able to.

Who am I kidding? I can't sleep in here. It's big, dark, and how do I even know that I'm alone? Anyone could be here, and I would never know.

After tossing and turning for what seemed an age, Catherine rose to her feet and stared at the surrounding darkness. She immediately felt better after lighting the candle she had kept close.

She walked to the rear door John and the boys had exited from a good while ago and wondered what they were doing. More than anything, she wished she was with them.

She didn't want to be in this big house alone.

Catherine wandered around the house, trying to find her bearings. Although she'd been here before, she'd never had the freedom to wander around and discover the house in her own way.

She wandered from room to room, marvelling at the

opulence of the wealthy earl. Every room looked like it was a statement of Robert Howard's power and wealth, and Catherine felt small and worthless as she peered at the expensive furniture that by itself was worth more than her entire family had possessed in twenty generations.

Catherine found herself back at the entryway at the rear of the grand house. A set of stairs ahead of her led to the upper floors, but these stairs were reserved for the Howard family and their wealthy guests. The stairs close to the kitchens were the ones used by the servants and other less deserving people like Catherine.

I'm Lady Catherine Howard, and I'm married to the future Earl of Coventry! I can use which ever staircase I desire.

Catherine repeated those words to herself over and over, but as hard as she tried, she didn't believe them. She knew she would never feel like she was the equal to the nobles she would be expected to meet in the future.

If we survive this night.

Her thoughts went back to John and the others. What were they doing? What would they find?

Catherine hoped they would find the proof they required to show that Carlyle owned the house, along with some other proof of his guilt. Anything that would bring this nightmare to an end and allow them to move on with their lives.

By the time she'd pulled herself from her thoughts, Catherine found herself staring down a long, dark corridor in the east wing of the large house. She knew this was the new extension Robert Howard had built that included his new study. Normally, nobody but Robert himself was allowed here.

Catherine gulped and forced back the feelings of shakiness in her limbs as she stared down the long, dark tunnel ahead of her. Every part of her body screamed at her to turn away and ignore this frightening corridor facing her.

And yet something pulled her towards it, like a moth to a flame. Catherine ignored her heart beating out of her chest and stepped forward, holding the candle high above her head.

I can do this. John would do it without a second thought. I can do this.

Catherine repeated this mantra to herself continuously as she passed empty rooms on either side of the narrow corridor. Her footsteps sounded as loud as an angry bear shaking a cage, as she tried every door she passed. Without exception, every room was empty.

Catherine turned around to look back to where she'd come from, and all she saw was blackness. She closed her eyes and shuddered. Then she repeated her mantra under her breath.

I can do this. John would do it without a second thought. I can do this.

After what seemed an eternity, Catherine reached the end of the long, eerie corridor. Two doors faced her, one on the left and one on the right. Instinctively, she tried the door on the right.

It opened.

Catherine crept inside and looked around. Shadows bounced off the walls, making her even more jittery than she had been before. The room had a desk and a chair towards the back wall, but other than that, it was empty.

Catherine placed the candle on the desk and tried the drawers one by one. They all opened, revealing nothing but empty space. Whatever Robert Howard had planned for this room, he hadn't implemented it yet.

There was nothing here.

Retracing her steps, Catherine tried the door to the

left. This one also opened, and once again, shadows danced off the walls, creating strange images that stimulated her imagination, forcing her to look away and repeat her mantra over and over.

This office was different. It was full of intricate paintings and expensive furniture. A large desk sat in front of the fireplace, and Catherine knew she had found Robert's private study.

Not really knowing what she was doing there, she searched around the tidy room. Nothing was out of place, and she imagined it looked as pristine as the day it had been built. She stepped forward, ignoring the shadow demons dancing in the candlelight.

The drawers in the desk were unlocked, and like the one in the other room, they were empty. A quill sat on top of the desk, along with blank paper and a container that was used for ink. Other than that, Robert's desk was empty.

Where does he keep his private papers, then? They have to be here somewhere.

A large cabinet stood against the wall to the right side of the desk, and Catherine tried the handles to see if they were unlocked.

They were.

As she opened it, she saw several sheaths of papers stored in an orderly manner inside the drawers. She pulled some out and laid them out on the desk. She was learning to read and write, so she could make out some words if she stared long enough and concentrated on them. The one thing she did notice was that the writing was the neatest she had ever seen. The letters flowed together so perfectly that Catherine had a hard time imagining how someone could be so good at it.

I suppose that's the difference between a noble and us. They learn to write from an early age, where all we do is learn our place and learn how to be good servants.

A few letters stood out as Catherine studied them. A, followed by a C, and then another C. Then O, U, N, T, S. She wasn't sure what it meant until she practiced them a few times at a faster speed. Then it hit her. Accounts! These must be his accounts.

Feeling quite proud of herself, Catherine returned the documents back to where she'd got them from and held her candle high as she peered around the room. Several paintings lined the panelled walls, and she went to get a closer look at some of them.

One was of a pretty young woman who resembled both John and Sarah in so many ways. This must be their mother, Jayne Howard.

Catherine sighed and tilted her head to the side. Life would have been so much different for all of them if Jayne hadn't died when she did. That monster, Margaret Colte, would never have entered their lives, and John would never have had to live like a beggar in London.

Catherine jumped back. *If John hadn't been in London that day, I'd be working in the brothels for Ren Walden!*

She shuddered again and put the thought to the back of her mind. She moved to another painting. This was obviously a portrait of Robert himself, and it showed a young, handsome nobleman stood proudly in his full regalia. It was a totally different world from the one in which she'd grown up in.

The next painting was hanging on the panels on the rear wall, behind the desk in the rear left corner as she looked from the doorway. She moved closer to get a better look.

The painting was of a baby laying in a crib. A man was bent over the far side of the crib, stroking the baby's head.

The baby was looking away from the painter towards the man stroking its head. A young boy and a younger girl stood behind the man, both staring at the scene before them.

Catherine stepped back and wiped a tear from her eyes. She felt a lump form in her throat as she realised what she was looking at.

The painting depicted John and Sarah stood behind their father as he comforted Arthur in his crib. Whatever Catherine had thought of Robert before instantly drained away as she saw the raw emotions of family love beaming back at her from the painting.

Robert Howard had feelings after all!

Catherine ran her fingers down the painting, and she felt the brush strokes that had been lovingly painted by who knows who. *What was that famous painter's name she'd heard of? Holbein, that's it. Hans Holbein the Younger, that's his name.*

Catherine stood for a moment imagining Holbein painting the beautiful scene that was depicted before her, and she felt her heart sing at the thought of one day having a loving family of her own with the man she loved: John Howard.

Her fingers ran down the painting onto the wooden panels below. Catherine felt the grain of the wood and allowed herself to imagine her and John living at Saddleworth Manor together with two children running around, playing in the well-stocked gardens. It was the most peaceful and beautiful image Catherine had ever experienced, and one day she hoped it might even become a reality.

Suddenly, she stopped. Her fingers caught a knot or something in the wood that the naked eye couldn't see in the dim candlelight. She pressed, and then gasped, as the panel silently swung open, revealing a large dark hole in front of her.

Instinctively, Catherine turned and looked around the room to make sure nobody else was there.

She was alone.

Holding the candle close to the hole, Catherine peered into the space behind the panel. There looked to be a hole large enough to store documents, or perhaps expensive gold and jewellery, but not much more. Her heart skipped a beat, as she put her hand inside and felt around the bottom of the hiding place.

Her fingers clasped around a sheath of papers, and as she pulled them out, she closed her eyes. *They couldn't be, could they?*

If they were the missing confessions, what were they doing here in Robert Howard's private study? Catherine pulled them out and laid them on the desk.

She couldn't read the contents, but even by the dim candlelight, she knew that the handwriting matched that of the confessions John had hidden in the crypts.

Catherine had found Margaret Colte's missing confessions!

Chapter 39

After kissing his beloved Catherine one last time, John led the way out of the rear of the house and down through the gardens towards the mighty River Thames. They kept to the cover of the wall that divided the Howard residence from the large house next door that had sat empty since the day it had been built.

They followed the wall to the end, where it stopped at the top of the banking before it angled sharply down towards the private docks that served the noble elites on the waters of the Thames. The river itself continued on through London and all the way out to the sea. Large sheets of ice were visible as the river struggled to flow, and although no longer frozen solid, the water moved at a snail's pace towards its ultimate destination.

A boat sat dark and still at the dock, but that wasn't unusual as most of the large houses along the Stronde had boats ready and waiting for their owners to use whenever they were in residence.

Keeping low to the ground, John went around the wall and entered the overgrown gardens of the house next door to their own. He ran to a large tree and stopped to assess his options.

There was scant cloud cover, and the moon and the stars were as bright as they could be. Their light reflected off the ice that covered the frozen ground, providing almost as much visibility as in daylight.

And it was cold. It was wretchedly cold.

The three men watched the house for any signs of life, but there were none. It looked as empty as it had always been.

"Do you think anyone's here?" Stephen whispered. "It looks empty to me."

John watched his breath pour out of his mouth and nostrils in a never-ending flow of steam. He blew on his hands, hoping some of the warmth would transfer to his frozen fingers.

"The best we can hope for is that we find the missing confessions that hopefully prove Carlyle's guilt. If nothing else, we need to make sure he doesn't have anyone here who means us harm."

"I hope he does." Steam poured out of Edward's mouth.

John led the way from tree to tree to avoid any watching eyes. Once they got to the last tree before the house, he halted them to assess the situation. The layout was similar to his father's residence, and the stables were in the same location.

John pointed to the building that backed up to the wall separating the two properties. "There are the stables," he whispered. "Let's go."

They ran one at a time to the stables and hid inside to catch their breath and take stock before they moved on to the house itself.

John pointed to the stalls. "Look," he exclaimed. "There are horses here. Six of them."

"Why would there be horses in an empty house?" Stephen asked before answering his own question. "There's somebody here!"

John's eyes narrowed. "This changes things. I expected it to be empty, but obviously Carlyle has men here watching my father's house. We need to take them alive so they can tell Sheriff Holley everything they know about Carlyle's plans."

Edward knelt in the doorway, searching the grounds in the moonlight. "It's clear. Let's go."

John allowed Edward to take the lead. He was a ferocious and experienced warrior, and John trusted him implicitly. If he ever commanded men to go to war, it would be Edward he would choose to be his general.

They reached the side of the house, and one by one, they filed around to the rear. Edward checked the windows and doors, but they were all closed and locked. He picked up a rock from the ground near his feet.

He moved away from the rear entrance and followed the house wall to the left of the doorway, all the way to the end. Turning the corner, Edward smashed the window, stood to the side, and waited.

Once he gave the signal, John and Stephen followed him into the dark house.

With their blades at the ready, the three men went from empty room to empty room on the east wing of the house. Cobwebs were everywhere, and it was clear that nobody had been in any of them since the day it had been built.

"Why build a house like this and never use it?" Stephen whispered.

"Knowing how Carlyle operates, he probably built it

for Margaret using my father's coin," John said. "So he wouldn't care if it got used or not."

Stephen shrugged in the darkness. "Makes sense, I suppose."

They fell silent again as the corridor opened out into the large entryway at the rear of the house. Moonlight streamed in through the many windows, illuminating everything so they could see clearly.

As it was in Robert's house next door, a staircase to their left led to the upstairs bedchambers, but Edward ignored them. He wanted to clear the downstairs rooms first.

Two hallways broke off past the stairs, both narrow and dark. One led towards the front of the house, and the other to the rooms along the west wing. Edward whispered that they should stay together and search the west wing first.

Room by room, they cleared each one carefully and silently, staying in the shadows and away from the moonlight pouring through the windows that penetrated the darkness better than any candle ever could.

Eventually, they reached the last two rooms at the west end of the house. These were the rooms, on the downstairs level at least, that were closest to the Howard residence, and John reasoned that if the owners of the horses would be anywhere, then this is where they would find them.

He tightened his grip on the hilt of his knife.

Edward huddled them all together so they could hear his words. "I'll take the room to the right. You two take the other one. Whatever happens, remain as silent as you can. We don't know how many men are here, or even if there are any at all, but going by the stables, there should be at least six."

John took a deep breath to combat the familiar feeling

of butterflies in his stomach. He shivered, but not from the cold. He'd forgotten that long ago. He shivered because the hairs on his arms raised, as the blood in his veins pumped at a ferocious speed.

He was ready.

Edward vanished into the room on the right, and John led Stephen silently into the other one. The door creaked, making John wince at the sound, but there was nothing he could do about it.

Moonlight streamed through the windows, and John made out the shapes of bodies leaping to their feet.

Two of them.

One of them shouted, but Stephen's knife flew through the air and silenced him forever.

The man fell to the floor with a thud.

John threw himself at the other man, who had taken longer to react. He was still on his knees by the time John had his knife at his throat.

"Make a sound and it shall be the last thing you ever do."

Stephen looked to make sure John didn't need his help and ran to Edward's aid in the room next door.

John could see the whites of his captive's eyes clearly in the moonlight. The man nodded. John relaxed his grip on his throat and whispered in his ear.

"Speak softly and tell me what you're doing here."

As John relaxed his grip, the man pushed the knife away from his throat and rolled away from John. He leapt to his feet and reached inside his cloak for his blade.

It was the last thing he ever did, because John was as fast as he was. As soon as the man broke away and reached for his weapon, John closed the gap and almost severed his neck with one violent swipe of his knife. Warm blood spurted all over John as the man fell to his knees, clutching his neck. He stared towards the ceiling with a blank expression on his face that was full of disbelief at what was happening to him. He gargled something that John couldn't decipher and fell face forward on the ground.

He was dead.

John took a deep breath and ran out of the room.

The scene next door was similar to the one he'd just left. Two men lay lifeless on the ground. Steam rose from large puddles of hot liquid as the blood drained out of their bodies, and Edward stood over them looking every inch the warrior that he was.

"He didn't need me," Stephen whispered.

"I told them to stay where they were and get on their knees," Edward whispered back at them. "They just didn't listen. All I wanted was for them to tell me if Gare was here or not."

John touched Edward's arm. "These men are obviously loyal to Carlyle, or he wouldn't have brought them here. We had no other choice than to kill them. What troubles me though, is why they were here. What were they doing? I guess we'll never know now."

Edward hurried out of the room and cleared the rest of the downstairs floor.

Chapter 40

The three of them quickly retraced their steps to the staircase at the rear of the house. They stopped, but all they heard was silence.

Keeping to the edges of the stairs to avoid creaking as much as possible, Edward led the way to the second floor. At the top of the stairs, the dark, narrow hallway split off to the left and right. Edward signalled they look at the rooms in the west wing that were nearest to the Howard residence.

As it was downstairs, every room they entered was empty until they reached the final two rooms. Also as before, Edward took the room to the right, leaving the other one to John and Stephen.

John's heartbeat was so loud that he was sure they would hear it at the city gates. He took deep breaths to try to control himself, but it didn't work. He pushed the door open and raced inside.

It was empty.

Edward was waiting for them in the hallway. His room

had been empty as well. They went back to the stairs and started on the rooms on the east wing.

A creaking sound from the stairs brought the three men to a standstill. Stephen, who was at the rear in the narrow hallway, turned and headed back towards the stairs. John and Edward followed right behind.

As they neared the stairs, a thud, followed by a groan, broke the silence. Stephen fell to his knees, making John stumble over him in his haste to stop.

Stephen fell backwards, trapping John against the wall, and as he struggled to free himself, a familiar voice boomed towards them.

"Do you think you could break into my home without me knowing?"

John would recognise that high-pitched, girl-like voice anywhere.

"Alexander Carlyle. We meet again."

John wriggled out from under Stephen, who struggled to his knees to show that, although injured, he could carry on. He pulled Carlyle's knife from his left shoulder and spat on the ground before standing unsteadily. Edward pushed past him, moving Stephen to the safety of their rear.

"Where did you hear that name?" Carlyle sounded surprised at the sound of his real name being mentioned.

"Everyone knows who you are, Carlyle, and everyone knows what you've been doing. The Sheriff has an arrest warrant for you, and you shall hang like you deserve."

Carlyle laughed. "On what grounds? You have nothing on me."

"Except a painting depicting you in full Yorkist regalia. From what I heard, King Henry was very interested when he saw that. Not to mention first-hand evidence that you sent a madman to murder an innocent baby and the good people that were raising him."

Silence.

"You're bluffing, and I have no time for your games. Asheborne isn't a reliable witness because he will say and do anything to save his own neck. He's the one who wanted the child killed, not me. Anyhow, I'm glad you are here because it saved me the trouble of having to break into your father's home to kill you there. It's time for you to die, John Howard. Both you and your thief of a father."

John stepped towards Carlyle's voice in the dark corridor, but by the time he reached the stairs, Carlyle was halfway down them.

"I have someone with me who has been dying to meet you again. He's here to kill you, John Howard."

"I'll leave Howard to you. I want Edward Johnson." The all too familiar voice came from the entryway at the bottom of the stairs.

"Gare!" Edward shouted. He struggled to force his way past John, but a hand on his shoulder from Stephen held him back.

"Wait," Stephen whispered. "It might be a trap. Wait until we're all together down the stairs."

Edward nodded. "Are you able to fight?"

"I think so. It's my left shoulder, so I am alright."

John turned and looked at his two best friends. "Let's end this. I want Carlyle to stand trial, but Gare doesn't leave this building alive."

He ran down the stairs.

A shadowy figure stood in front of the exit doors at the rear of the big house. The imposing, frightening figure of Oswyn Gare stood still, glowering at the three men who dared to challenge him.

"I don't run and hide. Edward Johnson, come and fight me like a man. You and I have unfinished business."

A deep, guttural growl emanated from Edward's throat, and he ran to accept Gare's challenge.

"Get Carlyle," he shouted as he ran past John and Stephen. "Leave Gare to me."

Shouts from the corridor to their west alerted John, and he ran down the corridor towards the high-pitched shouts of Alexander Carlyle.

"What do I pay you useless mumpers for? Get out here and fight, you cowards," Carlyle yelled outside the two closed doors at the end of the corridor.

"They're all dead," John said, closing the gap between himself and his prey. "You're on your own, Carlyle."

Carlyle kicked the door open to the room on the left and ran inside, slamming the door behind him. John ran after him, but Stephen stopped him at the door.

"Stop," he whispered. "He's luring you into his trap. Don't fall for his games, John, or he'll kill us both."

John could feel the burning heat from Stephen's body in the corridor's darkness. "Are you alright?" he asked.

"I'm fine," Stephen said. "I feel a little warm, but I'm able to fight. Just be careful, that's all. Fight with your brain, not your heart."

John turned to face the door. They were the most profound words Stephen had ever said to him, and he made a mental note to thank him later.

But not now. Right now, he had to concentrate on the guile and cunning of Alexander Carlyle.

"Get down," John whispered, and waited until Stephen dropped to his knees. Then he kicked the door open and dived inside, rolling over before rising to his knees in order to make as small a target as possible.

Stephen had been right, as he usually was. A knife flew

through the space where just a moment ago John had stood. It struck the wall and fell to the floor with a loud thud.

Stephen picked it up.

Carlyle was crouched on his knees on the icy ground outside the window that he'd climbed through. He got up and ran towards the river and the cover of the trees.

John ran after him with Stephen close behind. The night was so bright with the moon reflecting off the white-covered ground that John could see Carlyle clearly as he ran towards the trees.

He sprinted after him.

John skidded around the large tree he'd watched Carlyle disappear behind. He lost his footing on the icy ground and slid to the side, falling onto the cold, hard ground in a heap, face first.

In a flash, Carlyle was on him. Another knife flew at him, and this time it struck John on his left hip. He screamed as the knife penetrated his cloak and tore through his skin. He felt the grinding of the blade as it connected with bone, and for a moment, his world went black.

By the time he'd come to his senses, Carlyle was standing over his motionless body. He kicked the knife from John's hand and stood there with a smirk on his face that was so smug that it made John want to slap it out of him.

He struggled to get up, but Carlyle's foot smashed into his chest, knocking him down again.

"I win, John Howard. I always win. My victory has been a long time coming, but both you and your thief of a father shall die, and I shall rejoice from afar. You should have died last year, but I shall finish what Margaret Colte started."

John looked around desperately, searching for Stephen.

Where was he? He had been right behind him the last time he'd looked.

Carlyle had his sword in his hands, and as he raised it high above his head, he stopped and looked down at John.

"Do you have any last words, knave?"

"Go to hell." John closed his eyes and waited for the inevitable blow that would end his life. At least Catherine was safe, and he would die knowing that should Stephen or Edward survive this night, they would make sure she would be safe.

The fatal blow never came. Instead, he heard a groan and felt the sword clatter on the ground next to him. He opened his eyes and saw Carlyle swaying on his feet, the whites of his eyes so wide that he could see them clearly from where he lay.

Carlyle fell forwards towards John, but an arm grabbed him and pulled him back. It was Stephen!

"I wondered what had happened to you," John said, getting to his feet and groaning at the deep pain in his hip.

"Sorry. I must have passed out back there. I woke up, and you were gone. When I came to, this mumper was standing over you with his sword in his hands."

Carlyle dropped to his knees.

"Search him for any more weapons," John ordered, testing his hip, and wincing at the scorching pain when he tried to walk. He stepped forward and put all his weight on his injured side. He bit his lip at the sharp pain, but he knew he could function.

"I'm alright," he announced. "Let's secure him and go help Edward."

John reached down to grab Carlyle by the back of his hair, but as he did so, Carlyle lashed out with a fist into John's injured hip. Lightning bolts of white-hot pain shot through John's body, and he staggered backwards and collapsed to the ground.

Carlyle leapt to his feet and smashed his other fist into Stephen's injured shoulder, sending him into the same fits of agony that he'd inflicted on John.

He staggered towards the river, and John watched as he left a trail of dark liquid behind him from the knife wound inflicted on his back by Stephen.

Ignoring the pain, John rose to his feet and limped after him.

Carlyle wasn't getting away.

John caught him up by the river. Carlyle was trying to untie the boat that was moored to the docks at the side of the river. Stephen was right beside him.

"You won't get far in that," John said. "The river has too much ice on it."

"It will get me to where I want to go."

John drew his sword. "Enough, Carlyle. You no longer have any weapons and you're finished. You are coming with us."

Alexander Carlyle was stronger and quicker than his physical attributes suggested, and once again, he was too quick for John. He spun around and threw a rock, striking John on the nose, sending blood and stars in all directions. John fell backwards and slid towards the frozen river.

Stephen reacted and thrust his sword into Carlyle's side. Carlyle yelped and staggered towards the banking, losing his footing.

John, who had stopped his own slide down the icy banking by grabbing onto one of the mooring posts, watched as Carlyle slid past him.

Carlyle screamed as he entered the freezing river, and his arms flailed about on the breaking ice. John grabbed the mooring rope that Carlyle had untied and threw it at him. Carlyle grabbed it and held on tight as John and Stephen pulled him out of the frozen river.

Once he was out of the water, John reached forward and slapped him as hard as he could across his frozen face. Carlyle's eyes opened wide in shock before they clouded over in a mask of hatred. He shook his fists, but John ignored his gestures.

"That's for all the pain you've caused my family."

John used the mooring rope to secure Carlyle to one of the posts. With Stephen's help, he made sure Carlyle was secured and couldn't move.

"Surely you aren't going to leave me like this?" Carlyle shivered under his soaking, ice-covered cloak. "I thought you wanted me alive?"

"I don't care anymore," John said, and he meant it. "We're going to help Edward, and if you're dead when we return, then so be it. You'll answer for your crimes one way or the other."

Alexander Carlyle's screams and shouts could be heard all the way back to the house.

John was worried about Edward. As great a warrior that he was, none of them had ever come across anyone as remotely dangerous as Oswyn Gare. Even Edward wasn't sure he could best him, and if Edward couldn't, then John doubted that any man alive could.

Smashed glass lay all around the rear entrance, and deep red blood stained the entry hallway. John and Stephen hurried inside and stopped to listen.

Edward needed their help.

Chapter 41

Edward charged towards Gare, who stood his ground and stared at Edward with his dead, grey eyes. Not an ounce of fear spread across his face, and even though Edward had trained for this moment for all his life, he knew he was up against the most dangerous man he'd ever faced.

But Edward didn't care. Visions of his precious wife, Sybil, who had been due to give birth to their first child when Gare had attacked her at Burningtown the previous year, flashed through his mind. His blood pumped at breakneck speed through his body as the rage consumed him. Either he would die, or Gare would die. Either way, this was a fight to the death, and one or both of them were going to die this night.

They stood facing each other for a long moment, each sizing up the other as they circled around like tigers waiting to pounce.

"I've been waiting for this moment for a long time." Gare broke the silence and pointed to the scar running down the left side of his face. "You put this mark on me. And for that, I vowed I would enjoy killing you. I'm going to carve you open like a swan, and you are going to be alive while I do it."

Gare's eyes burned with intensity and pleasure as he spoke. This was the first and only time Edward had ever seen any kind of emotion from him, and he realised that crude violence was the only thing that stirred his soul.

"You are truly evil, Gare. Never have I heard of someone like you roaming around our stretes like the devil in a monk's robes. You killed my wife and unborn child, as well as my master and his wife. I, too, have been waiting for this night for a long time, and I vow you shall not see another dawn."

Edward was done talking.

He jumped forward with all his great strength and attacked Gare with his sword in his huge hands. The two men collided, equal in strength. The momentum of Edward's attack forced Gare backwards, and the ferocious energy of his hatred knocked Gare off his feet.

Gare fell backward into the glass panes of the windows near the doorway, and as he did so, Edward smashed his huge hand into Gare's face. Blood spurted from Gare's nose, and the force of the blow knocked him through the window.

Glass shattered all over the floor.

Gare stood up, his eyes burning with hatred and rage. He threw himself at Edward. He thrust his sword, but Gare was not an expert with his weapons. At least he wasn't an expert in the art of swordplay. His expertise lay in other areas.

Edward was a Master of Arms, and he parried Gare's crude attack and smashed the hilt of his sword into Gare's face. Gare staggered back, screaming in agony. The hilt of Edward's sword had hit him in the left eye, and the sheer force of the blow had shattered the bone around his eye socket, causing him blindness as his eye was lost in the heat of the battle.

Edward didn't let up his onslaught. He crashed another huge hand into Gare's temple, and then stood back and watched as he fell to the ground.

Blood spread all over the floor from Gare's wounds, and it mixed with the broken glass as it spread across the cold floor.

Gare picked up a piece of shattered glass and thrust forward, catching Edward in his leg. Gare hit him as hard as he could, and Edward saw the glass tear through the skin of Gare's hand as he stabbed him in his leg.

Edward screamed and staggered backward, his blood now joining Gare's on the blood-soaked ground.

Gare stood and ran towards the kitchens and the many knives he knew it contained. Edward limped after him. Gare wasn't getting away.

The bright moonlight lit up the kitchen area, and Edward watched Gare grab a long-handled carving knife. Blood streamed down the left side of his face from the wound where his eye used to be, but Gare seemed oblivious to the pain. He was an animal who thrived and survived on misery and suffering.

They stared at each other for a long moment in silence before Gare made his move. He jumped forward and thrust his knife at Edward's face, but Edward had trained his whole life for moments such as this.

He sidestepped the crude attack, and in a flash of graceful movement, he used the power of his hips to add force to his counter. His sword flashed down and severed Gare's right hand at the wrist.

Gare watched in disbelief as his hand separated from his arm and fell to the ground. As he watched, Edward moved in for his final assault.

Using the momentum of his body, he thrust his hips back around again and struck with all his might.

Gare gurgled, but whatever words he had been going to utter never came. Edward stood back and watched as Gare's head wobbled, and then fell off his shoulders, landing with a sickening crash on the blood-soaked floor. His body lurched, and then it too, fell forward and hit the ground.

Oswyn Gare was dead.

Chapter 42

Edward fell to his knees and roared, and as he did so, he felt hands touching his shoulders. He jumped up and span around to face his new attackers. Blood streaked his face and hair, and his eyes burned wild with controlled rage.

"Edward, it's us. John and Stephen."

Edward stared through his bloodshot eyes and lowered his sword. "I'm sorry. I thought you were here to fight me."

"From the look on your face, I wouldn't want to be the man facing you this night," John said. "We came to your aid, but obviously you didn't need us."

"I told you Gare was mine to deal with." Edward spat on the ground, close to Gare's head. "That's for Sybil and my unborn child. It's for James and Joan Stanton, and for John's baby brother, Arthur. And it's for the countless other men and women he murdered over the years. I hope your soul rots in hell, Oswyn Gare."

"Amen." Both John and Stephen echoed Edward's sentiments.

"Did you kill Carlyle?" Edward asked.

"No." John shook his head. "Although he might be

dead from either his injuries or the cold. He fell into the river, so we pulled him out and tied him up so we could come to your aid."

The three men embraced. "Friends forever," Edward said, and they all agreed.

John limped towards the river, leading the wounded trio of brave men to rescue Alexander Carlyle from his frozen hell.

"If he's still alive," John said. "At this point, I really don't care anymore."

Alexander Carlyle was still alive. Barely.

His eyes flickered open when John and the others approached. He flinched when he saw Edward with them.

"Gare?" he inquired, his normally high-pitched voice deeper and garbled, like his throat was parched and burned.

"Gare is in hell, where he belongs," John said. "And that's where you're going to join him."

"You have nothing on me other than the words of William Asheborne's useless son, and he's going to say anything to save his own neck. I know things about him that will send him to the gallows long before they hang me. I shall walk free, John Howard, mark my words, and when I do, you won't sleep well, because you know I shall never rest until you and your thieving father are dead."

"Shut up, Carlyle." John kicked him hard in the ribs. "You're finished, and you shall hang for your crimes. The painting alone is treason, but I'm sure you're aware of Sir William Kingston. Whatever you're not telling us now will be clear by the time he's finished with you."

Carlyle spluttered something unintelligible.

"Who's Sir William Kingston?" Stephen asked.

"He's the constable of the Tower," John replied. "And he's very adept at getting confessions from his prisoners."

Carlyle stared at John while he untied him and dragged him to his feet. As they limped their way to the Howard residence and the waiting Catherine, Carlyle regained some of his swagger.

"For one who evaded capture last year when all of England was after you, you really are a stupid boy," Carlyle taunted in his high-pitched voice. "Your father is even more stupid. You never saw what she did to you, and it was right there in front of your noses all along."

"Unless you are confessing your crimes, I don't want to hear your whining," Stephen said, smacking Carlyle on the back of his head.

"What did I miss?" John asked. "What did Margaret do that I missed? I think she made it very obvious what she was doing to me, and that's why she had to die, just like you shall."

Carlyle ignored John's threats and continued taunting his younger foe.

"You only saw the obvious. You missed the biggest disgrace she brought on your family, and I was looking forward to seeing the all-powerful Howard family brought to their knees when you found out about it. I can't go to my grave without knowing how she broke you."

"He's taunting you, John. Ignore him," Stephen said, holding his bleeding shoulder.

"Let him have his moment," John said. "Tell me, Alexander, what is so bad it will break us? Surely Margaret Colte did enough damage to my family before she died?"

"Not even close," Carlyle sneered. "Not even close."

By now, they had reached the rear doors of the Howard residence, and Catherine raced out to meet them.

"John!" she shouted. "You're all alive." She hugged John and kissed him. "I was worried about you all." She broke away from John and hugged Stephen and Edward.

Once they were inside and she could see them better with the light of the many candles she had lit, she gasped. "You're all hurt. Are you alright?"

"We're cut and bruised, but we shall recover."

"I'll get the honey, if there's any here." Catherine ran to the kitchens to search for the stash of honey she knew would be there somewhere. "I have something important to tell you, John. I found them!"

"You found what?" John shouted back, but Catherine had vanished down the corridor.

John turned to Carlyle. "You were telling me about Margaret's crimes?"

Carlyle's pale face creased into a wide grin. "Only if you give me some ale and a fresh cloak. I'm parched and I'm frozen."

John limped off and grabbed one of his father's cloaks, and when he returned, Stephen was forcing a jug of ale down Carlyle's throat, making him cough and choke.

"Drink, you knave. Drink and drown for all I care."

John threw the cloak at him. "Now speak."

Catherine returned and got to work with the honey, smearing it all over the many wounds on her beloved men. At John's request, she started on Edward first.

John turned back towards Carlyle, who was never an inch from Stephen's side. Stephen's gaze never left him, and he was making sure he didn't try anything else to escape.

"I don't trust him," Stephen said when John looked at him.

"Well?" John asked.

Stephen pulled the jug of ale away from Carlyle's head and watched him splutter and choke. John gave Stephen a look of satisfaction and smiled at him.

"He deserves it," Stephen said for the umpteenth time.

"I hope I live long enough to see your faces when you discover Margaret's greatest act of treachery against your disgusting family." Carlyle pumped his fists and shook them about as though he were throwing a childish tantrum.

"We're still waiting," John said impatiently. "Either tell us, or I'll have Stephen bind your mouth so tight you'll choke to death before we hand you over to the Sheriff."

"I'm not making it easy for you. If you can't see what's right in front of you, then you are even more stupid than I already thought. I'll tell you this, and I hope it is enough before I die. You found her confessions and yet you still haven't connected it all together. The answer to her past is in Speke. Go there, and you shall find what you have so glaringly missed. And it shall destroy your world."

Chapter 43

Once Catherine had finished smearing honey over all the wounds, even those of Alexander Carlyle, she wiped her hands and beamed at John.

"I found them, John. I found the missing confessions."

John blinked slowly. "You found the missing confessions? Where? How?"

Stephen and Edward stared as Catherine pulled the wad of papers from under her cloak. Even Carlyle stared open-mouthed.

Stephen kept his uninjured arm on Carlyle's neck the whole time to make sure he didn't try to escape.

"I couldn't sleep, so I wandered around the house. You won't believe me when I tell you where I found them."

"Try me," John said.

"What about him? Do you want him to know where they were? He might use it to escape or something."

"Good point. Tell me out there." John pointed to the hallway and walked away from the listening ears of Alexander Carlyle. "I'll tell you later," he said to the onlooking Stephen and Edward.

"I found myself in your father's study, and I got close to the wall to look at a painting of a man standing over a baby in a crib. I assumed it was your father standing over Arthur with you and Sarah looking on?"

John nodded. "That's what father said it was supposed to be when he had it painted."

"Anyway, I ran my fingers down it and touched the panel below. I felt a knot in the wood and pressed, and the panel flew open. The confessions were hidden inside."

"They were hidden in my father's study? Nobody goes in there except my father. Not even Margaret was allowed in there, although I wouldn't be surprised if she hid them there when he was with the king."

John kissed Catherine and held her close. "You and Sarah are the bravest, smartest girls I know, and you are both warriors. I love you to the ends of the world, and I am so proud of you."

Catherine beamed.

John headed back to the others and began reading the confessions to himself. His eyes widened as he read down the page.

"I think you all need to hear this. Especially you, Carlyle." John began reading aloud.

Andrew Griffiths purchased several houses in England on my behalf in case I ever had the need to escape quickly. Robert, blinded by love and lust, never knew what I was doing with his coin, and he never once questioned me about it. By the time I'd finished, Andrew had purchased a dozen properties for me in his name.

I have listed the properties on a different page, but they include the little white house in London where I hold my meetings with Ren Walden and his gang. I must confess to being quite fond of the little house, and I can see myself relaxing there once this is all over and I am cleansed of the disgusting Howards once and for all.

Andrew Griffiths is a clever man whose problem is that he thinks he's smarter than everyone else. He certainly believes he is smarter than me.

It is this flaw that shall be his downfall.

John looked up and saw the scowl on Carlyle's face. "Maybe you're not as smart as you think you are. Even Margaret saw through you."

Carlyle turned his scowl at John.

Andrew believes he has covered his tracks, and that nobody knows who he is, but William is the smartest man I've ever met, and he knows all about Andrew Griffiths.

If I'm giving someone as much coin as I gave Griffiths to hold for me, I'm going to know everything about them before I hand it over. And I, too, know everything there is to know about Andrew Griffiths.

Andrew's true identity is Alexander Carlyle, the Viscount Richmond of Yorkshire. Once anyone has seen Alexander, as he shall henceforth be known, his physical appearance makes it impossible to forget him.

Alexander keeps his secrets close, but I know them all. I know he has a home in a small village in Yorkshire that he calls Erikson Hall, after renaming it after the great Viking explorer Leif Erikson. He bought it for himself with my coin.

Alexander will one day pay for his treachery with my coin, but for now he is useful to me, so I let it pass.

Erikson Hall is in a village called Burton Agnes, which is close to Bretlinton in Yorkshire. In it, he proudly hangs a portrait of himself wearing the full Yorkist regalia, which by itself is an act of treason against Henry VIII.

In addition, Alexander has ambitions to replace Robert as the head of the Privy Council, so he has close access to the king. However, even that isn't enough for Alexander. He changed his name when he was young to Alexander, so he could compare himself to Alexander the Great, such was his ambition and conceit.

Alexander believes he is the rightful heir to the throne, and once he has the ear of the king, he plans to kill him and claim the throne for himself. If anyone in England is guilty of treason, it is Alexander Carlyle, for no man has committed greater sins against Henry Tudor than he . . .

John looked up. "I think that's enough. I doubt you are as confident of keeping your head now, are you?"

Carlyle continued to scowl, but John watched as the blood drained from his face.

John gathered up the confessions, that included a list of properties Carlyle had purchased, and placed them inside his cloak.

"Dawn is breaking, and curfew is about to be called. It's time to go to London and hand this traitor over to Sheriff Holley."

Chapter 44

As soon as John had handed over Carlyle to Sheriff Holley at the little white house, he left to retrieve the confessions from the crypts. Edward, Stephen, and Catherine accompanied him, and they dragged their damaged, weary bodies across London to the place they loved to hate.

It was the safest place they could ever find, but at the same time, it was the last place they ever wanted to be.

Once inside the storeroom in the rear corner of the small church on Britten Strete, it wasn't long before Edward, Catherine, and Stephen were fast asleep. John didn't blame them, because they were all exhausted.

John lit a candle and unlocked the door to the dark and eerie crypts and entered the darkness. Ignoring the familiar feeling that he was disturbing the resting place of people long forgotten, he made his way to the second tomb on the right-hand side.

At the rear of the tomb where the head lay near the wall, John pulled a stone away from the base and reached inside to retrieve his mother's jewellery box. He took it to the storeroom where he could see better in the light from the window.

He dropped the large number of confessions from the elaborate jewellery box onto the stone floor. His eyes felt heavy with fatigue and pain, but he forced himself to concentrate. There would be time to rest after he'd finished.

John spent the rest of the morning sorting through Margaret's confessions, taking out any that referenced Isobel, along with a few that might see his father hang if Cromwell got his way.

Once he'd finished, John replaced the ones he'd kept, and put the jewellery box back in its hiding place. Then he lay next to his beloved Catherine and closed his eyes.

Sleep came immediately, and it felt like only moments had passed when hands were shaking him, and someone was speaking his name.

"John, John, wake up."

It was Edward, although it took a moment for John's fuzzy brain to recognise it.

"What is it?"

"John, we have slept all day. Curfew will be called if we don't hurry, and you promised the Sheriff you'd hand over the confessions this day. If we don't leave now, we won't get through the gates in time."

John yawned and stretched. The last thing he wanted to do was walk all the way back to their little white house, but as his senses returned, he knew he had no choice. He got up and immediately grabbed at his injured hip.

"Take it easy," Catherine said. "You're injured."

John sighed. "I'm fine. Let's go."

The bedraggled quartet gathered their meagre belongings and headed back into the city.

Sheriff Holley was pacing around the corridor of the

house when they arrived. "Here you are. I was beginning to wonder if you'd changed your mind."

"Why would I do that?"

"Are they all here?" Holley eyed the large sheath of papers John placed on the table.

"Every one of them," John lied.

"Are you sure? You kept nothing back?" Holley tilted his head to the side and eyed John as only a Sheriff could.

"I'm sure." John held his gaze.

"Even the ones that reference Isobel and Speke?"

John's mouth dropped open, and for a moment, he was speechless. Then he realised what had happened.

"Carlyle. Carlyle told you about Isobel?"

"Not much. Only that once you discover her story, your family will realise the true treachery of Margaret Colte and William Asheborne."

"I might have lost those confessions." John's eyes widened as he looked at Holley. "I'm sure they're in there, but I couldn't say for sure. There are a lot of them, as you can see."

"Hmm." Holley shook his head and raised his eyebrows. "We'll look, but if you say they are all there, then they are all there. If any are supposedly missing, then I can only conclude that they never existed."

"Thank you, Sheriff." John bowed his head.

Holley read through a few of the pages and whistled to himself. "These are powerful letters, and they will bring down many of the nobles. I hope Cromwell uses them wisely and keeps them out of the grasp of the nobles at court."

"I'm sure he will," John said. "He will probably use them to gain even more control in the court and even more influence with the king. But that's up to him. Those confessions are poison to whoever holds them, and I'm glad to be rid of them. As long as they release my father as promised, then I am done with them."

"He shall be released. At least that was what was promised to me, but you know the world of the nobles better than I. It doesn't look good for Carlyle or Asheborne, though."

"What's happened to Carlyle?" John asked.

"Oh, he confessed everything. For some reason, he was terrified of meeting Sir William Kingston at the Tower. You wouldn't have had anything to do with that, would you, John?" Sheriff Holley's eyes twinkled.

John threw his arms in the air. "I don't know what you're talking about, Sheriff."

"There is more than enough to prove his guilt with the confessions and the painting," Holley said. "If what I've heard so far is anything to go by, William Asheborne is going to die alongside him."

"Regarding Asheborne," John said. "If it wasn't for him, we would never have caught Carlyle and Gare. It was he who told us about the priory, and it was he who showed me the painting. He has suffered more than most through the actions of his father, and the only thing he did was steal some of his father's wealth to make sure he had a life after everything he'd ever known was taken away. I'm assuming Carlyle stole that from him as well, so Asheborne has nothing. Surely that is punishment enough?"

"You would advocate for leniency for the man who plotted to kill you? You are indeed a nobleman, John Howard."

"I would. William Asheborne is as much a victim of his father's ambitions as I was, so I understand why he took the actions that he did."

"I'll see what I can do. Now, speaking of Gare. I sent my men to search your father's house after we arrested

Carlyle, and my men told me a disturbing story about how they found Gare. Or what you left of him."

"Sheriff, there has never been a more deserved death than that of Oswyn Gare. He was truly the evillest man that has ever lived, and his death should not be mourned."

"He was beheaded, John. I can't allow that to pass without investigating it."

"It was self-defence. He was about to kill Edward, and bearing in mind that he'd already murdered his wife and unborn child, Edward had no choice other than to defend himself and kill Gare."

"Did he have to behead him?"

"With one so evil, Edward had to make sure he was dead. For Gare was truly the devil himself, and normal injuries didn't seem to stop him."

"That's all I needed. I'll see the matter is closed. There was one other thing my men discovered."

"What was that?"

"Were you aware that Carlyle was planning to leave England after he and Gare had killed you? He was going to poison Gare after he'd used him to kill all of you, and then take a boat to France, where he has a large estate. He carried a large amount of gold and coin with him, most of it I'm sure belonging to Asheborne and your father."

"I wasn't aware of that, no. What did you do with it?"

"I handed it over to Kingston to hold as evidence, as I was supposed to have done."

John winced. "I doubt anyone shall see any of that ever again, then."

"Are you accusing Sir William of thievery?"

"Not at all, Sheriff. I'm accusing the nobles who will hold the trial of thievery. They'll find a way of taking it as their fee. Mark my words."

"As I said, you know the nobles better than I."

"So, what happens next?" John asked.

"There will be a trial, naturally, and I am sure they will find Carlyle guilty. Then he will be executed as the king orders. I will try to gain mercy for Asheborne, but I can't promise. I can say that after he heard all the evidence, he was full of remorse for what he's done to you and your family."

"I don't care about his remorse," John said. "But I do care about justice for him. He's suffered enough. What about my father?"

"I expect Lord Cromwell to honour his word and release your father in the morn once he's seen the confessions. Then it will be several weeks before Carlyle's trial takes place. You know how it works."

"Good. I have to leave London for a while, but I'll be back before the trial. I'll wait until they release my father before I leave."

"You're going to Speke?"

"Perhaps it's better you don't know."

"Maybe, but I'd like to remain informed of your movements just the same. You can trust me, John, and I hope you know that by now. I have never been your enemy."

"I know that, Sheriff, and I am very grateful for all you've done for me. Meet me in the graveyard at the rear of the small church on Britten Strete by Aldersgate after curfew lifts the day after tomorrow. Assuming they release my father in the morn, that is when I shall be leaving."

Sheriff Holley nodded.

Chapter 45

As promised, Cromwell issued the order to release Robert Howard from the Tower the following morn. The king directed him to stay with his brother, Thomas Howard, the Duke of Norfolk, at his London residence until after Carlyle's trials.

Thomas Howard sent for John in the afternoon, and he duly arrived in the carriage his uncle sent for him. Memories flooded back from the previous visits he'd taken to his uncle's residence when he had been on the run and desperately needing help. Although they had a fractious relationship, if it hadn't been for Thomas Howard, John would surely have been executed as a common criminal and murderer.

After the steward showed John to a smaller room than he'd seen on his previous visits, he waited patiently for his father to show up. Thomas Howard had expressly forbidden John to bring any of his "ruffian friends" as he called them, and in deference to his uncle's nobility, he had complied and gone alone.

The door opened and his father walked in. John immediately noticed that he looked gaunt and tired after his ordeal.

"Hello, Father. It's good to see you again."

Robert sat in the chair opposite his son and looked at him. "You and I have had our differences, but I owe you my life. If you hadn't turned over the confessions, I would have been executed, but I am concerned with the contents of what Margaret wrote. If she implicated me in her wild schemes, I am worried that once Cromwell reads them, the king will order my arrest again and execute me. I am strongly considering going to France where I will be safer, as my life here is surely over."

"Father, I may have told the Sheriff that I'd handed all the confessions to him, but that doesn't mean that I actually did. I'm not stupid, and I kept back most of the ones pertaining to you. I told Sheriff Holley that all the ones that referenced you had already been handed over last year, when I was trying to prove my innocence."

Robert Howard blew out his pale cheeks. "John, you have proven yourself to be more of a man than I could have ever hoped. I heard about what you did to the monk in that house."

"Gare deserved it, and in any case, it wasn't me that fought him. Father, I'll get right to the point. I found the missing confessions that referred to Carlyle hiding behind a panel in your study. Did you have them?"

Robert bit his lip. "I won't lie to you, John. Sheriff Holley told me you had found them, but I had no idea they were there. I'm guessing Margaret hid them when I was away serving the king."

"Would you have told me if you did have them?"

"Probably not, for the same reason you wouldn't give me the ones you had. I didn't trust you."

"At least we got that straight between us." John stood to leave.

"Please, sit down. I have other news to tell you." Robert gestured to the chair.

John obliged.

"They released me, but I am ordered by the king to remain here until the trial of Alexander Carlyle is over. The king has removed me from the Privy Council and banished me from the court. He also stripped me of the Order of the Garter. I am a broken man, John."

"Did he allow you to keep your lands and titles?"

"That much he granted, or at least most of it. He said it was for my past loyalty."

"Then you have lost little, Father. They didn't throw you out onto the stretes without coin or home, and you still have your nobility to hide behind. I'd say you have got away with this lightly."

"I suppose I deserved that. Is there anything I can do for you in return for my life?"

"Is Stephenson still in charge of Broxley? And is Sarah still there?"

"It looks like I shall lose Broxley. The king is confiscating it to give to Stephenson as a gift. Sarah is still there, but not for much longer. I haven't been told yet for certain, but it looks like I shall have but a few weeks to vacate Broxley and hand it over."

"Where shall you live? And what will happen to Sarah?"

"We'll all live here in London until I find another suitable residence."

"That's all I wanted to know. Stay here, Father, and I shall return with Sarah."

John walked away.

Chapter 46

The following morn, John, Catherine, Edward, and Stephen gathered around the unmarked grave of their fallen friend, Isaac Shore. Gamaliell Pye, their friend and saviour, joined them. Without his help, they would surely have perished. The only man missing was Sheriff Holley, who had promised to be there after curfew had lifted.

After a long wait in the freezing grip of winter, footsteps crunched in the ice and the familiar face of Sheriff Holley appeared alongside another man John knew he'd seen before but couldn't quite place.

Platinum hair fell from beneath his head covering, and his slender figure glided across the ice. Recognition dawned on John.

"Father Kirk, it's good to see you again."

"It's good to see you again, Master John. I hope you don't mind, but the Sheriff invited me along in case you needed my guidance."

"We're very glad you are here, Father, and we could certainly do with your guidance. This is the grave of our dearest friend, Isaac Shore, who shared many adventures with us until he was struck down last year. Before we leave London, we came here to say the Lord's prayer over his grave. These were Isaac's favourite words, and they always brought him comfort in life. We hope they also bring him comfort in death. I always spoke the prayer, but I am but a mere friend. It would mean so much more if you would do us the honour, Father."

"I would be delighted to say the prayer for your friend."

John gathered everyone together by the hand and closed his eyes. Father Kirk began reciting Isaac's favourite prayer.

Pater noster, qui es in caelis,
sanctificetur nomen tuum.
Adveniat regnum tuum.
Fiat voluntas tua,
sicut in caelo et in terra.
Panem nostrum quotidianum da nobis hodie,
et dimitte nobis debita nostra,
sicut et nos dimittimus debitoribus nostris.
Et ne nos inducas in tentationem,
sed libera nos a malo.
Amen.

John wiped the frozen tears from his cheek before raising his head. "Thank you, Father Kirk. I cannot tell you how grateful we are for your words."

"It is my pleasure, John. From what the Sheriff tells me, you've all had a torrid time these past months, and it is my fervent wish that life treats you kind from here on in."

"Thank you, Father. We have one more journey to make, and then we hope the violence will be behind us, although only time will tell, of course."

"I know where you are going, John," Sheriff Holley

spoke up. "And I hope you find what it is you seek. Is there anything I can do to help you on your way?"

John shook his head. "Thank you, Sheriff, but we have what we need."

"Carlyle's trial will be in three weeks, so make sure you are back by then."

John bowed his head. "We will be back."

After Sheriff Holley and Father Kirk had left, Gamaliell Pye turned to John and pressed a bag of coin into his palm. "I know you don't need this now, but please accept it as a sign of my friendship. I wish you a safe journey, my young friends, and please be sure to tell me what you discover when you return."

"We will, Gamaliell. We will."

John clutched the bag of coin and watched as their old friend disappeared from view.

Chapter 47

The journey north to Warwickshire was fast and furious. John exchanged the horses at regular intervals so they could keep up their breakneck speed. In the end, the journey from London that normally lasted a week or more only took them three days.

John was in a hurry and didn't have time to dally around.

They arrived at St Michael's Church, close to Broxley Hall, late into the night. Catherine had been here before, when they had dragged Sarah and Margaret Colte's son, Mark Colte, from their beds, and dragged them down to London to help clear John's name.

After tying the horses at the rear of the small church, including the extra one they had picked up for Sarah, John led the weary travellers inside and closed the doors so they wouldn't be seen from Broxley Hall a short way away at the bottom of the hill.

John gathered them at the front of the altar and closed his eyes. "Lord God, please accept our presence here as a token of our gratitude for taking care of our brother, Mark

Colte, who bravely gave his life when he defied his mother to help clear my name. Lord, we pray you look down upon us and grant us your blessing this night, and guide us with your compassion to our destiny. Amen."

"Amen."

John sat down and addressed the others through the dull moonlight shining through the stained-glass windows. "Wait here and rest until I return. If all goes to plan, I shouldn't be long, and then we'll leave for Speke at dawn."

"I still don't know why you don't just go to the front gates and demand to enter," Stephen said for the thousandth time on this journey. "It's your residence, and Sarah isn't a prisoner, especially as your father is now a free man again."

"I could, but I fear Stephenson won't allow me access. He would move Sarah to a location where I couldn't reach her, and he wouldn't believe me if I told him that my father had been freed. He won't have heard the news yet, and as Robert Howard's son, he won't take my word for it. If I try reasoning with him, he'll not only keep Sarah there, but he would have his men arrest me and lock me inside until he hears from London, which might be another week or more. Stephenson wouldn't be in any hurry to release me, and he would make sure I missed the trial, knowing that Cromwell has ordered me to attend."

John looked at his friends one by one. "Stephenson is no friend of ours. I have to get Sarah out without them knowing, just like I did last time."

"I am coming with you," Edward said. "And I am not asking." His huge hands grabbed John's shoulders and pulled him forward. "I know you said it's easier if you go alone, but Stephenson will have guards on patrol, and it's too dangerous for you to go alone."

John sighed. "We've already been through this. I know

Broxley like the back of my hand, and I can be in and out before they know it. If you come with me, there's more chance Stephenson's men will see us."

"I'm not asking." Edward stood his ground.

"I'm with Edward," Catherine said. "You'd better do as you're told for once, my love." She reached forward and kissed her husband on the cheek.

"I'd rather go alone, but if you insist, then I won't fight you over it."

"Good, because you will lose." Edward smiled, but John knew he meant it.

"In that case, Stephen, you're in charge. Remain alert until we return. I'll knock on the rear windows before approaching the doors, so you'll know it's us. Be ready to leave at a moment's notice."

"What if you're not back by dawn?"

"Go back to London and wait for me there. Don't try to rescue us, because there will be too many of them, not to mention you're injured."

"So are both of you," Catherine exclaimed. "You all are."

"We're fine," three voices spoke at once.

With one last kiss with Catherine, John was gone, with Edward right behind.

BROXLEY HALL LOOKED massive in the moonlight, and John fought back the memories from his childhood as they flooded into his mind. He shook his head and concentrated on the task at hand.

Although still frozen solid, the ice wasn't as thick as it had been in London. Winter was slowly loosening its grip on the landscape, and spring wasn't far away. John was happy to look forward to the sun warming his back once again and seeing the end of the frozen stretes and hills.

He shook himself. *Concentrate, or you shall fail.*

They stopped behind a tree close to the rear of the house. Broxley Hall was old, and like most old houses, it contained secrets. Secrets that only people very familiar with the residence would ever know about. People like John and Sarah, who had spent their entire childhood finding them.

John and Edward watched for guards patrolling the outside of the house, but none were to be seen. They ran across the drawbridge over the moat and huddled at the side of the walls surrounding the grand residence.

Content that nobody was watching, John climbed over the wall and lowered himself on the other side. A few moments later, Edward joined him, and they ran quietly through the courtyard towards the kitchens that served the magnificent house.

Guards patrolled in pairs, and John curled his top lip when he saw them. *Broxley is mine, and even though the king is giving it to Stephenson, one day I shall get it back, no matter how I do it.*

Once the guards had cleared the area, John led Edward through the courtyard and into the kitchens, heading straight to the large fireplace that now sat cold and still. He touched his hands to the left of the soot-filled fireplace wall and slid the small latch that was hidden in plain sight.

After a soft click, a large black hole appeared in the wall. This was their secret passage into the inner sanctum of the house.

John and Sarah always kept candles hidden inside the secret tunnel so they could see whenever they used it, so after Edward closed the door behind him, John lit one and led the way into the depths of the house.

The passage ended in the library, and John was careful to listen for noise as they entered the house. Satisfied, he led the way up the stairs, being careful to avoid causing creaks and groans along the way.

John knew every step like the back of his hand, and Edward followed carefully to make sure he didn't give them away.

At the top of the stairs, John quickly found Sarah's bedchamber, and, with his heart thundering in his chest, he entered the room. Edward followed and closed the door behind him.

Unlike the last time he'd rescued Sarah, she wasn't fast asleep. She was sat in her bed reading by candlelight, or at least she was until two strange men entered her room.

Fourteen-year-old Sarah Howard, soon to be fifteen, with her shoulder-length brown hair falling loose, and her slender body barely covered by a thin nightgown, leapt out of bed and threw her book at John. She opened her mouth to scream, but John spoke first.

"Sarah, it's me, John! Don't scream."

Sarah's expression changed from one of fear and horror to one John recognised all too well. Her mouth dropped open, and her eyes grew wide. "John?" she whispered. "Is that really you?"

"Yes, it's me. And my loyal friend, Edward."

Sarah threw herself at John. "John, I can't believe you are here. What are you doing? How is father? Are they going to execute him? Lord Stephenson keeps me prisoner and enjoys telling me how he will soon be in London, witnessing our father being executed. He tells me you are going to be executed with him, and that Broxley will be his."

"Sarah, calm down," John whispered. "None of that is true. Well, most of it, anyway, but we've got to get you out of here. I'll tell you everything once we are free of Stephenson."

"Brother, you smell."

"Ahh, the same old Sarah." John hugged his beloved sister.

Sarah hugged Edward. "I'm sorry, Edward. I didn't mean to ignore you."

Edward bowed. "I understand, Lady Sarah."

Sarah dressed quickly while John and Edward respectfully turned around, and she gathered a few warm clothes. Then she grabbed four bags of coin her father had given her, and she was ready.

John led the way back to the library, and as Edward closed the door so they wouldn't be seen entering the secret passage, hurried footsteps ran towards them in the corridor outside. Edward drew his blade and waited by the wall. John did the same on the other side, with Sarah by his side.

The door burst open, and two men ran in, blades in hand. As they ran, Edward sprang into action. In a flash, he crashed his massive hand into the lead guard's face and stood aside as he crumbled to the floor.

John used the hilt of his blade to add weight to his strike, and he hit the second guard as hard as he could on the side of the head. He fell on top of his fellow guard, and John once again curled his lips at the sight of Stephenson's guards roaming around his house.

Ignoring his inner feelings, John pushed Sarah towards the secret passage and hurried through the narrow, ancient tunnel.

When they exited in the kitchens, Edward listened for any signs of disturbance, but the men in the library must still have been unconscious, so John led the way and ran to the wall surrounding the rear of the house. They ran over the drawbridge, and to St Michael's Church as fast as they could.

John tapped on the rear window, and almost immediately the door burst open, and Catherine ran outside and hugged John.

Sarah grabbed Catherine and hugged her tightly. "Catherine, it's so good to see you again."

The two girls hugged for a long moment before John stepped in. "We've got to go. Two guards saw us and must have raised the alarm by now. We've got to get out of here. Sarah, I promise I'll explain everything once we get a safe distance away from here."

They jumped on their horses and galloped into the night.

Chapter 48

They rode all night and most of the next day, until they found themselves in a small market town called Market Drayton in the Midlands.

"This is as far as we ride today," John announced. "The horses are exhausted, and so are we. We'll find an inn and exchange the horses. Then tomorrow, we continue."

Sarah wouldn't leave John alone. "You still haven't told me anything. You dragged me from my bed and halfway through England and I am still no wiser. Is father still alive? Is that why you won't tell me anything? I'm not leaving here until you tell me everything."

"Calm down, sister. I aim to tell you once we're safely in the room at the Inn. Then we can talk and rest."

Stephen and Edward took the horses to be exchanged while John, Sarah, and Catherine found an inn on the main strete that went through Market Drayton. Then they bought enough food and ale to feed a starving army and waited for Stephen and Edward to join them.

Once they had taken their fill, they dragged their

weary bodies to the room John had paid for and laid down on the straw-filled pallets on the grimy floor of the small room.

Edward took first watch, while Stephen and Catherine fell asleep almost immediately.

"I'll take first watch," John said, looking at Edward. "Sarah and I need to talk, so there's no need for you to be awake as well."

Edward shook his head. "You need to concentrate on informing Lady Sarah about what happened and where we're going. I'll concentrate on what's going on outside."

Sarah pulled a face at John. "Edward is so serious. Is he always like this?" she whispered.

"I am a warrior, Lady Sarah. I was trained to be like this."

"I'm sorry, Edward. I didn't mean to offend you. We are so much safer when you are with us."

"Thank you, Lady Sarah."

Sarah turned to her brother. "Tell me everything."

John told her what had happened in London, and how he'd turned over the confessions to save their father. He also told her of his travels to Yorkshire, and how they'd rescued William Asheborne, and he ended with what had happened at the Stronde. He left nothing out.

Sarah turned pale and sat quietly for several minutes while she absorbed what John had told her.

"So, father is a prisoner at Uncle Thomas's residence although he's a free man? That doesn't sound right, John. Then the king confiscated our home so he can give it to Lord Stephenson? How can he even do that to us? And I don't even begin to understand what is awaiting us in Speke. Do you have any idea?"

"None at all. Whatever Margaret did, it must have been bad if it's worse than anything she's done to us already. All I know from her confessions is that she drowned a young girl named Isobel, who was the daughter of the Lord in Speke."

"That's bad enough," Sarah said.

"I agree. As for father having to stay at Uncle Thomas's residence, I believe it is so father doesn't leave for France, which is something he mentioned to me when I saw him. Once Carlyle is executed, I expect the king will grant him his freedom again."

"Except he's no longer allowed at court? That will hurt father more than losing Broxley."

"That's why he did it. He tired of the constant drama surrounding our family, and he believed we caused danger to him. So, he removed father from the court."

"I guess when you put it like that, it's understandable why the king did what he did. But why take Broxley away from us?"

"To punish father for trying his patience too many times. Being king, he can do whatever he wants."

Sarah sighed. "I don't know if I want to find out what Margaret did in Speke."

"I feel the same, but if it affects us, we need to know."

TWO DAYS and several wrong turns later, the weary travellers rolled into the small village of Speke. The sun was setting, and the late afternoon shadows were forming when they pulled into the only inn they could find.

After securing their horses in the stables, they paid for a room and took their fill of ale and food.

The locals were more than helpful once John told them he had business with the Lord of Speke Hall, and they gladly gave directions to its location, although they informed John that he wouldn't be able to miss it once the sun rose in the morning.

And they were right. The massive stately home loomed into view as John and Sarah drew closer. They had decided it was better if just the two of them went, as they were nobles of equal status to Lord Gordon, who owned Speke Hall. Until the previous evening, neither John nor Sarah had ever heard his name before.

Speke Hall sat a short distance from the River Mersey, one of the largest rivers in the north, according to the proud locals who had given their visitors a thorough description of the wonderful area where they lived. After the sun had risen that morn, John felt inclined to believe them.

The massive house, with its black and white painted framing came into view, and it was a sight to behold. Four triangular archways separating the front of the house from the roof gave it a unique, mystical kind of look, or at least it did to John. Four chimneys bellowed smoke from the rooftops, signalling that the house was alive and thriving.

And warm.

John and Sarah trotted their horses down the long road that led to the red brick archway that allowed access to the massive mansion. When they reached the gate, two guards blocked their way. John bent down to address them and spoke in his best nobleman's voice. He felt strange because he hadn't spoken like this for some time, and it didn't feel like him any longer.

But today it served a purpose, so he was happy to use his status as the son of a famed earl.

"What's yer business here, sir?" a guard asked, eyeing up the bedraggled travellers.

"Please inform Lord Gordon that Master John and Lady Sarah Howard are here to see him. Please inform His

Lordship that we are here on a matter of extreme urgency."

The guard raised his eyebrows when John spoke. By the look of him, he'd probably assumed the two travellers were poor beggars searching for work.

"Is the Lord expecting you?" the guard asked.

"No. We have ridden from London with barely a stop, and we are tired and weary. Please inform your Lordship immediately."

The guard bowed and opened the gate to allow John and Sarah passage. The other guard ran towards the house to inform his Lordship of their arrival.

Two stable boys took care of the horses, and the steward, who introduced himself as Longmead, ushered them into a plush sitting room. While they waited, Longmead provided them with ale and bread.

They didn't have to wait for long. A short while later, an ageing man who had seen better days, shuffled in and surveyed his visitors. Although his body was portly and stooped, Lord Gordon's eyes looked as sharp as those of a man half his age.

If, indeed, this was Lord Gordon.

"For what do I owe the pleasure of a visit from Earl Howard's famous son? For if I'm not mistaken, you are the infamous John Howard, are you not?" Lord Gordon's voice was soft and cultured, and the generations of nobility in his heritage shone through his words.

John rose to his feet. "Indeed, I am, Lord Gordon, although I trust you also know that I was never guilty of the accusations made against me. Please allow me to introduce my sister, Lady Sarah Howard."

"Please, sit. I know all about your story. Everyone does. It makes for a good after dinner conversation." Lord

Gordon chuckled. “I hear your father has fallen foul of our great king?”

“They released him from the Tower, and he is now a free man.” Sarah spoke against the wishes of her brother.

“Indeed, and I’m glad to hear it. I know why you are here. I’ve been waiting for you to pay me a visit for a long time.”

John looked at Sarah and furrowed his brow. “How would you know we would come all the way to Speke to see you?”

“Let’s drop the pretence. There is only one reason John Howard would come all this way to see me. It’s regarding Margaret Colte, isn’t it?”

John’s gaze wandered around the opulent room for a moment while he gathered his thoughts. “Yes, Sir James, we’re here regarding Margaret Colte. I assume you know the story of how she married my father and forced me out of the family?”

“Your story is legendary, John Howard. People will speak of it for generations to come. Of course I know what she did to you. Everybody does.”

“You speak as though you know Margaret. May I ask how you knew her?” John held James Gordon’s gaze until Gordon looked away at the ground.

“What is it you want to know?” he avoided the question.

“Sir, we know everything we need to know about her actions after she married our father. What we don’t know is what made her become the evil woman that she was when we knew her. She even killed her own son, Mark Colte. Were you aware of that?”

James Gordon nodded his head slowly.

“I found the confessions she left behind, and she mentions her time here when she was a young girl. I have brought some with me so you can see for yourself what she wrote."

John pulled the confessions that had haunted him for so long from under his cloak. His hands trembled as he handed them over to Lord Gordon, with the words of Alexander Carlyle ringing in his ears.

What had she done that was so terrible?

James Gordon took the confessions and began to read. His eyes clouded over, and his arms trembled as he studied the letter.

My confessions begin in April 1520. I was thirteen years old, and I remember it was only a handful of weeks before I turned another year older.

On the day my life changed, I was walking along the banks of the river, enjoying a rare dry day after the heavy recent rains. The small path along the side of the now-raging river soothed my soul and made me feel alive. More importantly, the solitude I found by the river's edge calmed the inner anger that was never far from the surface, and it helped me hold my tongue when I returned to the village and the normal life that I detested so much.

I deserved more, and I knew that one day I would have all that I wanted, and more.

I remember singing to myself as my feet sank in the muddy, waterlogged path. Thick filth clung to my shoes, and I watched it climb up my legs like a dark shadow. I love remembering this moment because it reflects the most personal, innermost feelings that have haunted my mind since I was a young child.

I was lost in my own little world, enjoying the solitude I so craved, when a voice I was all too familiar with startled me so much I almost tumbled down the banking into the raging waters.

"What are you doing here?" Isobel snarled at me. She might have only been ten years old, but she hated me with the passion of a thousand suns. I thought only I was capable of such deep hatred, and yet

here she was, sneering at me yet again, her mere presence reminding me how superior she was.

Except she wasn't. She wasn't even my equal, and we both knew it.

"Shouldn't you be cleaning out the privies or something?" Isobel taunted me.

I thought about turning away and ignoring her, and I tried. I honestly tried. But my heart had had enough of this little bitch, and we were alone.

It was time to teach her a lesson and show her I was more than her equal.

The first words I ever spoke against the likes of her happened on that very day, and the more I think of them, the prouder of myself I am for standing up to her.

"You might get away with that back at the Manor House, but out here where it's just you and me, you can't. You're a spoiled little girl who needs a good slapping."

Those are the exact words that will remain etched into my heart for the rest of my life.

I felt alive! I had finally stood up to one of the two sisters who made my life so miserable. Even though I knew I would pay for it later, not least with my own mother, I knew I had crossed a line I could never go back over.

Isobel yelled and screamed at me, and all I did was stand there and take it. Until she told me that my mother would pay for my insolence. That's when I truly crossed the line and began the journey that brought me to the woman I am today.

Strong and firm.

I raised my fist and slapped Isobel as hard as I could across her face. The look of shock was worth a thousand lashings, especially when I saw the red finger marks down the sides of her cheeks.

"You will hang for this, or your mother will. Nobody strikes me, not even my father."

Isobel ran past me, but by now the mists of rage had taken control. I grabbed her and pulled her back towards me. Isobel struggled, and the next thing I knew, she had lost her footing and was sliding down the banking towards the rushing water.

Isobel pleaded with me to help her as she grabbed for all she was worth at the undergrowth, but the river was too ferocious this day, and she wasn't strong enough to haul herself out of the strong current.

Her anger changed to fear. I could see it in her eyes, and I admit I was enjoying it. She grabbed my hands after I offered them, and I stood as if to pull her up.

Then I let go.

I felt joyful as the raging river dragged Isobel deep into the rapid, muddy waters. The last thing I saw was her face as it disappeared beneath the surface.

I stood there, frozen to the spot for a long time, before I gathered myself together. I had never felt such a powerful feeling before, but I knew I had to act quickly if I was to save my own life.

She slipped down the banking. I tried to save her, but it wasn't my fault. The river was just too strong.

To make things believable, I found a sturdy branch overhanging the river's edge and gripped tightly so I wouldn't join Isobel in her watery grave at the bottom of the river. I lowered myself into the water as far as I dared and made sure the water soaked me to the skin. I held on as the water washed away all my sins, but I was tired.

My fingers slipped, and water was rushing up my nose and into my mouth. I panicked and had lost control.

What had I done? I was going to die, and I didn't deserve to die like this. My life was only just beginning, and yet I felt myself being washed away to my demise. My back thudded into a large rock, and the back of my head cracked open as it collided with the heavy stone. I was pinned to the rock by the fast current, and water poured over my head in torrents. I reached up, convinced I was going to die, and grabbed hold of another overhead branch. With one almighty heave, I pulled myself towards the riverbank with the last strength I had, and I collapsed onto the muddy banking, glad to be alive.

I lay there for what seemed an age before I gathered myself and got my story straight in my mind. My head ached, and I was cold and tired, but the thrill was something I wouldn't feel again for a long time. Not until Malton, but that's a confession for another day.

I ran as fast as I could back to the village and played the best part I have ever played. Everyone believed me, and everyone felt sorry for me. Everyone, that is, except Isobel's mother and sister, who both hated me as much as Isobel did.

At least now they had good reason for that hatred . . .

Lord Gordon placed the confession on the table and sat in stunned silence. Tears ran down his face and John felt incredibly sorry for him.

Sarah reached forward and touched his arm. "We're sorry if this upsets you, Lord Gordon, but we need answers, and you are the only person who can provide them."

James Gordon looked up and took a deep breath. "I'll tell you everything you need to know."

Chapter 49

Lord Gordon grabbed some ale and dismissed Longmead. "What I have to say is for your ears only."

Once the room cleared of servants, Lord Gordon cleared his throat and began to speak.

"What do you know of Margaret's past? Not much I'm guessing, if you are here to see me."

"We know about her life in Malton, Yorkshire, and her times in Horsham in the south," John said. "In both places, she brought nothing but death and misery to those who cared for her. Although we don't know what she did here, we know it was something similar."

Lord Gordon sat back in his chair. "Did you know that Margaret's father was the best carpenter I ever had? Francis Shipley was his name, and he built the triangular arches above the windows at the front of the house. It was a sad day when he left the household."

"We heard he died fighting for the king in France," John said. "We learned that in Malton last year."

"Yes, indeed. A sad loss. Her mother, Joan Shipley, was the fairest looking woman I ever saw. Margaret was attractive from what I heard when she grew older, but nobody came close to her mother's beauty when she was young."

James looked at the ground, his gaze fixed on the thick rug under his feet.

"Who was Isobel?" John asked.

James sighed. "Isobel was my daughter. She was only ten years old when she died. My poor wife never got over her death, and she died of a broken heart only a year later. Although Margaret's story seemed reasonable at the time, I always suspected her of Isobel's murder. Now I know for sure."

Tears streamed down his face.

"Why would Margaret murder Isobel? And why would it be so important to her years later? After all, by then she had murdered several others, but there was something about Isobel that haunted her memories." John pressed the grieving lord.

"That would be because Isobel was Margaret's sister." Lord Gordon looked John in the eye. "Her half-sister, to be exact."

John stared at James Gordon, his hand pressed to his mouth. Sarah gasped audibly beside him.

"Although Francis raised Margaret as his own, Margaret was my daughter. You see, Joan Shipley was my mistress for many years, and I loved her dearly. I adored Margaret when she was young, and I wanted to raise her as my own. I would have, too, if it hadn't been for the objections of my wife. Instead, we came to an agreement that Margaret would take the Shipley name, and I would provide for her upbringing. I showered her with coin and clothes, and made sure her family was well fed and cared for. I loved Margaret."

"What made her so resentful that she would drown her own half-sister?" John asked.

"Margaret always felt left out and resented the fact that Isobel and her sister lived here in Speke Hall as a Gordon. She hated it when we had parties and guests, and she had to stay away while the other two dressed for the occasion and played the part of a lord's daughter."

James sighed and looked down again.

"Margaret grew to hate me as she got older. And my, how she hated her sisters."

"Who was her other sister?" John asked. "Margaret mentioned her in the confessions, but never named her. What happened to her?"

Lord Gordon stared at John before turning his gaze to Sarah. He sighed.

"You knew her sister very well. Her name was Jayne Gordon, who later became Jayne Howard. Margaret's other sister was your mother."

John shot to his feet, suddenly feeling cold and clammy. His chest felt heavy, and he struggled to breathe. Sarah fell to her knees and cried out loud.

"No. No. Please say that isn't true."

"I'm afraid it is true, and that is why I have carried the shame with me ever since. I'm sorry."

"Did my father know he married Jayne's sister?" John asked through the fog of confusion.

"How could he?"

James shook his head. "Margaret was a Shipley. Nobody knew of her past here. Isobel's death was put down to an accidental drowning, and although Margaret was not suspected of drowning her, my wife couldn't stand to see Margaret around after Isobel passed, so we sent them away so we wouldn't have to see her again. Her name was banned from ever being mentioned in our household from that day forward."

James bowed his head once again. "Who would have

predicted that she would turn out the way she did, killing people everywhere she went? I swear that if I'd known, I would have killed her myself the day she drowned my poor Isobel."

"Margaret was our aunt? She must have known that she was marrying her sister's husband, and yet she did it, anyway?" Sarah battled to force the words out.

"And then she set about destroying us," John added. "She knew alright."

"Of course she knew," James Gordon said. "How could she not know? I'm so sorry to have to tell you, but that is why you came here, is it not?"

John gathered the confessions and grabbed his sister. Alexander Carlyle had been correct all along. Margaret had saved her ultimate betrayal for them, and she knew that one day it would destroy the Howard family.

That day was now.

Chapter 50

The weather was lousy as a crowd gathered on Tower Hill to watch the latest execution of a nobleman.

John, Catherine, and Sarah stood to the side of Robert and Thomas Howard, with Edward and Stephen right behind them. Sheriff Holley stood close by, along with Father Kirk. Rain and sleet had fallen earlier, but now it had been replaced by a strong wind that whipped through the scaffolding as though it was telling the executioner to hurry and get it done.

John couldn't agree more. He felt sick to his stomach, and he'd barely eaten since he and Sarah left Speke Hall. Sarah was even worse, and she looked visibly drawn and sick. She, too, had barely uttered a word since they had discovered Margaret's ultimate act of deception against them.

The crowd, which was large given the terrible conditions, stirred. Men were walking onto the platform, and it was time for Alexander Carlyle to face the justice of the axe.

John took no pleasure in what he was about to see. In

truth, he felt nothing either way. He was numb to death after all he'd seen and done, and one more didn't affect him at all. Not that Carlyle didn't deserve to die, because he did. Everyone present knew it, even Carlyle himself, although John doubted that he'd ever admit it.

Carlyle walked out onto the scaffolding, and the people gasped at his unusual physical appearance. Some laughed and mocked the condemned man, while others took pity on him.

John did neither.

Carlyle's eyes searched the crowd until he found the Howard family stood together, and when he knelt before them in his final moments, he smiled at John, obviously taking the satisfaction of what he'd helped bring about to his grave.

John ignored the taunting expression and held Carlyle's gaze. When given the chance to speak his last words, Carlyle shook his head. He knew his high-pitched, girl-like voice would only bring more ridicule, so he refused. Instead, he just glared at John Howard with a look that said, even in defeat, Carlyle felt like he had won.

He had got the ultimate vengeance on the hated Howard family.

The axe struck, and Carlyle screamed in agony. Again and again, the executioner struck Carlyle on the head, neck, and shoulders. Men and women in the crowd threw up at the grotesque spectacle in front of them, as the poorly trained executioner went about his ghastly business. Eventually, he succeeded, and Carlyle's head fell away from his body.

Alexander Carlyle was dead.

John turned around and caught the eye of William Asheborne, who gently nodded back at him. While they would never be friends, they had at least a new understanding between each other. Both had been played by their fathers and Margaret Colte, and both had paid a heavy price. Sheriff Holley had got back at least some of the wealth Asheborne had sent to Carlyle, which gave him a modest chance of life after this.

In his graciousness, King Henry VIII pardoned William Asheborne and gave him his freedom. Asheborne had a chance at life again. Just not a wealthy one.

The crowd thinned as fast as it had gathered, because nobody wanted to be out in the driving wind and sleet any longer than they had to be. John and his small group hung around as the last ones to leave.

Sheriff Holley shook hands with everyone, leaving John until last. "It has been a pleasure knowing you, John, and I wish we could have met in better circumstances. You now have the chance of a full life, and I beg you to take it with both hands."

"I shall, Sheriff, and I feel likewise. Take care, and I hope our paths cross again in better times."

As Holley turned to leave, John stopped him. "I fear the confessions shall continue to haunt the nobility of England, and I am glad to be no longer a part of it."

"Cromwell has summoned me to a meeting in the morn already. I am sure he is acting on those confessions, so I don't blame you for getting away. Just take care of yourself and watch your back."

John bowed his head and turned to his father, who had approached from the other side.

"John," he said, grasping John's hand with his. "I'm so sorry life turned out the way it did for all of us. That woman should never have got near us, and for that, I shall blame myself for the rest of my life. I swear I did not know she was Jayne's sister, or I would never have married her."

"I know, Father, and I don't blame you for that. She deceived all of us. Tell me, what shall you do now?"

"I shall stay at the Stronde until I find somewhere more suitable in the countryside. I may have lost Broxley, but I have gained the large house next to our residence on the Stronde. It is yours if you want it, or Sarah's. I shall restore it and make it available to you whenever you need it."

"Thank you, Father, but I have enough with Saddleworth. That's where you shall find me in the years ahead."

"I'm glad, John. Go and enjoy your life in Saddleworth Manor with your wife and your friends. Make sure you hold your children, when you have them, close, and never let them down as I did you. I'm proud of you, son."

"Father, why did you never tell us about our grandfather in Speke?" Sarah asked. "Neither John nor I had ever heard of Lord Gordon until we went to see him."

Robert Howard sighed. "Like I already told you, your mother never spoke of her childhood, and she refused to visit her father in Speke. Lord Gordon never liked Jayne marrying a Howard, and he in turn wanted nothing to do with us. So, we never told you about them. I swear to you both, I had no idea that Margaret was Jayne's sister, or I would have never gone near her. Marrying her is the biggest regret of my life."

Sarah frowned, and her sad eyes gripped John's heart. He squeezed her hand and bowed his head.

After one more embrace, Robert Howard was gone.

John turned to Edward and Stephen, who were hugging Catherine and Sarah one last time. "I wish you would come with us. We could do with your help in setting up Saddleworth, and you shall always have a home with us, no matter how much time passes before we see you again."

They embraced for a long moment. "Our place is out there, fighting injustice and serving a higher cause,"

Edward said. "But we shall always be there should you need us, and we will stop by from time to time. I wish you all the best, John Howard, for you are the bravest man I have ever met, and it has been an honour to have served you."

"I'm the same." Tears clouded John's eyes as he bade farewell to his two greatest friends that still lived. The other lay in a grave outside a small church on Britten Strete in London.

John threaded his arms through Catherine and Sarah's, and together they made their way to the carriage that would take them to the new life that awaited them at Saddleworth Manor in Horsham.

For John Howard, it was over.

THE END

Please Leave a Review

If you loved the book and have a moment to spare, I would really appreciate a short review.

Your help in spreading the word is gratefully appreciated and reviews make a huge difference to helping new readers find the series.

Please click the appropriate link below to leave your review:

Amazon USA

AMAZON UK

Other Amazon Stores

Thank you!

Get a FREE Book!

Before John Howard found sanctuary on the streets of London, Andrew Cullane formed a small band of outlawed survivors called the Underlings. Discover their fight for life for free when you join J.C. Jarvis's newsletter at jcjarvis.com/cullane

More Books by J.C. Jarvis

John Howard Tudor Series

John Howard and the Underlings

John Howard and the Tudor Legacy

John Howard and the Tudor Deception

Fernsby's War Series

Ryskamp

Alderauge *Coming Soon...*

About the Author

J.C. Jarvis is the author of the breakout John Howard series.

He makes his home at www.jcjarvis.com

Email: jc@jcjarvis.com

Printed in Great Britain
by Amazon